Advance Praise for Gina Chung's

Sea Change

"*Sea Change* tugged at my heart and refused to let go. . . . Between giant Pacific octopuses and humans, this remarkable debut reminds us that we are not so different—all of us hoping to be witnessed, all of us striving to surface through our loneliness to connect, even when we know nothing is permanent." —Elaine Hsieh Chou, author of *Disorientation*

"A wild blessing of a debut. Gina Chung's curiosity, precision, and grace have created a world both strange and recognizable, the kind of place you can find a version of yourself you did not know existed and call her home."
—Mira Jacob, author of *Good Talk*

"From the first page, *Sea Change* stole my big weirdo heart. . . . With her debut, Chung has proven she is a true original, the rare kind of writer who can be simultaneously witty and deeply sensitive, confident and devastatingly vulnerable."
—Jean Kyoung Frazier, author of *Pizza Girl*

"Weaving deftly between humor and longing, Chung's masterful prose interrogates what it means to be alive—and all of the growth, heartache, love, and friendship at the center of it. Marvelously original, tender, and moving, *Sea Change* will stay with readers long after they've surfaced from its pages."
—Qian Julie Wang, *New York Times* bestselling author of *Beautiful Country*

"Soulful, evocative, and wise. *Sea Change* is a powerful meditation on grief and healing, as well as family, immigration, and intergenerational trauma."

—Daphne Palasi Andreades, author of *Brown Girls*

"Tender, perceptive, and sumptuously original. . . . *Sea Change* is a novel of vast empathy, flickering between humor and vulnerability as deftly as our beloved octopus Dolores changes her colors. A glittering debut."

—Crystal Hana Kim, author of *If You Leave Me*

"Absolutely stunning debut. . . . Full of longing, mystery, fear, and hope. I loved this book to pieces!"

—Frances Cha, author of *If I Had Your Face*

GINA CHUNG

Sea Change

Gina Chung is a Korean American writer
from New Jersey currently living in New
York City. A recipient of the Pushcart Prize,
she is a 2021–2022 Center for Fiction/Susan
Kamil Emerging Writer Fellow and holds an
MFA in fiction from the New School. Her
work appears or is forthcoming in *Kenyon
Review, Catapult, Electric Literature, Gulf
Coast, Indiana Review,* and *Idaho Review,*
among others. She is also the author of the
forthcoming story collection *Green Frog*
(Vintage). *Sea Change* is her first novel.

Sea Change

Gina Chung

VINTAGE BOOKS
A DIVISION OF PENGUIN RANDOM HOUSE LLC
NEW YORK

A VINTAGE BOOKS ORIGINAL 2023

Library of Congress Cataloging-in-Publication Data
Names: Chung, Gina, [date] author.
Title: Sea change / Gina Chung.
Description: New York : Vintage Books, a division
    of Penguin Random House LLC, 2023.
Identifiers: LCCN 2022023368 | ISBN 9780593469347
    (trade paperback) | ISBN 9780593469354 (ebook)
Subjects: LCGFT: Bildungsromans. | Novels.
Classification: LCC PS3603.H8534 S43 2023 |
    DDC 813/.6—dc23/eng/20220523
LC record available at https://lccn.loc.gov/2022023368

Vintage Books Trade Paperback ISBN: 978-0-593-46934-7
eBook ISBN: 978-0-593-46935-4

Book design by Nicholas Alguire

vintagebooks.com

Printed in the United States of America
1st Printing

For my family

All life from the ocean, is a sure thing.
Even when time divides us, *(please)*
laugh triumphantly and call them waves.
                    —Haolun Xu, "Reverse Takoyaki
                    (How to Uncook an Octopus)"

Sea Change

CHAPTER 1

This morning, Dolores is blue again. She's signaling her readiness to mate, her eagerness to mount the rocks and corals of her tank and push herself against a male octopus, who will insert his hectocotylus into her mantle cavity and deposit sperm packets inside her until she is ready to lay the eggs. Unfortunately for Dolores, there is no bachelor octopus around ready to father her orphan eggs, and so when she turns that milky, almost pearlescent blue that I know means she is in the mood for love, there is no one but me to see.

Dolores can turn herself as flat as a pancake or puff up like a mushroom, and when she propels herself through all one thousand gallons of her tank, air bubbles dance around her like they're laughing with her. When she undulates her arms through the clean, dark water, she looks like a storm of ribbons. She can be cranky, like any old lady, but she loves seeing me come in with a bucket full of shrimp and fish for her. I could swear that sometimes she waves at me.

So this morning, when I wished her good morning and told

her how the weather was outside and she responded by turning blue, I didn't bat an eyelash. "You and me both, Lo," I said before turning the radio on and mopping up the floor. It was eight a.m., and I wasn't about to empathize with a thirsty octopus over her sexual needs when I hadn't gotten laid in months.

This is my own fault, I know. After Tae left, I basically coped with it by not coping at all. I've been broken up with before, but never because the guy in question was actually planning on leaving the planet.

Tae never liked my working at the aquarium. He couldn't understand why I had "tethered myself to a sinking ship," as he said. No pun intended probably, knowing Tae. And it's true that we don't get too many visitors these days, especially with more and more of the animals being bought up by wealthy investors who want to be able to gawk at a giant endangered sea turtle in their at-home aquarium. The exhibit hall feels ghostly sometimes during the off-season, like an abandoned carnival ground.

But Dolores is still here. She has been one of the aquarium's crown jewels since I was a kid pressing my nose against the glass to marvel at her shimmering colors. She's probably one of the oldest giant Pacific octopuses in the world.

"Look at the size of her," Apa would say. "Isn't she a beauty?" He was a marine biologist and a consultant for the aquarium, tasked with making sure that the tanks replicated the animals' natural environments as much as possible. Umma always said, not really joking, that she wouldn't be surprised if he left her for Dolores someday.

My manager, Carl, walks in, all hair cream and business. Dolores immediately turns inky dark and makes herself scarce. I don't blame her. Carl is the kind of guy who thinks everyone is happy to see him and always talks like he's wearing a headset. He's both fairly harmless and extremely irritating.

"Morning, ladies!" he says, radiating caffeinated goodwill.

"Morning, Carl," I say, not looking up from my mopping.

Carl pats the glass like it's a flank, and somewhere in the water I see one of Dolores's huge eyes open, a horizontal pupil flashing as she watches the movement of his fleshy pink hand, but Carl doesn't see her. "Cheryl's out today and Francine's got a field trip. Mind overseeing cleanup in Tide Pools, Ro?"

I open my mouth to tell him no, and he hastens to add, "There might be a day off in it for you. I'd do it myself, but I can't stay late tonight."

"Hot date?" I say, and then wish I hadn't, because the smile that spreads across Carl's face is the kind of smile that announces it's got something to say and it won't let you go till it's been said.

"Her name's Christina. Since it's our first date, I thought we'd—"

"Fine." *Just stop talking to me, please,* I don't say.

Days off used to mean something to me, back when Tae was still around and I had a life in which I did things outside of work. We used to plan weekend trips to towns we picked at random, either in Upstate New York or down in South Jersey. Tae always took care of all the logistical details, but I was the one who planned out what hokey roadside attraction or niche museums we'd go see, like the wooden clog collection we found once in a town we breezed through on the way up to Hudson. Tae liked our jaunts, my propensity for seeking out the strange. "I get to see more of the world with you," he told me once after I'd forced him to go to a jug band concert played by animatronic squirrels somewhere outside Albany.

But who says I can't take trips on my own, now that Tae's gone, somewhere in the Arizona desert? It's been months since I've had a break of any kind.

Carl is surprised by my acquiescence. "Super!" he trills. "See if you can get Dolores to come out and say hi later this afternoon when the field trip comes by. The kids always love her." As if in response, Dolores waves one pale arm through the water in his direction, which startles a yelp out of him. I suppress my laughter at the idea that anyone could get Dolores to do anything she doesn't want to do.

Dolores is somewhere between eighteen and twenty-five years old, so technically, she's younger than me. But by sea creature standards, she's practically nonagenarian. In addition to being one of the last known giant Pacific octopuses in the world, she has the prestige of having been spawned in one of the most polluted zones of our warmed-over oceans, the Bering Vortex, where my father disappeared fifteen years ago on what was supposed to be a routine research trip.

I've saved and studied just about every known photo of the Vortex. I've made notes on the sheen of its waters, which are red and green and violet with toxins and spills from the refineries in Alaska. I've imagined going there myself, to look for my father.

Officially he's listed as "missing, presumed dead." I don't know if that last part is true, though. Sometimes I get calls from unknown numbers or numbers with area codes I don't recognize, and when I pick up, I swear I can hear waves of sound, spray and roar, or breathing, a voice that sounds like it's trying to break through. When I first told Umma about the calls, she said it was just perverts or spam, but I can't shake the thought that it might be Apa. That somewhere out there he might still be trying to find his way back, and that the calls are his way of checking in. Of letting me know that he's thinking about me, wherever he is.

The Bering Vortex isn't on any of the Alaskan cruise stops. The only people who go there are pollution tourists or researchers. The creatures that have managed to survive, mutate, and breed there, passing on their irrevocably altered genetic material over the last few decades, are biblical in size and shape and hard to see or catch. Climate scientists and marine biologists alike haunt the Vortex, hoping for a sight of them, for a chance to discover what's allowed them to continue living under such harsh conditions.

When Dolores was first caught, she was about fifteen feet long and still growing, and powerful and smart enough that they had to lid her tank with iron. Now there's more than twenty feet of her, and her round, wicked eyes are the size of classroom globes, the kind I used to spin and place my finger on when I was a kid, trying to guess where I would land when the spinning stopped.

"The women of our family have never had luck with men," Umma said when I told her Tae had broken up with me. She cites my grandfather's untimely death, which widowed my grandmother at the age of thirty-two, as well as the fact that her younger sister was never able to find a husband as further examples of this bad luck. She's not the type of mother to whine about my never calling home or visiting, or to say things like "between us girls." But every once in a while, she comes out with pronouncements like these that make me realize there is a person with feelings somewhere underneath her usual veneer of chilly poise and disapproval.

Umma actually liked Tae, couldn't believe that her daughter had finally gotten herself a boyfriend who was not only Korean but also smart, handsome, and had a real job. In a way, he legitimized me, made me into a girl she could finally start to understand the shape of. I've never brought anyone else home to her before, so it's highly possible she thinks he was the first person I've ever dated or slept with. Umma never told me about sex, and when I was a kid, I imagined that I must have been born from sea-foam, a tiny pearl that bobbed to shore that she and Apa had scooped up one day.

Tae wasn't supposed to leave on the Arc 4 mission. He was just one of thousands of volunteers on the waiting list, waiting to hear the results of a lottery that would determine who'd get to join the crew for years of spinning around in the dark toward Mars, to build the first human colony out on the red planet. I hadn't taken his interest in the mission seriously, dismissing it as one of those fantasies that scientifically minded boys always have, about saving the world by leaving it.

"So what, if you get picked, then it's off to Mars?" I said skeptically when he first told me he'd signed up for the lottery. He shook his head.

"It doesn't work that way," he'd said. "I have to get picked, then pass the fitness and aptitude tests, and then there's a training program out in Arizona. A simulation, to see if we can take it." By the time he started going into the different initiatives and goals of the program and the types of people they were looking for (apparently there were diversity and inclusion quotas that Arc 4 was supposed to be fulfilling), I had already stopped listening. The vast darkness of outer space—which is totally unlike the darkness of the ocean, where even the most unfathomable, seemingly inhospitable depths still glimmer with signs of life, the kind of life you can see and touch—has never interested me much.

When Tae finally got into the program, he waited until two weeks before he was supposed to leave for the desert to break the news. "Ro, I have to tell you something," he said one night over bowls of green curry at his place. My stomach dropped, because nothing good has ever happened after someone says that they have to tell me something. It was how Umma had told me that Apa's ship had gone missing and that there was no sign of him or the rest of the crew.

So I steeled myself and watched my curry grow cold as he showed me the confirmation and plane tickets they'd sent him, and the glossy welcome packet he'd received in the mail with the gold Arc 4 logo embossed on it.

"I'm sorry," he said after I'd failed to say anything in response. He took his glasses off and polished them, the way he always did when he got nervous. "But I can't turn this down."

"Can't you?" I said, my throat as dry as sand. "What's out there that you can't find here? Why is this so important?"

"Ro," he said gently, as though I were a child. "The planet is dying. Arc 4 is about finding solutions to an untenable problem. I've wanted to be part of something like this since forever."

"What about me?" I asked, my voice becoming high and strangled the way it always did when we fought. Tae hated that. "What am I supposed to do? Just wait until you come back?"

He was quiet, and then I knew that he wasn't going to come back for a very long time, if at all. Tae had told me, back when he'd first signed up, about all the mission preparations, beyond the usual necessities: seeds, water purification kits, even condoms, in case the crew got lonely—but also ovulation kits. Europa, the company funding the mission, wasn't being subtle about the fact that if the crew of Arc 4 should want to start populating Mars with a new generation of humans, they should feel free.

I told Dolores about it the next day at work. I shook her breakfast into the water and watched her unfurl herself like the world's scariest beach umbrella and devour the silvery fish with her sharp beak while I told her about Tae and cried. Once she'd finished eating, she slowly turned maroon, which I decided to take as a sign that she was trying to be supportive.

I would have told my best friend first, made her come out to drinks with me after work, but she's always too busy now. Yoonhee and I have known each other since we were kids. Now we work at the aquarium together—I'm in animal husbandry and she's in development. But since her promotion to assistant deputy of funding, she's been hard to get ahold of. My texts to her usually go unanswered, and then she responds days later, her messages peppered with exclamation points and offers to "catch up soon."

When I finally got a chance to talk to her about what was going on with me and Tae, it was almost like old times, though I could hear a hint of judgment behind the sympathy in her voice.

"What?" I said. We were drinking in my apartment, the air conditioner whirring. I was having a sharktini, which is just Mountain Dew with copious amounts of gin and a hint of jalapeño. Yoonhee and I invented them one day when we were both bored at a bad party in college. We were so drunk then, I don't even remember why we decided to call them that.

Yoonhee was having wine from the one unshattered glass I had in my apartment, each measured sip making her cheeks get pinker. "Nothing," she said. "It's just that—it's not like you didn't see it coming, right? It takes two to make or break a relationship."

"Are you saying it's my fault that my boyfriend is breaking up with me to go to Mars?"

"No, but maybe it's the best thing for you both, you know? We're not in our twenties anymore. It's time to, like, get serious about our lives. Manifest the reality we want."

"I guess," I said, cranking up the air conditioning. Yoonhee talked like an Instagram caption sometimes. I watched as she set her glass of wine down on my coffee table and angled her phone over it, taking three or four pictures before deciding which one to post. I wondered what she'd say in her eventual post, whether she'd think to tag me or not. She used to just post the drawings she was always working on, funny little doodles or watercolors she did in her spare time. She even sold prints of them online before, but now her feed is just lifestyle content, full of light-filled squares featuring her meals, her clothes, her vacations, her accessories. Since she got engaged, her follower count has ballooned. She posts about everything, from the types of cakes she and her fiancé, James, are trying out to the cream-colored invitations she showed me at one of our increasingly infrequent lunches one day.

This morning marked three months and three weeks since Tae left. The Arc 4 Instagram account has been posting updates about the training facilities, preflight preparations, and the simulation exercises the crew have been undergoing. Today they posted a group photo of the crew and the volunteers, all dressed in silvery coveralls. Tae was on the side, sandwiched between two girls whose names are, according to their tagged profiles, Sandhya and Bree. Despite months of desert life, their skin looks moisturized, their hair full and lustrous. I zoomed in on Tae's face on my phone while I was still in bed, hating myself for doing it. His hair is long now, and it looks like he's trying to grow a beard.

Tae still texts me sometimes, in a manner of speaking. The whole crew has to use special encrypted apps that Europa devised, and I can't bring myself to delete mine. A few days after his arrival in Arizona, he sent me a photo of the desert landscape, seen through the plexiglass window of his bedroom, the red of the earth and the blue of the sky both so bright they seem unreal. "It's beautiful out here," the message said. I didn't reply.

"Do you miss me at all?" I wrote to him once, in a more vulnerable moment, after I'd had a sharktini or three alone at home. When I'm at work, the phosphorescent blue-green light of the tanks soothes me, makes me feel submerged and suspended in a kind of watery relief. But at home, in my shitty apartment where the ceiling leaks sometimes and the bathroom door doesn't stay shut and the fridge always smells of spilled yogurt no matter how many times I clean it, everything comes back, so vivid it hurts: sunlit mornings when I woke up to the smell of coffee brewing, Tae reading while sitting cross-legged on the floor, looking up to smile at me when I finally dragged myself out of bed; afternoons when we'd disappear into each other; evenings when he'd cook me something complicated while I drank a bottle of wine and did impressions of the animals in the aquarium to make him laugh; all the sunrises he made me wake up obscenely early for, because he loved morning walks. What a nerd.

"I do," he wrote back after two days of silence.

I really should delete the app. I work up the nerve to do it every once in a while, but I lose my resolve whenever I think about Tae's smile or the way he muttered my name sometimes in his sleep. How embarrassing it is, to be so undone by such small things.

After Carl leaves to go refresh his inbox or whatever else he does in his spare time, I check on Dolores's pH levels and provide her with her daily puzzle. I put a small crab from her food bucket inside a hinged box that I drop in for her, and then I let my arm linger in the water for a bit. She curls one of her own arms around mine, and I feel the strange sensation of her suckers tasting my arm, curious, before she releases it so she can turn her full attention to figuring out how to open the box.

I wonder if Dolores misses the pull of the open ocean, or if the crabs and fish we feed her here pale in comparison to the six-finned salmon or winged cod that are rumored to be thriving in the Bering Strait now. Humans aren't strong enough to stomach Bering fish, but for a full-grown giant Pacific octopus born and bred in those waters, they're probably a delicacy. I watch Dolores pry at the lid of the box for a few minutes before I go check on the other halls.

I pass Francine's group on my way to the tide pools. It's a class of elementary school kids, all wearing matching T-shirts and lanyards. Francine's good with kids, which is why she gets all the field trips, and she gives me a wink when one of them, a little girl whose T-shirt is way too big for her, wanders off and has to be steered back to the herd by one of the teachers. "And who can tell me what a group of otters is called?" she asks. The children stare up at her blankly. "A family?" one of them says, and this makes me stop in my tracks for a second. I take a breath and remind myself to keep walking. As I round the corner, I hear Francine's voice say, "That's right! You can also call them a bevy or a romp, because they're so playful."

My own family was never particularly playful. Love was portioned out, something to be both carefully guarded and left alone in the hopes that it would grow on its own overnight, like cultures in a petri dish.

I always felt like I was competing with something for Apa's attention. He loved teaching me how to do things, explaining how to pick out constellations in the night sky or the best way to parallel park into a tight spot on the street, but he would immediately throw up his hands with exasperation and cut me off abruptly whenever I took too long to get what he was trying to explain. Umma, who studied voice in college and is now the conductor of the choir at her church, where she spends five out of seven days each week, taught me to fold myself up into prayer to ask for things she couldn't give me, like forgiveness or patience. I think there must have been a time when they loved each other, or at least liked each other, but whatever it was that had brought them together initially had curdled into something much more volatile by the time I came along.

I used to count all the ways that I had been good in a given week. I gave myself points for everything I'd managed to get done without having to be asked, like making my bed or clearing the table or finishing all my homework before dinner. On Saturday nights, I'd add up all the points on report cards I made for myself, to determine how much I should have been loved that week. I made my parents sign off on each of them, and then I'd file them away in a box I kept in my closet.

When I got old enough to have boyfriends and sneak them over to our house when my parents weren't home, I thought love was the tiny purple geodes on my neck that I didn't even attempt to cover; hot breath in the back seats of cars; crying alone in an empty parking lot when I inevitably got dumped for someone new, someone easier to deal with and not quite so desperate. In my early twenties, I thought love was the taste of sweat, pooled below a collarbone on a warm hungover morning, letting boys come inside me—sometimes without a condom; sometimes because I wanted it, sometimes because I didn't know if I wanted it—feeling their heat inside me until it felt like my own. Love was paring myself down, again and again, until I was as smooth as a block of new marble, ready to become whatever the next one needed me to be.

But Tae was different. Right away, he told me he wasn't going to sleep with me until we were sure of where things were going, which of course offended and fascinated me in equal measure. "You can just tell me if you don't like me," I said.

He didn't laugh. He stared at me, his eyes round and serious behind his gold wire-frame glasses. "I've rushed things before, and I don't really see a reason to do that with you."

The first time we finally had sex, two months later, after a series of increasingly frustrating dates over coffee, wine, art shows, movies, evening talks (all Tae's suggestions), I was so nervous that I was sweating all over. I was so slick with sweat that I worried I'd slide off the bed and down the hallway in a snail trail of shame and longing. Sweat pooled below my armpits, behind my knees, below the curves of my stomach. And because I have never had any game, I told him this, standing in front of him in the middle of his bedroom.

"I'm so sweaty," I said. Outside, it was raining, the sound of water pattering against the roof and windows of his apartment, which was clean and spare, just like everything else about him.

Tae didn't say anything to that. He took off his glasses and folded their temples neatly over each other, and when he looked back up at me, his eyes were as naked and trusting as a dog's. He reached over his shoulders to tug his shirt off, that way boys always do, his skinny wrists and elbows flashing in the dim light of his bedroom. He pulled me over to where he was standing and placed my hand on his chest, where his heart was beating so fast I worried for a second that I'd have to call 911. "I'm nervous, too," he said before he kissed me.

He undressed me slowly, his hands encircling my belly and waist and breasts as though they were afraid to leave me alone for too long. He kissed me like a sailor about to go away on a long journey. It was a kiss of salt spray, breaking waves, pink horizons. I thought of dark water and sun-warmed surfaces as we rose and fell, again and again, bobbing against each other like two small boats in a storm. By the end of it, we were both gasping and he was as sweaty as I was, the room sharp with the mingled smell of us.

Afterward, I lost my mind and told him I thought I loved him, and I lost it again when he told me he loved me, too. I felt a happy quiet settle into my bones, so alien that I almost didn't even recognize it, before it was followed swiftly by fear. *Oh no,* I thought to myself, watching his chest rise and fall as he slept. *Here's another thing I could lose.*

It was like that all throughout our relationship.

The tide pools are the petting zoo of the aquarium. They're brightly lit, noisy, smelly. Red starfish and purple sea urchins dot the brackish blue-green waters, and in the background, some genius has decided to pipe in the sounds of shrieking gulls and waves crashing. Francine's tour group will be here soon enough—kids go nuts for the tide pool, because they're allowed to scoop up and touch some of the mollusks—so I'm here to check on the water temperature and oxygen levels before they do, to minimize whatever cleanup Carl needs me to oversee later.

I notice that one of the new hermit crabs, just shipped in from the Caribbean, looks a little pale. Dolores loves hermit crabs—they're sweet and juicy and probably taste like candy to her. This one doesn't look so great. It's tottering around like a drunk girl looking for her purse. I'm about to reach in, to lift it out of the pool and onto the sand so it can rest, when I hear Yoonhee call my name.

"Hey, you!" she says, her eyes crinkling into a smile. For a second, it's like old times with her, like she's about to ask me what I'm doing for lunch or tell me about something annoying that happened today. But then she lowers her voice. "Did you get my email?" she asks. Before I can answer, she continues, "You should really be better about staying on top of your inbox. I just looped you in on something big." She seems excited but wary, like she's watching me for my reaction.

"I honestly haven't had a chance to check. Crazy morning," I say, affecting the tone she uses whenever she doesn't get back to me.

"Right," she says, eyebrows raised. "Well, I might as well

be the one to tell you. There's interest in Dolores from some higher-ups right now. They want to sell her."

"What?" It's like she's told me that they're planning on selling the moon. "They can't. That doesn't even make any sense."

"Private buyer. They're looking to send her over by the end of the month. I've been asked to tell you to write up a memo of items we'll need to include in the shipment." *I've been asked.* The thing I hate most about the new Yoonhee is her penchant for the passive voice, as though whatever she's talking about is totally outside her control. It's the way Tae told me about Arc 4, too. *I've been selected, Ro. I'm being picked for the chance of a lifetime.*

But I don't have time to get fully angry before I realize, feeling gut punched, that I should have seen this coming, should have known something was up when Carl asked me a few weeks ago if Dolores was always "shy."

"It's a good thing, Ro," Yoonhee says, softening her voice. "I know she's important to you. But it's good for Dolores and for us. The buyer wants to open a private aquarium—he has enough money to get her a bigger tank, nicer facilities. Are you okay?"

I have to sit down. I find my way to a bench and focus on the hermit crabs. They live in colonies, unlike some crab species. A collective of crabs is known as a cast. Tae told me that one Christmas, when he presented me with a pair of socks that had different crab species embroidered on them—hermits, fiddlers, ghosts, spiders, blues. He collected information like that. A parliament of owls, a quiver of cobras, a zeal of zebras, a clowder of cats.

A week before he told me he was leaving, I found a Russian blue kitty online that I had already named Pavlova in my mind, that I was going to ask him if we could adopt together, as a prelude to his finally moving in with me. As a prelude to staying together. I must have felt him slipping away from me even then.

"I'm sorry, Ro. I know she means a lot to you." Yoonhee's hand on my shoulder feels heavy and hesitant at the same time. I shrug it off.

"How can they do that? This place has been her home for the last decade," I say.

Yoonhee sighs. Her phone blips and she pulls it out, taps the screen a few times before putting it away. She takes her time before she responds. She once told me that a trick for making yourself seem more interesting to others is to take little pauses before you speak. "It makes people lean in, pay attention to you," she said. "Notice how all the directors here do it."

"Well, you didn't hear this from me," she finally says. "But more cuts are coming. And Dolores, while she's always been a draw for the aquarium, is eating into our budget. What this buyer is offering to pay would help us restock our Grand Hall. Revamp our marketing budget."

I try to remember to pause before I respond, but my words come rushing out one after the other, choked and tangled. "The marketing budget? There won't be anything to market if they keep—"

"They could close the aquarium," she says.

I stare at her. "What do you mean, they could close it? We're state-funded."

"The state has a lot of funding priorities. The aquarium isn't one of them," Yoonhee says. "And again, you didn't hear this from me, but if we don't start liquidating our assets, we're not going to survive the year as is. That includes most staff, a lot of our programming, and we'd probably have to slash the food and maintenance budgets." She says this all like she's giving a presentation, her calm eyes trained on me, watchful in case I make any sudden movements.

"What's going to happen to all of them if we close?" I say, gesturing around wildly. "What about the animals that aren't lucky enough to be bought up by rich investors?"

"They'll be let go, probably. Maybe to sanctuaries," Yoonhee says, a rising note of impatience in her voice. "I don't know. But this sale is important, Ro. It'd be a real win for us. I'd think you'd want to help save the aquarium."

Dolores swims through my mind. Her intelligent, cunning eyes. Her suckers gently palpating my arms. Her legs moving like strands of kelp in the water.

"Anyway, let me know if you need help on that memo," Yoonhee says, standing up. "I have a meeting in five, but let's catch up soon, okay?"

I don't hear her walk away. I wonder if Yoonhee was always like this. Maybe I just never saw it, the way that she could prize efficiency and bottom lines and "wins" over being a person.

I stare into the blue of the tide pools and try to remind myself that it's wrong to feel proprietary over Dolores. She's an animal, after all, a collection of nerve endings and instincts, driven by hunger. But then I think about the way her eyes widen whenever I wear orange or pink, how she seems to dance in the tank when her water is changed, how she always takes her time with the puzzles I give her—not, I suspect, because she can't solve them, but because she enjoys doing them.

The anemic-looking hermit crab has hoisted itself onto a flat rock, where it watches me from its new vantage point.

Its fellow crabs are hard at work digging in the sand. I wonder how much they know about the falseness of their world, whether any of them have any inherited memories of real sand and real ocean, and if they're capable of wishing for or imagining anything else.

CHAPTER 2

Twenty-one years earlier

The very first time I ever set foot in the aquarium, I was nine years old and cranky. *In a mood,* as my mother would say. It was a hot day in July, the sidewalks bubbling with heat. Our air conditioner and fridge had stopped working, and my parents were fighting. I'd covered my ears with my hands, but words like *costs, always,* and *your fault* slipped through. My mother, her hair clinging to the sides of her face in sweaty pieces, gesticulated in our kitchen as she screamed at my father, asking him how he could have forgotten to pay the electricity bill during the hottest time of the year.

A few years ago, my father left his low-paying research position at the local university to work for the aquarium at the Fountain Plaza. Umma made me avert my eyes whenever we drove past. She usually took local routes to avoid driving by the mall, which she claimed was so ugly it hurt her eyes, but it was so large it bisected one major highway and another main road, and so sometimes passing the Fountain Plaza was inevitable. It was large and sprawling, like a pale spider, with exterior walls that were coated, occasionally and inexplicably, in orange and blue tiles.

The aquarium was on the second floor of the mall. Umma refused to take me and wouldn't let me go on my own, saying that I was too young and besides that we shouldn't encourage my father's folly. She never forgave him for leaving the university, for turning his back on the respectability of academia to become what she called a glorified zookeeper.

That day, the sky shimmered with heat and the air felt like a wet towel pressed around my nose and mouth. It was so bad that even the flies that snuck into our house had no energy to do more than buzz fatalistically against the windows.

Finally Umma stopped yelling. She slammed their bedroom door shut, where I soon heard the whirring of a fan, its blade futilely chopping up the dead air. Apa knocked on my own bedroom door. "You okay in there?" he said, the door ajar.

My father was not a handsome man, but there was something about him that put everyone at ease. He still had all his hair, and he had a broad, cheek-splitting smile that seemed, based on the old family photos we had, not to have changed at all since he was a child. He played tennis with his friends and colleagues in the evenings and on weekends, so he was always walking around in his tennis gear—thick white socks, turquoise shirts, sweatbands around his wrists. Umma used to tease him about it, asked him if he was going to Wimbledon. He tried to teach me how to play once, but I could never seem to make the ball and the racket connect.

"Fine," I said.

"I'm sorry you had to hear all that, Acorn," he said. It was his pet name for me, a reference to when I was much younger and confused the word *daughter* with the Korean word for acorn, *dotori*.

"Is Umma mad at you?" I asked. I hated when they fought. The days after a big fight were the worst—everything so quiet and tense that it felt like the smallest thing would set off a trip wire. Umma was always extra critical of me after she got into a fight with Apa, as though whatever had happened could be fixed if I were just a little quieter, a little smarter, a little more attuned to her needs.

"You could say that," he said as classical music began blaring from their room. My mother loved Beethoven and blasted his symphonies whenever she was in a temper.

He sat down on the edge of my bed. It was a difficult operation, because I never had any fewer than ten stuffed animals lined up on it at a time. I had about thirty in those days, and I would rotate their positions periodically so that none of them would feel neglected.

He picked up Noreen the Narwhal. "Noreen," he said, addressing the stuffed animal instead of me, "how would you like to go on an adventure?"

I felt my cheeks warm with embarrassment. Apa was always acting like I was much younger than I was, as though I had never stopped being four years old for him.

"An adventure?" Noreen said in my father's voice, but higher. I looked away.

Apa stood up. "Well, how about it?" he said in his normal voice.

The drive over to the aquarium was longer than it should have been, from what I remembered. Out the window I watched the highway dribble by, the midday weekend traffic a slow crawl. I fell asleep several times. My father listened to a recorded lecture on his phone, and the voice of his old mentor, Dr. Forrest Pendent, filled the car in sonorous waves. "We are living in unprecedented times of crisis," he said. The lecture had been recorded ten years ago, before I was born. My father, a young PhD student at the time, must have been in the audience the night of Dr. Pendent's lecture. "Our planet's oceans have never been warmer. Our climate will become, within our lifetimes, completely unlivable. It is at this point that we must turn to our fellow creatures and look to their examples. Our research team is currently launching several studies into the giant Pacific octopus, particularly several noted specimens in the Bering Vortex region . . ."

My mother didn't like to listen to Dr. Pendent's talks. "What's the point of hearing all this doomsdaying?" she would say. But my father always maintained that it was important to pay attention, to note even the parts of our world that we couldn't save.

"Is the Earth going to explode?" I asked.

He considered this as he changed lanes. "No. It won't explode. Not for a very, very long time."

"But what's going to happen to us?"

"I don't know," he said. "But we're going to go see one of the animals that Dr. Pendent was talking about. She's a very special animal that we're trying to learn from."

"We have to open our eyes to what the natural world is trying to show us," I said.

He swiveled his head to look at me, surprised. "Why, yes. Where did you hear that?"

"You're always saying it," I said.

He laughed. "Guess you really are listening to me when I'm going on."

We pulled into the Fountain Plaza parking lot, which was packed. The sunlight shone on the windshields and hoods of all the cars, making them look like so many shiny beetles. Apa used his staff pass to pull into a reserved spot not far from the entrance, and then we walked inside, enduring the mind-melting heat for just a few seconds before we could feel the cool relief of institutional air conditioning.

The ceilings of the mall were high and vaulted, as though we were inside a church. Giant potted plants and trees, some real and some fake, interrupted the flow of traffic across the floors, forcing the rivers of people to part around them. Gaggles of chokered and eyelinered teenage girls, their hair ironed straight and their midriffs winking in the light, roamed past us, laughing like birds, while store windows, shiny with Windex, advertised sales. I shivered with the sheer delight of looking at everything. Even the headless mannequins seemed jaunty and inviting.

We took an escalator up to the second floor, where a neon sign welcoming us to the Fountain Aquarium lit up the polished tiles of the mall floor in a wash of color. There was already a line out the door of adults and small children, many of them younger than me, but we walked up to the front of the line, where my father flashed his staff pass at a girl with green hair who waved him in. I stared at her face, fascinated by the tongue ring I could see flashing at us from inside her mouth, and she gave me a practiced glare.

Inside, the aquarium was dark and quiet, and lit with blue, as though we were all suspended in the heart of the ocean. A giant papier-mâché eyeball glowered at us from the ceiling. A sign nearby proclaimed that the eyeball was an approximation of what the eyeball of the fabled Kraken would look like. "Is that who we're seeing?" I asked my father. "The Kraken?"

"I taught you better than that. Krakens aren't real. But Dolores is," he said, grinning.

We walked past the guards and down the grand exhibit

hall, taking a quick right and then a left to where a crowd was gathered outside a giant single tank, in a darkened room lit by violet-colored light. A guide was speaking in front of a large crowd of tourists, mostly old men wearing belts to hold up their khaki shorts and old women wearing visors. "The *Enteroctopus dofleini* is the largest known cephalopod," she said. She had purple lipstick and seemed to be chewing gum. "Who can tell me what a cephalopod is?" The visors and the belts looked askance at her. One man took a picture of the dark tank, and the white star of his camera flash rippled across the dark screen. "Sir, please do not," started the guide. But then we all saw what was inside the tank, and a gasp ran through the crowd.

A cluster of red-purple arms and suckers waved at us, like flames in the dark water. The octopus pushed herself off the bottom and drifted lazily through the eddies and bubbles of the water. She was a volcano, a flower, a starburst. She seemed curious to see us, but at the same time completely indifferent. She finally settled herself on the floor of her tank, where she lay like a giant curled hand and watched as everyone stared. She turned banana yellow, then silver, then an iridescent green.

"What is it?" I asked my father. I had reached for his hand without realizing it. Back then, I was always trying to avoid holding on to my parents, the old instinct to cling to them fighting against a new one, which was to seem as detached from them as possible.

"This is Dolores," he said. He had the same glazed, dumb-bright look in his eye that he got whenever he had a second beer after dinner. He was staring at Dolores with rapt attention. I had rarely seen him look at anything like that, let alone me or my mother. It was always hard to get my father's attention. Most of the time, he drifted through our house like a messy ghost, leaving behind a storm of papers and half-filled coffee cups.

"Isn't she beautiful?" he said. As if she could hear us, Dolores ballooned back up toward the top of the tank. She soared through the water like a kite, leaving a trail of bubbles in her wake.

Once the tour group had moved on, we stayed behind while my father spoke with the large, muscled man who came by to feed Dolores. His bald head was as shiny as the polished floors of the mall, and he wore navy coveralls that had the Fountain Plaza's logo embroidered on the back and on the chest. He flipped open the lid of Dolores's giant tank and casually tossed in bits of raw fish and shrimp from a bucket.

"How's she doing, Bruce?" Apa asked.

"She's fine, just fine. A little fractious this morning. She's like one of my dogs, can't seem to settle down when she thinks food's around." I watched Dolores eat, her beak stretching open like a tiny trapdoor that seemed to grow bigger and bigger as the chum disappeared down her gullet. Her eyes looked into mine with a calm friendliness. An ancient intelligence lingered behind her eyes, despite the fact that my father had told me she was younger than me.

"Hi," I said, putting my hand against the glass.

"Well, hey there, little lady," said Bruce, even though I hadn't been talking to him. "Coming to work for us someday?"

"This is Aurora, my daughter," my father said. It was odd hearing him say my English name. At home, I was always Arim, or Bae Arim, my full name, if I was in trouble.

"Like Sleeping Beauty?" Bruce said, producing a cellophane-wrapped hard candy from his pockets and winking at me.

"Like the northern lights," I said, taking the candy from him, even though I didn't want it. "It means 'goddess of the dawn' in Latin. But you can call me Ro. Everyone does."

Bruce laughed, in the way of adults who are determined to find everything kids say amusing. "Well, Ro, Dolores here certainly seems to like you just as much as she likes your daddy."

My father was watching Dolores again, a faint smile on his face. Satisfied from her meal, she seemed to be drifting along in the waters of her tank, her yellow eyes closed.

After we'd said goodbye to Bruce and Dolores, we walked through the rest of the aquarium. I liked the penguins and the seals the best, and the coral reef second, but Dolores was the one that stayed in my mind long after we'd left.

"Did you find Dolores that time you went away?" I asked him in the car on the way back.

I felt my father's surprise. I kept my face turned toward the window, avoiding his glance. "Yes, I was part of the research team that found her. Why?"

"Why did you go for so long?" I said. Without any warning, hot tears suddenly clouded my vision. I stared out the window, willing them to go away. I focused on reading the exit signs. *You are not a baby,* I told myself. Other people's cars whizzed by us, while our ancient Toyota puttered along in the right lane.

"We talked about this," he said. "I needed to work. I got that research grant, remember?"

I remembered that particular fight between my parents as if it had happened yesterday. How my mother had seemed to collapse into herself, like a dying star, when he told us. "A year?" she said, her voice a rasp. "What are we supposed to do for a year while you're gone?"

He never seemed to know what to do when my mother was upset with him, even though it seemed like she was always upset with him. "It'll be over before you know it," he said, trying desperately to smile.

In the end, of course, he'd gone, after the long campaign of silence Umma had waged failed, after the series of fights that exploded in our house once the silence ended. I took to heading straight to my bedroom when I got home from school, to avoid getting caught in the cross fire. When Apa threatened to leave Umma for good, she screamed back that he should, and I heard a shoe make contact with a wall. She told him that he'd be doing her a favor. That she regretted marrying him. That she should never have left Korea. During their fights, sometimes I covered my ears and got under the covers, and other times I pressed my ears to the walls or the floor, feeling sick to my stomach but compelled to listen to everything, so I would know if Apa really was going to leave us, if this was the end of our family. I woke up every morning in knots, waiting for him to disappear forever.

The morning he left, I watched as Umma packed his things away silently. At the airport, she handed him a sandwich in a brown bag. All around us other people hugged and wept as they held each other and said their goodbyes, as though it would be the last time they would ever see one another, while Apa stared at the ground and Umma stared straight ahead, just past him. Finally he gave me a quick hug and disappeared into the crowds beyond the security line.

While he was away, he sent us photos of his research team,

the boat he'd be living on for the next couple hundred days. He emailed us short, vivid updates. *Today we saw a whole pod of humpback whales. The sky was green tonight. Jupiter especially bright. Getting colder as we near Bering.* He sent us blurry photos of the boat, his workstation, and the ever-changing colors of the sky, which reminded me of shimmery gasoline puddles—all iridescent purples and electric greens and filmy blues swirling into one another. During his infrequent calls home, his voice on the phone became increasingly animated and harder to hear as they reached the Vortex, the crackling in the background growing louder and louder as they ventured past where cell phone towers could reach, toward what he referred to as the northern edge of the world.

At home, the year passed almost like any other, even though the knots in my stomach never subsided. I stopped eating the breakfasts Umma prepared every morning because I kept waking up with stomachaches—stabbing pains that sometimes didn't subside until noon. Umma scolded me for wasting food, though I noticed that she rarely ingested anything other than black coffee.

I was in second grade, until I was in third grade. I lost two teeth and buried them in our backyard, waiting, with bated breath, for something to grow from them. "Stupid," Yoonhee said, "you're supposed to put them under your pillow for the tooth fairy so you can get money." "Stupid yourself," I said. "The tooth fairy isn't real." We fought viciously. The next day we made up like nothing had happened. Umma bought new orange plates that I hated. Two hurricanes made landfall near us that September, and the power went out both times during dinner. Umma and I lit candles and she let me sleep in her bed, as the weather lashed itself into a fury outside. Sometimes I woke in the night to hear her crying in the bathroom—soft, muffled sobs that sounded like the whimpering of a wounded animal.

When Apa came back home, the knots in my stomach undid themselves, though I kept a close eye on him, certain he would disappear again if I didn't remain vigilant. He walked through the front door as though he'd been gone for only a week, kissed my mother on the cheek, and handed me a stuffed otter he'd probably picked up in the airport. "How are my girls?" he said.

He disappeared into his study every night for hours, to write up his findings from the trip. He wasn't allowed to share too much of what he'd discovered with us, but I stole glimpses at his research notes when he wasn't in his study. I pored over his things, hungry for any and all details of what had kept him away from us for so long.

The Bering Vortex is one of nature's puzzles, a rare example of what happens when man-made folly and natural resilience collide, began one entry. I could barely make out some of his handwritten notes, written in his large, slapdash handwriting that always slanted downward, in a mixture of Korean and English.

But there was something else in his notes, too. One day I found a faded Polaroid, clipped discreetly to the back of one of the small leather-bound notebooks he had filled during the trip. It was a picture of a woman leaning against a tree, a white woman with long, dark red hair. She was glancing away from the camera and laughing, and the way the light fell across her face and neck made the shot look like a film still.

I realized, flipping through the pages of my father's spiky handwriting, that he had also written about me. *Ro lost two teeth today. Can't believe she was so small I could hold her with one arm once.*

Then: *Crew morale strong after we found giant octopus (F). Never seen anything like her before. We've named her Dolores. Laura very interested in her color patterns, possible she's trying to communicate something to us?* Was Laura the red-haired woman? I wondered.

I came across one more picture of Laura and my father, taken presumably by one of the other crew members. They were standing on the deck of the ship, against the strangest backdrop I had ever seen. The sky behind them was an opalescent, shimmering green. It almost seemed to breathe in the picture, and without thinking, I touched the photo at the place where the sky met the water, which was a deep ruby-purple. I wondered what it would be like to swim in those waters, to feel the swirling currents and eddies all around me while sea creatures the size of Dolores swam just a few hundred meters below the surface. The waters of the Bering Vortex were not safe for humans to swim in for long. Scientists still didn't know what prolonged exposures to the Vortex's waters could do to the human body, what mutations the chemicals could cause. Did Dolores miss being back in her waters? Did she have a father, a mother, a family?

In the photo, Apa's arm was around Laura in a kind of half embrace. She was smiling and her mouth was open, like she was about to say something to the photographer, but Apa was looking into her eyes, his face turned toward her, like he couldn't bear to look away for even a second. I had never seen my parents so much as hold hands. I resisted the urge to tear the photo and instead slipped it back into the envelope I had found it in. Afterward, my hands burned, as though I had dipped them in acid.

Apa hummed tunelessly while he switched lanes. His eyes caught mine in the rearview mirror. "Now wasn't that something?" he said. He was smiling from ear to ear, as though he'd forgotten that he had taken me out of the house and to the aquarium purely to get away from my mother and her rage. I nodded, even though he couldn't see me, even though I wanted to ask him now, as I hadn't back when I'd found his journal, who Laura was, if he was still seeing her. It was so like my father to not just try and act like nothing was wrong, but to actually come to believe his own version of the truth.

CHAPTER 3

After talking to Yoonhee, I have trouble focusing for the rest of the day. I pull out my phone, fighting the old impulse to call Tae. *He's not yours anymore,* I tell myself.

During my lunch break, I visit the Tropical Reef Habitat hall. The sight of the fish, their muted reds and blues and oranges gliding past the rocks and reeds as if they are all on their way to somewhere, usually calms me. Their scales glisten in the dim light, and the sounds of people talking and walking by seem muted here.

The walls of the tanks extend almost up to the ceiling. It's dark, the blue glow of the water the only thing lighting up the long corridor. This was Tae's favorite part of the aquarium. When I brought him here early on in our relationship, he had been impressed, even paying attention during the guided tour led by Francine.

"This exhibit is meant to represent the Blue Corner of Palau, in Micronesia," Francine said. "It's one of the most beautiful diving spots in the world."

"I'll take you there someday," Tae said to me. "I'm serious," he said when I rolled my eyes at him. "I've always wanted to go diving." We never ended up going, but every once in a while he'd send me articles or photos of the Blue Corner, until he became an expert on why it was one of the most sought-after diving spots in the world. "It's the currents," he told me. "The smaller fish travel along with the currents, which attracts predators. You just dive in and drift toward the bottom, and you get to see all of these fish following each other." It was something I both loved and found annoying about Tae, his tendency to get obsessed with something once he decided he was interested in it, until he considered himself an authority on the subject. It was what made him a good teacher and an occasionally infuriating boyfriend.

I watch a gray reef shark cut through the water like a slow knife, while a gasp goes up through a group of kids. A few of the braver ones walk up to the tank and take turns touching the glass as the shark moves past them, before chickening out and running back to the main group. Their teacher gives them a warning look, but they don't seem to care. Two of the girls hang back from the others, whispering and giggling to each other.

"That one's me," the taller and prettier of the girls announces, pointing at a blue angelfish as it swims by. Its pectoral fins dance in the water like cat whiskers. "Now you have to pick one."

"Can I be that one?" the shorter girl asks. She points at a small zebra fish darting behind the blue angelfish, its black and white stripes shimmering.

"No, that's so boring!" says the first girl. She spies another angelfish, a pale gold ghost. "That's you," she says triumphantly.

They watch as the two angelfish float past each other, change course, and begin swimming in the same direction. "Look, they're friends," she says. "Just like us." And at this, the second girl smiles, her small face aglow in the dark of the hall.

When Yoonhee and I were teenagers, old enough to come to the mall on our own, we'd hang out for hours in the food court downstairs, splurging on endless cups of frozen yogurt. We'd pick out people in the crowds and make up stories about them to each other.

Yoonhee always picked couples. "She's upset, but she's trying not to say anything," she'd say about a couple in their thirties with a shopping bag from Zales, both picking at their sandwiches and not talking to each other. "She thought he was going to surprise her with a ring, but it turned out he just wanted advice on a present for his mom."

"What about that guy?" I asked, pointing at an old man with liver spots on his hands, dressed in a blue sweater and bright white sneakers. He was alone and didn't seem to be waiting for anyone or even eating. He was just sitting there, his hands folded on the table in front of him, staring straight ahead at nothing.

"He's a widower. His wife died a few years ago, and he comes here to remember her because she used to love coming to the mall just to look around. They wore matching sneakers to power walk and tracked their steps together," Yoonhee said, sighing at the imagined tragedy of her own made-up story.

"Is that all you think about? Love and relationships?" I said.

Yoonhee was always going on in those days about being single and wanting a boyfriend.

"I mean, yeah," she said, her mascaraed eyes widening. "Relationships are the most important thing in the world. Don't you want to get married someday and have kids?"

"I don't know," I said. "Maybe the married part, but kids—it seems like a lot of work to have one."

"Guess you'll just have to be the fun aunt to mine, then," Yoonhee said airily. Yoonhee was the youngest of three girls, and her house felt like an endless slumber party. Whenever I got home after being at her house, our own felt that much quieter and emptier. Yoonhee's mom was incredibly glamorous. I almost never saw her without a full face of makeup. While Yoonhee and her sisters didn't look exactly like her or each other, they all bore a striking resemblance to one another, particularly around their eyes and noses. Together, the four of them looked like Russian nesting dolls. Yoonhee seemed to fight with her sisters a lot, but I envied their closeness, the constant laughter and shouting and teasing that seemed to go on at her house. It was a welcome change from home, where the near-constant silence was punctured only by my parents' fighting, when they exploded at each other with all the things they didn't know how to say.

When Yoonhee and I got ready for our senior prom at her house, her sister Yoonkyung did our hair and makeup, curling our eyelashes, dusting glitter over our eyelids and across our cheekbones, and spraying our hair into curlicues and ringlets. I was hesitant about the glitter and the curls. I never wore makeup and was convinced I'd look foolish, as if I was trying too hard, but Yoonhee was adamant, swearing up and down that she would make us both stay at home if I didn't at least try to make an effort.

"See?" Yoonhee said when our transformations were complete. We stared at each other in her bedroom mirror. "We look so good."

Yoonhee was like that. She always had a way of making me feel like I was beautiful by association, and that beauty wasn't something magical the way I'd always thought it was, but something that could be attained with just a little bit of polish and elbow grease.

I decide to leave work a little early. Before I sign out, I linger in front of Dolores's tank, watching her curl herself around her second puzzle. Not for the first time, I wonder what she thinks of me, of the aquarium. Does she ever get tired of being so confined? Does she think of trying to escape? I read on the internet once about an octopus in New Zealand who had managed to move the lid of his tank, sneak out through a small opening, and slither down a drainpipe to the open ocean. "You could probably do that," I tell Dolores. "If you really put your mind to it." She narrows her eyes at me, as if to say, *Don't you think I've thought about it?*

In the mall parking garage, my phone buzzes. It's a text from my cousin Rachel—a photo of her kid, Hailie, in a sea of cardboard boxes in the middle of her living room. She's sitting in the largest one, a huge grin splayed across her little face. "I told her it's a spaceship," said the accompanying text. "Call me when you get a sec?"

Rachel is six years older than me. A few months ago, she left her husband and moved out of their three-story house in Tenafly to a small apartment across town. She shocked everyone when she did it, because divorces just don't hap-

pen in our family. You find a way to deal or you resign yourself to being unhappy in silence forever, at least according to
my mother, who was scandalized by the whole thing. "You
can't just turn your back on a marriage," she'd said. As if her
own husband hadn't done that, too, as if people didn't do it
every day.

I get into my old Camry and sink into the heat of it, melting into my seat. It's only April, but it's sweltering outside. I
remember springs when I was a kid being cool, chilly even.
For a moment, I pretend I don't have a skeletal system, that my
body is rapidly turning into warm liquid, which isn't too hard
to imagine. Some days, wandering through the aquarium's
blue halls, I start feeling like maybe I don't exist, like my body
is just this translucent membrane for water and light to rush
through, day in and day out, just like all the other creatures
here. It's felt that way ever since Tae and I broke up. I have
to remind myself to go to sleep, to wake up, to eat, to keep
breathing in and out.

I call Rachel while driving home, and she picks up on my
second try. The background noise sounds like she's inside a
carnival, bouncy electronic music, probably from the TV.

"Haven't heard from you in a while, missy," Rachel says. I
picture her wide smile, her nose ring flashing at me. The jury
is still out, according to Rachel, on what broke her mother, my
aunt, more—the divorce or the celebratory nose ring she got
after leaving her husband.

"Hey, Rach," I say.

"You sound off. Did you delete that space app yet? You
know it's not good for you to keep looking at that. You guys
need a clean break."

"Deleted it yesterday," I lie.

"So what's up? How's work?"

"They're selling Dolores," I say, then wish I hadn't, because the next thing she says is, "Who?" and now I have to explain to her what I mean, even though that's the last thing I want to do right now.

"Dolores. The octopus Apa found." I bite my lip. I never got good at talking about Apa after he disappeared.

There's a pause. Something clatters to the floor while Rachel curses under her breath. "Shit. Sorry. I'm trying to do ten things at once and doing them all badly, as per usual. So they're selling her? Can they do that?"

"They've already found a buyer. Some rich dick building his own home aquarium."

"Maybe it's a good thing if he can afford to give her a nicer place to live? You're always complaining about them cutting costs."

"But this is where she's lived the last decade of her life." It feels like there's a hole in my throat and my voice is leaking out of it.

"Hold on a sec, sorry. Hailie, put that down. I said, put that down." When Rachel comes back, she sighs and puts on the Class Mom voice, the one she uses when teachers or other parents try to talk down to her or Hailie. "Okay. That sucks. I'm sorry. Do you want advice, or do you want to vent?"

This is one of the many things I love about Rachel—she never tries to make things seem better than they are or does the thing Tae always did, where he'd ask me a bunch of questions about whatever I was upset about, to try to "find a solution." Sometimes the last thing you want to do is figure out a solution to a problem, especially when the problem should never have existed in the first place.

"I don't know. Got a half million lying around you could donate to the aquarium?" I say. "Apparently they might close."

"You think I'd still be living here if I had that kind of money?" she says.

"How are you? How's Hailie?" I ask. There's a brief silence on the other end.

"We're okay." Her voice is lower, like she's ducked into a hallway or a side room. "She keeps asking when we're going to go home and see Daddy, so you know, that's been heartbreaking."

Rachel's ex-husband, Simon, is a surgeon, and according to her, taking people apart and digging into their insides all day must have warped his mind. When I asked her what went wrong, all she could bring herself to say was, "There's no reasoning with someone who thinks everything can be taken apart and put back together again."

They fought constantly through all six years of their marriage, until one day he pushed her in front of Hailie, who was four at the time. The next day Rachel packed a bag and took Hailie and the car and left him, just like that. "I don't want my baby growing up thinking that's okay," she said. She's still embroiled in ongoing proceedings with Simon because he doesn't want to pay alimony and is insisting on full custody, even though he doesn't have the time to look after anyone but himself.

"Auntie Ro!" Hailie screams in the background. "Today I learned how to make a fart with my armpit!" I smile as Rachel tells her to hush. "Don't interrupt," she tells her amid a cascade of fart noises.

"As you can hear, we're doing fine otherwise. I just don't want this whole thing to mess her up or give her daddy issues. I don't want to be dealing with that when she's a teenager."

"It's kind of inevitable, you know. You screw them up, even when you love them."

"Maybe so, but that's no kind of attitude to have about raising a human being. I have to at least try to do better than what I got," she says. Her voice sounds brittle, and I start to feel shitty before she shifts into Class Mom mode again. "Listen, I texted because I need a favor. Can you watch Hailie on Saturday? I have something I have to take care of."

"Sure," I say. I'm not very good with kids, but I like Hailie. She's a little weirdo, which I can appreciate. I hear her making fart noises in the background while also, it seems, pretending to be a bus.

"Great. I'll drop her off then," Rachel says, relief flooding her voice. "Have you eaten?" I suppress the urge to tell Rachel she sounds like one of our moms now, asking what we've been eating or are about to eat. It's one of the first things Umma always says to me, instead of "How are you?" "Have you eaten?" is code for so many things in Korean families.

I pull up at a stoplight, and in the car next to me, there's a couple, a guy and a girl, sharing a bag of fries. Their windows are rolled down. The girl is driving and telling the guy some story while he laughs. I remember how good it felt to make Tae laugh. How sometimes I felt like I'd do anything just to hear it, to watch that smile break across his face.

"Ro?" Rachel says. "You there?"

"I'll call you back," I say. "I just remembered I have a thing."

"A thing," she says. "Okay. Listen, don't worry about Dolores. She'll be fine. I want you to focus on you right now."

"I'm okay, Rach. I'm doing much better."

"Yeah, right. You didn't even eat lunch, did you?"

I haven't, I realize, and my stomach mutters something sour

at me. She sighs on the other end. "Go eat," she says gently. "I'll talk to you later."

Back at home, it's so humid in my apartment I can hardly breathe once I walk in through the front door. I open a window and feel the soggy evening air slap my face. One of my neighbors from across the way has their air conditioner going. Every year, it feels like we have to start preparing for the heat a little earlier than usual.

I consider the contents of my fridge, which holds little more than a few condiment bottles, some beer, and some old leftovers I haven't looked at in probably weeks. I think about getting into the tub with a cup full of ice and gin and forgoing dinner entirely.

I used to wonder if we would take better care of our bodies if our skin was transparent, if every little thing we did and said and ate was observable. If every hurtful or careless thing we ever said to one another manifested itself visually in the body. Would we be any different than how we are now? Would we do more to protect each other, ourselves?

Before, Tae was the one who reminded me to eat. He used to cook elaborate meals at my apartment, bringing over ingredients from markets he'd had to go all the way to the other side of town for. "You don't have any spices," he'd say incredulously. "What kind of Korean person are you?"

He'd commandeer my kitchen, coax my temperamental oven to life. I don't know how he made the things he made over my tiny grease-flecked stove—curries, stews, soups, even barbecue. "Cooking's not so hard," he said. "You just have to know how to improvise and how to trust the process. That's what'll give you the confidence to try new things, throw random ingredients together, trust that they'll work out. And if not, you can always start over."

It felt like graduating to some next level of adulthood once I started living alone, even though it was only because Yoonhee had moved out to live with her boyfriend and I was staying in the leaky, cramped unit we'd been sharing for years. But it was Yoonhee's plants, framed art pieces, and rugs throughout the apartment that had made it feel like a home, and now that they're gone, the apartment feels smaller, worse. The one thing she did leave me was the ancient yellow couch that she'd inherited from one of her older sisters, which had been the scene of many a drunken wine-and-movie night together. There are more than a few mystery stains and blotches all over it, and it's hideously uncomfortable, but I like the buttery yellow color of the upholstery, the way it seems to absorb all the sunlight in the room and reflect it back to me.

I decide to microwave a freezer-burned Hot Pocket that I unearth from behind a bag of pot stickers in my freezer. I heat it up on a plate, watching it turn inside my microwave like it's on a merry-go-round, and burn my tongue on the melted cheese. I sit on the couch and thumb through Arc 4's Instagram. There are two new pictures of Tae, one of him tending to some seedlings in their greenhouse and another of him running on the treadmill. *Tae Park, one of our youngest crew members, gets in a few miles before breakfast.*

I consider pivoting to fitness, just for the hell of it. Becoming the kind of girl Tae probably always wanted me to be, the kind of girl who gets in a few miles before breakfast and knows how to cook and take care of herself and isn't so consumed by her own bad brain that she forgets to turn the oven off or wash her moldy towels or pick up her dirty laundry off the floor. He was often appalled by the way I lived, but I think he secretly liked that I was such a disaster compared to him. I was a project he could focus on, a mess he could clean up. Sometimes I think he loved me the way a mathematician might love a particularly complicated equation.

"You were more than that for him," Yoonhee said to me when I first confessed this to her, that I thought I was just a novelty for him. She pointed out all the things I'd told her about, how I helped him with problems like misbehaving kids in his classes, listened to his band's demos and offered my thoughts, soothed him back to sleep when he woke from night terrors, which he had often.

I make a half-hearted sharktini that's mostly gin and drink it in what feels like one fizzy gulp. I make another and then another. Outside, the dull roar of the highway interrupts my thoughts and I think about my mother saying how the women in our family have no luck with men, and about how I can't believe it's been almost ten years since Yoonhee and I first moved into this apartment together. How the first time Tae sat on the yellow couch, he laughed at how uncomfortable it was, but then later pulled me close while we were nestled on it and kissed me.

I plug in my headphones and listen to the last thing I have from him, a voice mail he left me just before his plane took off. "Ro," he says, his voice calm and resonant, the way it always was when he was about to try and have a difficult conversation with me, "I hope someday you'll forgive me, but I understand if you don't want to. Be good to yourself."

I stare up at the ceiling. I count the number of stain marks

I see, including one dark mark that looks an awful lot like Dolores. The last thing I picture before I fall asleep is Dolores crawling out of her tank, all eight of her arms moving over one another across the shining tiles of the aquarium, headed toward the open sea.

CHAPTER 4

Twenty-one years earlier

One afternoon, a few months after that first visit to the aquarium, Umma came to pick me up from school. I could tell from the way she gripped the steering wheel and stared straight ahead when she told me to get in the car and stop dawdling that something was wrong. It was October, and I was holding a gluey paper pumpkin, covered in orange and gold glitter, that Umma took one look at and ordered me to put away in my backpack. "You are not getting glitter all over this car, Arim," she said.

I knew better than to talk back or protest when Umma was like this. Umma is small—she always made a point of telling me that her waistline and wrists were as slender as mine—but she expands when she gets angry. Even the neatly combed strands of her bobbed hair crackle with energy when she yells, using the full power of her clear soprano to express her displeasure with me or Apa, about how slow or lazy or selfish we are. Umma often lumped my failings in with Apa's whenever she really got going, so eventually it was hard to disentangle which mistakes were mine and which were Apa's, the fault lines in our personalities intersecting with one another until they formed a spiderweb of cracks and fissures, a radial network of sins.

The ride home from school usually took less than ten minutes, but that day it felt longer. We drove past the park, where I often rode around aimlessly for hours on my bike on the weekends; past the street that had four pale blue houses all in a row; the laundromat run by the Chos, who kept a jar out front full of chalky strawberry candies wrapped in foil; the liquor store that always seemed to be open, its parking lot comically large in comparison to the store. Umma didn't even bother trying not to pass the Fountain Plaza, and I watched as it flashed past my window, wondering what Dolores the octopus was doing.

Apa had told me that Dolores rarely slept. Instead of closing her eyes and drifting along in the currents and eddies of her tank the way I had imagined she might, she was the first octopus of her kind who rarely seemed to require any kind of REM activity. She was almost always doing something, he said, even when she was resting. She seemed to enjoy floating, suspending herself in the water or crouching among the rocks at the bottom, as though she was playing hide-and-seek with herself. He had never seen an octopus with such a capacity for play. "We think it might be because of where she grew up," he said. "The Bering Vortex is a fascinating intersection of all the harshest environmental conditions you could think of, but it's led to the birth and flourishing of a lot of creatures like Dolores—beautiful anomalies."

"What's an anomaly?" I asked.

"It's anything that deviates from what's expected. That defies understanding or logic." He made me write it down on an index card and practice spelling and saying it out loud, the way he always did whenever I asked him what a word meant. He was self-conscious about his accent, the way people heard his r's and l's and his inflections first before they could hear what he was saying. He had three degrees—a bachelor's in biology, a master's in economics, and a PhD in marine biology—but he would never be listened to in the same way his white colleagues (who, he never failed to point out, had all gone to inferior institutions) would. "It's not enough to be as good as them, Arim," he always said. "You have to be the best."

At the end of Sycamore Street, where we would normally have made a left and then a right to get home, Umma suddenly wheeled the car toward the right lane, pissing off a white Jeep and a blue Subaru in the process. "Umma?" I said. "Home's the other way." But Umma ignored me, turning in the opposite direction toward the highway.

I sat back and watched as Umma began going faster, merging onto the highway like a pro. Normally Umma was timid and indecisive behind the wheel, but she was driving like a race-car driver, speeding and swerving until we were careening down the river of traffic that was Route 4 just before rush hour. "Where are we going?" I asked.

"I need to think," Umma said. There was a strange light in her eyes, as though she was excited about something. But it was a queasy-making excitement, a feeling perched on a knife's edge, right up against something so big and so overwhelming that she seemed afraid it would catch up to her if she slowed down at all. She maneuvered into the left lane, tailgating a silver Benz until it got out of our way, and then floored it until we saw signs for the George Washington Bridge.

I began to grow frightened. "Umma, we have to slow down. We're going to get pulled over," I said. Sure enough, red and blue lights began to dance in the rearview mirror, and we heard the angry howl of sirens. Umma muttered something under her breath, and for a few terrifying seconds, I thought she would ignore the sirens and continue gunning it until we wound up in the papers. LOCAL WOMAN CAUGHT SPEEDING WITH CHILD ON BOARD, I imagined the headlines saying, with our faces in black and white. Then Umma would go to jail, and I would be sent away to military school or an orphanage or wherever else they put the children of mothers who had broken the law, and somehow it would all be my fault.

But Umma finally brought the car to a stop, pulling over onto the shoulder of the road. We were by one of those improbably beautiful grassy medians, dotted with late-blooming wildflowers, their yellow and pink and purple heads bobbing among the tall weeds. I often wondered if people ever picnicked on them and what would happen if you tried to. I was drawn to small, unlikely pockets of greenery, little bubbles of secret solitude and beauty.

As the cop made his way out of the vehicle, Umma flipped the sun visor down and checked the mirror, investigating the shine of her teeth and swiping off some lipstick that had trailed past her upper lip. She smoothed the hairs back from her face just as he tapped against her window. "License and registration," he intoned, his deep voice making the glass vibrate. I stared straight ahead, my face burning, as Umma rolled the window down. The back of my neck prickled and the contents of my stomach wriggled like a basket of eels. I hated getting in trouble, the scrutiny and embarrassment of it.

"Of course," Umma said, the frenetic urgency of her earlier

movements gone now as she reached into the glove compartment and pulled her wallet out of her purse. The gold bracelet she always wore, a present from my grandmother, brushed against my knee.

"Ma'am, your license is expired by four months," the cop said in a bored tone after he had thumbed through the papers. He had a bristly mustache that reminded me of a sea slug Apa had shown me in the aquarium.

"My husband usually makes sure to remind me of those things," Umma said. "He's away." I stared at Umma. Why was she lying?

"Away, huh?" the cop said, the bored amusement in his voice falling away to reveal something murkier that made the eels in my stomach hiss. He leaned farther into the window, his mirrored sunglasses reflecting back tiny replicas of Umma and me. I could see him noticing the pulse jumping in Umma's throat, her small hands. His eyes traveled back to her face, took in her features. I had never thought of Umma as being anything other than my mother, but I could see now, through the cop's eyes, that she could pass for a much younger woman. Suddenly the straightforward beauty of her face, which I had always taken for granted—her long, narrow nose and large eyes, her full mouth, none of which I had inherited—felt dangerous.

"Yes," she said, and it was as if she'd made some kind of decision. She straightened her spine and smiled. "I get confused sometimes when he's not around."

"You should be more careful," the cop said.

"It's because of me," I said, butting in before Umma could reply. I didn't like where the conversation was going, didn't like that they seemed to be talking now about things I didn't understand. The cop turned to look at me. "I told my mom I really had to go the bathroom. It's not her fault."

"Do you have any idea," he said, ignoring me and fixing his gaze back on Umma, "how fast you were going?"

Umma shook her head, like an abashed schoolgirl. I wanted to vomit.

"You were doing 85. In a 60-mile-per-hour lane," said the cop. Outside, the sky was a series of pink and orange smears, and blue and black and white lines of other cars on their way home streaked by. He began to reach for his notepad, to write out what our crimes were on it.

"Please," Umma said, "can't you just let me off with a warning?" Her teeth glinted back at us in the cop's sunglasses, and she began to finger the gold cross that hung on her necklace, something I knew she did whenever she was trying to get in touch with God, asking him to intervene. It was always like this with Umma. The only person she ever let inside was God. I felt abandoned whenever she closed her eyes to talk to him.

"Everyone else was going fast, too," I said. "Why didn't you stop them?"

"Arim, shut your mouth," Umma warned me in Korean.

The cop lowered his sunglasses. His eyes were surprisingly small, the whites slightly bloodshot and his irises a watery blue so pale they made me uncomfortable. The expression they held was one of complete and utter blankness, with a layer of watchfulness just below the surface. "You should teach your kid to be quiet when adults are speaking," he said.

In the silence that followed, I thought I could hear the sound of my own blood coursing through my body.

"I understand. It won't happen again." She said the words in her lightly accented English, speaking slowly so that he wouldn't ask her to repeat herself, the way people always did. "We're sorry to inconvenience you," she said.

The cop studied her, and one of the corners of his mouth tilted upward in an approximation of a smile. His mirrored sunglasses went back up over his red nose, covering up those terrible eyes. "Fine," he said, sighing as though he were doing us a great favor. "I'll let you off with a warning this time. You people are good at following rules, right?"

I didn't understand what he meant, but Umma's smile stayed on, like it was painted. It was the same smile she wore whenever someone called during one of her and Apa's fights. She would iron out all the ragged rage and pain in her voice and answer the phone brightly, cheerfully, as though she hadn't just been telling him how much she wanted to die, how much she wished they had never come to this country.

"Make sure I don't catch you out here speeding again," the cop said. He patted the top of the car before he walked away, his gait heavy and measured.

Umma rolled the window back up. We sat there for a while, even after the cop peeled off back into traffic. She slowly turned on the ignition, and as the engine roared to life, I wondered what the cop had meant by *you people*. Did he mean our family? I wanted to ask Umma, but I knew that she either wouldn't want to answer or wouldn't know how to.

Umma steered the car back onto the road, and this time we stayed in the right lane. Umma was still so distracted from our encounter with the cop that she forgot to turn off her turn signal, paying attention to the clicking only when I pointed it out to her. We drove on as the sky grew darker, from pink to a grayish lavender, punctuated only by the amber glow of the streetlights.

She took an exit into a park that faced the Hudson River, just before the lanes leading onto the bridge and into New York City. She stopped the car on a hill overlooking the rest of the park, the well-manicured greenery falling away to reveal the wide sky and water beyond. I had been to New York City only once before, to see the lighting of the tree at Rockefeller Center on my birthday. It was when I was much younger, young enough to think that the tree was being lit especially for me. It still got cold during the winters then, sometimes.

Umma and Apa had argued about paying for parking. By the time we had wormed our way into the crowds around the rink, our breath like clouds in the late fall air, they were angry with each other, but their bickering had ceased during that electric moment when the tree was lit up, its branches filled with thousands and thousands of multicolored stars. Afterward, we got big bowls of hot oxtail soup in Koreatown to warm ourselves up, and on the drive back home, I fell asleep in the back seat to the sound of their voices, soft and amicable again.

Umma got out of the car without looking at me. She walked over to a picnic table overlooking the view and sat down. She folded her hands, her fingers interlacing with one another, and stared out across the grassy field that opened up below us. I stayed inside the car, watching her. I wanted to get out, to tell Umma that we needed to get back in the car and turn around and go home before Apa came back from work, but I felt as though I couldn't move, the seat belt pinning me in place.

A group of joggers passed by, dressed in bright-colored exercise clothes, and a line of bicycles followed soon afterward, everyone getting in one last lap before night fell. I opened the car door. "Umma?" I called.

Umma straightened up, startled, as though she had forgotten I was there. Her eyes were red, but her face was calm. "What's wrong?" I asked.

Umma finally looked at me then. "It's nothing," she said. "Let's go home."

The erratic energy that had propelled Umma earlier seemed to seep out of her during the drive home. I watched her the whole time, uncertain of what to do or say. I felt I was too young to be of any use and too old to try to act like nothing had happened.

Umma scolded me if my hair was parted on the wrong side, complained incessantly if I left my socks on the floor, reminded me constantly that anywhere I went I would have to be well-behaved, so that people wouldn't form a bad opinion of our family. The woman Umma had been earlier that afternoon—bold, reckless, even flirtatious—was someone I didn't recognize.

As soon as we got home, Umma locked herself in Apa's study, where I heard her rummaging through his drawers and file folders. I stood outside the door, more frightened by Umma's silence than I had been by her wild driving. Had Apa forgotten to pay the bills again? Or was it something else?

Apa arrived home just an hour later, his cheery "I'm home!" booming through the house like a clock striking the wrong time. "Where's your mother, Acorn?" he said when he saw me sitting alone at the kitchen table, trying to do my homework.

"She's in your office," I said, feeling guilty.

A frown creased Apa's forehead. But he didn't say anything and instead started boiling water for tea. He was a tea fanatic, drinking at least ten cups of strong black tea a day. There were used tea bags all over our house, because Apa would dunk one in for a minute at a time and fish it out. He left them on old napkins, magazines, newspapers, and sometimes even the windowsill, claiming he was "saving the tea bag for later." It drove Umma crazy.

"You're home," Umma said. We both looked up to see her standing in the doorway of the kitchen. She was holding Apa's travel journal, the one I had found and read snippets of.

"Have you been going through my things?" Apa said. But he looked like a kid caught doing something he shouldn't have been, his eyes wide and scared.

"How could you do this to me? To our family?" Umma said. I closed my eyes and heard something fall to the floor and shatter. She had thrown the journal across the kitchen and it had knocked something over.

Apa's face turned in on itself. I could see him thinking what to say next, how to react. "You've finally gone crazy," he said. "You don't know what you're talking about. You know nothing of my life outside this house."

"I'll leave you," Umma said in a high, thin voice that scraped my heart. She was crying now. "I'll leave you if you don't stop seeing her."

"You're crazy," Apa kept repeating.

"I'll go back to Korea," Umma said. "I'll leave you."

"You think you'd get that far on your own?" Apa said, a coldness in his voice that I had never heard before. "Just try it. You don't even know how to book your own airplane ticket."

Umma was going to leave us both, and it was all my fault. I should have hidden my father's journal, burned it, thrown it out. I began to cry.

"Now look what you've done," Apa said. "Are you happy now? Acting like this in front of our daughter. *Michin saram.*" It was like if he kept on calling Umma a crazy person, he wouldn't have to pay attention to what she was saying.

I got up and left the house, clattering out the front door, my sneakers barely on. Just before the door slammed shut, I could hear Apa calling my name, but neither of them came after me. I sprang open the gate into our backyard.

One of my favorite places in the world was a corner behind the shed in our backyard that held rusting bikes and old appliances, which normally went untouched except on the rare days when Umma got Apa to mow the lawn. One day I ventured behind the shed while playing and found, to my delight, an old tree stump on which were carved the letters *J + P 4EVER,* left over from whoever had lived there before us. With my fingers, I traced the letters carved into the stump, wondering who J and P had been. I didn't tell my parents about the discovery, and I visited the crawl space behind the shed whenever I could, spreading out a blanket on top of the stump and curling up in the green shade of the mugunghwa bush next to the shed, which Umma had planted when she and Apa first moved in. The mugunghwa was the national flower of Korea, Apa told me, and its name meant "eternal blossom."

I sat down on the *J + P* stump, hugging my knees and shivering in the dark. Two runnels of moisture began to leak out of my nose and mingled with my tears. I fought back sobs and tried to focus on my breath, the way Apa had taught me to when he showed me how to swim, by drawing air into my nose and releasing it through my mouth, as though I was dipping my head in and out of water. Gradually I began to calm down and to feel drowsy. I curled myself up onto the stump and fell asleep.

When I woke, the moon was high and white in the sky, and Apa was calling my name. I stood up, pins and needles in my arms and legs. "I'm here," I said, emerging from behind the shed.

Relief broke in Apa's voice. "What on earth were you doing back there?"

I looked at him. "I'm not stupid, you know," I said.

My anger surprised him. "I never said you were," he said.

I wanted to ask if they were okay now. If he was going to stop seeing that woman. But I didn't, and instead I crossed my arms and stared straight at the wall behind Apa's head, the way I'd seen Umma do so many times before.

Apa sighed. "It's time for you to go to bed."

"I haven't even had dinner yet," I pointed out.

In the kitchen, the smashed remnants of Apa's favorite tea mug were on the floor. It was the lumpy green one I had painted years ago for Father's Day, with *World's Best Dad* in dripping yellow letters around its circumference. When I saw the fragments on the floor, I felt like crying all over again, but I held myself together as I watched Apa sweep them up, muttering to himself.

"Where's Umma?" I said. Normally, after a fight, Umma would lock herself in the bathroom or in the bedroom, blast Beethoven, and not come out until she was ready, her face as placid and unruffled as though nothing had happened. But I didn't hear the familiar sound of water filling the bathtub or the usual strains of classical music coming from upstairs.

"She's going away for a few days," Apa replied.

"What?" I said.

Apa gathered me in his arms as I drummed my fists against him. "I hate you. You made her leave," I said.

"She's just staying at a hotel for a few days," he said. "Now calm down."

"You made her leave," I repeated. "You're a bad husband and a bad dad." To my surprise and delight, the look on Apa's face when I said those words was one of pain. "You're a bad man," I said, relishing my newfound ability to hurt my parents in the same way they so often hurt each other and me.

"That's enough," Apa said. "You can go to bed without any dinner at all if you're going to behave that way."

So I did. I put myself to bed, changing out of my school clothes and folding them neatly, slipping into my pajamas, brushing my teeth, and even remembering to brush my hair one hundred times, the way Umma had taught me to, to make it shine. "You and I are blessed with thick hair, but it's important to take care of it," she always said. "It'll get bushy if we don't."

Umma was gone for a week. I carpooled home from school during that week with a girl named Amy who lived one street over and whom I didn't like, because she was always asking me stupid questions about homework and why I didn't have any brothers or sisters. Amy had two younger brothers, one older sister, a dog, and a guinea pig. "You don't have any pets at all?" Amy said.

"I have a pet octopus," I told her. "Her name is Dolores and she is rainbow-colored and as big as a house."

Amy's eyes narrowed. "I don't believe you," she said. "No one's pet can be as big as a house."

I shrugged. "She doesn't live in my house. She lives in the aquarium, and she's super smart. She's so smart she could probably eat you if she wanted."

"Let's be nice to each other, girls," Amy's mother said from the driver's seat. Amy sulked for the rest of the car ride home.

After they dropped me off, I would let myself in and fix myself a sandwich, watch TV, and do homework. I kept the TV on low so that I could listen for the phone ringing or the doorbell, just in case Umma came back. The house felt emptier without her. All Apa and I ate was pizza and Chinese takeout, and I felt tired all the time. *Please come back,* I thought, staring at the phone or at the front door and thinking of all the ways I would be better, be so good that she would never leave us again. *Please, please, please.*

As for the shattered mug on the kitchen floor, despite Apa's best efforts at cleaning up the mess, we continued finding small ceramic shards here and there as the days went by. No matter how closely we looked or how thoroughly we swept or vacuumed, there were always more tiny pieces of green shrapnel hidden in the corners of the kitchen, like the remnants of a battle or the artifacts of a lost civilization.

CHAPTER 5

The next morning, I wake up feeling awful. I assume it's the alcohol I consumed until I remember what Yoonhee told me yesterday about selling Dolores. I push the thought to the bottom of my brain and drift back to sleep, until my various phone alarms start screaming at me to wake up.

After hitting snooze, I'm blearily brushing my teeth when I see a text message from my mom, a long string of Korean, flash across my screen. I don't want to read it, to sit and parse through the letters that always take me a few minutes before I can fully comprehend their meaning, so I don't. *If it was an emergency, she'd call,* I tell myself to try and assuage the wrenching in my gut that inevitably happens whenever I think about my mother.

I rush through the rest of my morning routine—splashing cold water on my face to look more alive, slathering on toner and serum and whatever else Yoonhee made me buy a year ago when she insisted I couldn't just slap body lotion on my and comprehend at about the level of a fourth grader, which is good enough most days.

I study the blocky letters, the circles and squares and lines making up the paragraphs, until they come into focus and resolve themselves into words. I make out, after the first long preamble of words about the weather, how work has been, and which of her friends at church are fighting with which other friends, that she wants me to come over for dinner. *I hope you're doing well,* the text ends, as formal as an email. *It would be nice to see you for dinner if you're available later this week. Let me know . . .*

I don't want to talk to her. The thought rises to the top of my mind, like a whale breaching on a far-off horizon, unmistakable and un-ignorable. At the same time, guilt coats the inside of my mouth as I sip my coffee. The guilt sits on my tongue like a thick oily sheen, a reminder that nothing I do or say can free me from my parents, no matter how far away or how gone they feel, until it chokes everything else inside me. I often thought, growing up, that if my mother and I were to meet as two people around the same age, completely unconnected to each other, we would not get along. She would go her way and I would go mine, and in essence, this was how things went once Apa disappeared. "You are your father's child," Umma always said when I was growing up. When I was little, she would hold her hand up to mine, comparing my thick fingers to her own slim ones, and say, "You are nothing like me."

I ignore the text, pour the rest of my coffee into a mug, and leave the apartment. I'm about to be late, and Carl has made it abundantly clear that despite his friendly I'm-a-nice-guy attitude, he doesn't appreciate what he referred to, in my most recent annual review, as my "consistent tardiness."

It's unexpectedly beautiful and still out. The sky is a bright blue so sweet it almost hurts to look at it, and unlike yesterday, there is just the tiniest bite in the air, almost enough to make me go back in and get a light jacket, but I decide to savor the chill. We don't get many real spring days like this one anymore.

As my car starts and I feel the coffee work its magic, peeling back the layers of tired from my brain and massaging my skull back into working order, I feel my phone buzz in my pocket, with another text. This time it's from Yoonhee. *Do you want to get lunch later today?* I don't answer her, either. Instead, I put the car into gear and enjoy the feeling of my driving instincts taking over, easing my Camry into the stream of traffic already piling up on the avenue. It's almost nice, to feel like a small part of something so much larger than myself, even if it's just rush-hour traffic.

I bought the car a while back, when Yoonhee moved out and I couldn't use her Accord anymore to run errands or ask her to drop me off or pick me up at places. She complained about the fact that I always forgot to chip in for gas, but I think she liked being able to commute and make grocery runs together, because while she'd never admit it, she didn't like spending time on her own. She used to text me in a panic sometimes when she went shopping, my phone abuzz with dozens of messages in a row, just photos of the same sweater in five different colors. "Which one?" she'd ask, and it was my job to respond within minutes, to consider the pixels with great deliberation and text back *emerald, teal,* or *lavender.* She usually ended up picking something different from what I had chosen, but she always seemed to get a sense of satisfaction from my deciding for her, as though her desires and preferences had to be held up against mine in order to make sense.

Things changed when she started dating James, whom she met on an app called Comb. "That is a truly frightening name for a dating app," I said. "And why is this any better than any of the other ones?" I had given the apps a shot, only to quit them for good after one date with the first and only person I had bothered to respond to. He called me Rory the whole night long, talked about his ex-girlfriend too much, and insisted that we share an appetizer instead of getting separate ones. "Maybe you should have given him a chance," Yoonhee said afterward. "Rory's kind of a cute nickname for you."

Comb was the first dating app of its kind. It analyzed all the data available on your phone—including your online shopping history, text messages, photos, and so on—and paired you with someone they guaranteed you'd have at least a 95 percent compatibility rating with, based on your past internet searches and hits, message history, and lifestyle. If you had apps that tracked your steps or sleep habits, you could connect it all to Comb. And no profile was required. You just signed up, gave the app complete access to your data, and waited to be assigned a potential soulmate. Once you'd started dating someone through Comb, you could even keep the app on both your phones, switching it to Honey Mode, where it would track, for a low monthly fee, all your significant other's evolving likes, dislikes, interests, and preferences, even pinging you on birthdays, anniversaries, and other special occasions about what presents to get them. When I told Yoonhee that the whole concept creeped me out, she dismissed me, saying that you could choose how much information you wanted to share with the app. "Besides," she said, "don't you know our information is out there already?"

Yoonhee and James hit it off right away. On their first date, he took her to a nice rooftop restaurant in the city, and three months in, on her birthday, she got a bouquet of pink and cream sweetheart roses, her favorite kind. "He's really the perfect guy for me," she said without a trace of irony. And when I finally met him, I could see that he really was. James Yu was exactly four inches taller than her, good-looking, Korean, and clean-cut without being overly fashionable—all her checkboxes ticked off. The kind of guy Yoonhee was always fated to end up with.

When she got engaged, I found out on social media before I heard about it from her. Celebratory emojis littered the comments of her announcement post, which featured their hands, intertwined against the backdrop of a flowery field. "Happiest when I'm with Yu," the caption said, with a corresponding hashtag.

Happy, happier, happiest. It's not that I don't want Yoonhee to be happy. Other people's happiness just takes up so much room, involves so much heft and weight. Other people's joys have always seemed more solid to me than my own. I've never trusted happiness, have trouble with the very notion of it. It doesn't seem like the kind of thing you should try and pin down or rank or quantify or even declare, because you never know when it might disappear in the night, leaving you with nothing but questions and an unending ache.

The aquarium is quieter than usual today. I head to the kitchen, where I chop up the thawed-out squid and shrimp for the penguins. Francine's already in there, measuring out vitamins into the food mixtures for her tanks. "Hey, stranger," she says in her soft midwestern drawl. She looks up and sees the bags under my eyes. "Second coffee kind of day, huh?"

"Just having trouble sleeping," I say, not wanting to give her much more than that. Francine, a tall, stooped-over girl with hard blue eyes and the kind of hair that would be called flaxen in an Irish ballad, is what Yoonhee would call an emotional vampire. Men tend to like her (Carl has nursed a small crush on her since her first day), and although she is allegedly married, to a man named Toby whom she refers to often but whom none of us have ever seen, she indulges them and flirts back. She is oddly confident for someone who, when you get up close to the math of her face and leave the factors of her blond hair and blue eyes and height out of it, isn't actually all that pretty. Francine sniffs out other people's troubles the way some therapy dogs can sniff out cancer and gravitates toward them like a shark hones in on blood. She calls herself an empath, which I think is meant to be an excuse for why she's so goddamn nosy.

She tuts. "I'll get you some St. John's wort from my garden. I brew this tea with it, and then I'm just out like a light." She says this like she hasn't told me about this miracle tea at least three times already.

"Thanks, Francine," I say. "You really don't have to do that."

"You must be so busy helping out Yoonhee with the wedding and all," she says.

"Yep, real busy," I lie.

In reality, Yoonhee hasn't asked me to plan anything with her. In the old days, I would be on the phone with her 24/7, going over swatches of tablecloth fabric and different kinds of curly gold calligraphy font, but ever since Tae and I broke up, she's steered clear of me, as if heartbreak is catching. I assume she's transferred her wedding anxieties over to one of her sisters, and while I'm not exactly the type of girl who goes nuts for details like floral arrangements or balloon clusters, it does hurt, in the way a cut you didn't even notice getting can start bleeding out of nowhere.

"I remember when Toby and I got married," Francine says dreamily, which makes me wonder what kind of backyard Mason jar fiasco Francine and Toby's wedding must have been. "It took forever to get everything right. But, like, I get it, because you just want it to be perfect, right?" She leans over each of the plastic bowls, counting out scoops of white powder. Sometimes I think it must look like we're running the weirdest restaurant in the world, with only cocaine and raw seafood on the menu.

I continue cutting up the shrimp and squid without saying anything, their translucent bodies like slivers of light on the cutting board. It occurs to me occasionally how messed up it is to be working at an aquarium, caring for sea creatures by feeding them other sea creatures, but I guess that's the way it goes in the wild. "Nothing in nature gets wasted," Apa always said. "Even animals whose purposes we haven't yet figured out have a role to play in the ecosystem."

He delighted in finding aberrations in the system, learning about inherited traits that didn't initially seem compatible with survival, like how some penguin species mate for life. "On the one hand, it doesn't make much sense, evolutionarily, for any animal to mate for life," he said. "Limits your opportunities to pass on genetic material. And yet on the other hand, it's a way of limiting the amount of time you might have to spend on finding a mate and keeping one. Streamlines the choices you have to make."

I shuffle the chopped-up squid into a bucket for transport, then hesitate before walking back out. "Have you heard anything about these sales, by the way? To private owners?" I say to Francine casually, as though I've just thought of it.

"Yeah, but I thought they stopped doing that," Francine says, not looking up.

"They're selling Dolores," I answer.

I know what I want, even though I also know I won't get it—some kind of moment of solidarity with Francine, maybe, who doesn't usually talk to me except to try and gossip about Carl or Yoonhee or what she thinks the maintenance staff get up to. Some glimpse of my own deep-rooted anger at the unfairness of it all, reflected in someone else for once. I envision the two of us, Francine and me, passing out petitions and flyers and rallying a crowd of people in the vast entrance hall of the aquarium, coming up with slogans to stop the sale of the animals. I imagine Dolores and me ending up on the nightly news, and how Tae might even see it if the campaign gets big enough. I think about Dolores herself, her large eyes and strong arms, how it feels when she wraps one of them around mine and gives a friendly tug, as if to say, "Hey, look at me, looking at you. Isn't this weird?"

But of course, none of that happens. Francine just looks confused before she shrugs. "I guess they need to make money somewhere."

Coda, one of the royal penguins, isn't eating. She's been upset ever since her mate, Arpeggio, left her for another woman, Sonata. *So much for mating for life,* I think as I open the penguin enclosure and watch all twelve of them look up at me, their bright eyes like small jewels. There used to be fifteen of them, but after baby Harmony died, her parents, Tempo and

Presto, started fighting with each other, biting to the point of bleeding, and they had to be separated. Tempo was sent to a zoo in San Diego, while Presto went to Cleveland.

"Wait your turn, bro," I tell another penguin, named Forte, who nips at Coda in his haste to get to the food bucket. Coda slinks away toward the water, not interested. I wait till the other penguins have finished eating before I try to entice her with a nice bit of untouched squid. She usually goes crazy for squid, her eyes widening at the sight and smell of it. "C'mon, Coda, I know you're hungry," I say. But she just looks at me, as if to say, "Really?" while Sonata and Arpeggio preen each other ostentatiously in front of her. "Knock it off, you two," I say, but they ignore me.

I want to tell her I get it, but I don't, really. Coda and Arpeggio have broken up and gotten back together so many times by now that I've lost track. Royals are monogamous, but the drama among the Fountain's penguins is unparalleled. There's an actual chart of the penguins' relationships with one another somewhere in Carl's office. We use it to keep track of how often these fights and reconciliations happen. They're like actors in Hollywood, all dating from the same pool of ten to twelve other people.

Yoonhee never understood how we could tell the animals apart, even after I explained to her that they wear beaded bracelets showing how long they've been here and how old they are. But it goes beyond that. After a while, you just start to know from watching them, noticing the way they tilt their heads or eat their food or slide belly first into the water. "Most of the job is paying attention. And it's in paying attention, in noticing, that we come to understand what the animals need, sometimes before they know it themselves," Apa always said.

It's my job to notice as much as I can, to get to know all the animals and their habits. To take in the small details, from the way a fish might swim up to me some days and not others, to how bright the colors of a starfish turn depending on temperature fluctuations in its water, to what kind of treats a broken-hearted penguin might be persuaded to eat.

Each of the royals has a crown of wavy yellow hair, which looks like bizarre antennae or an eyebrow dye job gone wrong, depending on how you look at it, and when they walk, they look, like most penguins, absolutely ridiculous. But in the water, it's a completely different story. Their dense bones make them as sleek as torpedoes when they swim, and their golden feathers stream behind them like comet's tails. It makes me think of how Apa used to say that everything is beautiful when seen in its natural element.

I leave Coda her bit of squid and note in the log back at my workstation that she still hasn't touched anything. *Coda is still not eating enthusiastically,* I write. *Recommend medication or separation from the other penguins if she continues to worsen. Stress response?*

People like to laugh at penguins or think of them as small humans in tuxedos. And for a while I did, too, dismissing them in favor of the larger, much more interesting animals at the aquarium, like Dolores or the sharks or the moray eels or manta rays. But there's this moment in a Werner Herzog documentary about Antarctica that Tae made me watch once. We'd gotten some good weed from a friend of his and we were in his apartment, watching the smoke drift up from our mouths toward the ceiling, when he got the idea to show me *Encounters at the End of the World.* "That's a really uplifting title," I said.

"You'll see," he said. "It's one of my favorites."

And he was right. I watched, riveted, for all ninety-nine minutes of the documentary, while Tae watched me watching it, the way guys do when they're anxious about wanting you to like something they like but are trying to play it cool. In one scene about penguins, Werner Herzog asked a researcher, "Is there such a thing as insanity among penguins?" The question, and the matter-of-fact yet deeply serious way he asked it, made me laugh out loud, louder than I would have if I weren't high. "Could they just go crazy because they've had enough of their colony?"

The researcher seemed confused by Herzog's question. The camera panned across the colony of penguins, the fat black and white ovals of their bodies gleaming in the sun. "These penguins are all heading to the open water to the right," Herzog intoned. "But one of them caught our eye, the one in the center."

A lone penguin, a mere dot on the field of white tundra, appeared, waddling away from where the others were. Instead of going toward the water or where his fellow penguins were sunning themselves, he moved, awkwardly but with increasing speed and urgency, toward the interior, where, Herzog informed us, "he's heading toward certain death."

The camera zoomed out, moving away from the penguin to show us the vastness of the white ice surrounding him and the blue mountains in the distance, as if to confirm the penguin's fate. "Even if we caught him and brought him back to the colony he would immediately head right back for the mountains. But why?" Herzog said.

When the scene was over, I was crying, my body shaking and heaving with the violence of my sobs. Tae looked over at me with alarm. "Are you okay?" he asked. Throughout our entire relationship he'd seen me cry only a handful of times, maybe if we'd had a bad fight or something. The weed made his voice sound high and faraway, like it was being piped in from the ceiling. He stared at me, his eyes wide and glassy, and I felt so completely alone that I almost couldn't breathe. I felt my body compress itself into the shape of a comma as I curled into his blankets and cried and cried. Watching the penguin's tiny little body disappear into the mountains of Antarctica made me feel like I was watching myself dissolve and disappear, too.

Tae wrapped his arms around me, stroking my hair until I quieted down and fell asleep, and in the morning, when he asked me if I wanted to talk about it, I said nothing, just pulled him close until I felt him harden against me and we fucked the way I always wanted him to and the way he almost never did, where he pulled my hair and put his fingers in my mouth and I sucked them, the taste of his salt and iron sweat a comfort, an incantation against anything leaving me ever again.

Umma's text burns in the back pocket of my jeans all day while I feed the rest of the animals on my rotation. I tell Dolores about it as she chomps down on her breakfast. Once she's done eating, she just watches me, like she's bored by my problems.

She seems lethargic today, her large eyes closing into narrow yellow slits, in what I can describe only as a judgmental stare. I watch the red-purple shimmer of her as she floats around the tank, a lump in my throat when I think about how soon I won't be able to see her at all. I give her some extra squid because I don't know what else to do. *Maybe she'll be happier in her new home,* I think to myself.

"It's important not to get attached," Apa told me whenever he talked about his work. "The animals don't live as long as we do, and we can't learn as much from them if we're busy thinking about how they might be like us." But he broke his own rule all the time, often showing me the new tricks that he'd taught Dolores, the special puzzles he got just for her. "She's about as smart as a ten-year-old," he told me when I wasn't much older than that. "In fact," he said, "she's probably smarter than you." This was right after I'd had to ask him to sign one of my math tests, the shameful red 70/100 encircled on top of my paper like a billboard announcing to the world how dumb I was. Apa said things like that a lot, not thinking how they might sound to other people.

"That's what happens when you spend too much time with animals," Umma always said. "It's not good for a person to spend so much time apart from people." But Umma was the same, in her own way. She didn't really have friends outside of church, spent most of her time at home in the garden or reading or going over sheet music for choir practice. I always thought she just didn't like to do anything else when I was growing up, and it didn't occur to me until much later in life that perhaps she had been lonely, living in a place far from where she'd grown up, with a man who seemed obsessed by the sea and its secrets.

What's limiting about being a kid is that it takes so long to realize just how weird your own family is, the full extent of their failings or pluses or quirks. When I was little, I thought everyone's parents went long stretches of time without talking to each other, and that every dinner conversation was mostly silence punctuated by occasional requests to pass the salt or a napkin. That everyone's parents had fights that could turn explosive quickly, turning the house into a minefield.

Carl walks in when I'm back in the kitchen, cleaning up the prep bowls from this morning. He acts like I'm doing him a huge favor any time he sees me cleaning, telling me I'm "a rock star" or "such a team player," instead of just thanking me or asking someone else, like Francine, to do it instead. I know I'm part of the problem, that I could just stop. But at this point, everyone already expects me to do the washing-up, and it's just easier to keep on doing things the way I've always done them.

He tries to tell me about his date, going on at length about the restaurant he took her to, what she does for a living, even what they ordered. I wonder if Carl is really lonely, or if he's just like this with everyone else in his life, or both. He thinks that he and I are friends, which I guess is both endearing and a little sad, depending on how you look at it.

"Any plans for the weekend?" he asks me before starting to tell me about his own. I consider telling him the truth, which is that I'll probably drink alone until I pass out in front of the TV, wake up at six a.m. to throw up, and then go back to sleep until two p.m. or so. I think about yelling at him, telling him I don't care about his stupid date or his weekend plans. I wonder how Carl would react if I ever confronted him about any of the shit I know. Like about Dolores leaving, or about how Francine gets paid more than me even though she's been here for less time and makes mistakes with the animals' dosages. I almost want to just for the look of shock that would cross his stupid face.

But it's not really Carl's fault, any of it, I think. He's just as trapped as I am. For all his smugness, Carl isn't really that hateable. There's something about him that screams "kid who was always picked last for things," and I know, from what I've overheard when he's on the phone and thinks no one else is listening, that he has a younger sister in AA and a relative whose medical bills he's helping out with. When managerial salary cuts started happening last year, Carl was one of the few to take it in stride, instead of trying to find other ways to cut from our department's budget. He's a goober, but he's not so bad. The wave of irritation I feel inside my stomach dissipates, and so I tell him I don't have any plans, that I'm hoping to take it easy.

"No plans are the best plans," he agrees.

There's a green cactus-shaped clock that pulses with neon over the bar at Hattie's. I order a margarita that comes with a plastic cowboy boot inside it, small enough to fit a Barbie's foot. I sip it slowly, the salt and lime hitting the back of my throat and the tequila so strong it makes the hairs on my arm stand up. Instantly it makes the world around me feel soft and blurred, like I've taken out my contact lenses, and the lights over the bar wink at me like we're all in on some secret together. It doesn't take away the heaviness I feel inside.

Hattie's is on the far edge of the mall, the cursed side where the boutiques and restaurants often go out of business, only to be replaced by nearly identical storefronts. Even the kiosks don't do well here, the Dead Sea skin-product booths followed by miracle hair straighteners, followed by make-your-own candle kits. But Hattie's has endured, its crowds almost always made up of "girls' night out" groups, lone middle-aged men huddled over their beers, and the occasional cluster of teens trying to tough it out with their fake IDs.

Yoonhee and I used to come here sometimes after work. We liked it because it was roomy, the booths deep enough and separated enough that you could feel like you had some modicum of privacy. Plus the bartenders liked Yoonhee and sometimes sent over free shots. "Oh no," she'd always pretend to groan whenever they arrived. She loved the drama of shots, even though she didn't drink much. It was always me who could keep going even after our third or fourth round, who was usually still steady enough even after a night of drinking to drive us both home.

It's relatively busy tonight. The clusters of men drinking alone—*where do they even come from?* I wonder; none of them look like the usual crowd at the Fountain Plaza—have been replaced with older couples on dates, probably waiting for tables at the steak house across the parking lot, and a few women in suits or work dresses drinking with other women in similar getups. There's an office park on the other side of the mall, so Hattie's gets the occasional happy hour crew. The air smells like corn chips and menthol, from the smokers outside. The floor underneath my sneakers is sticky with spilled liquor, crunchy with mystery crumbs and stray pistachio shells.

"They should really make this place over," Yoonhee would always say. "It could be so cute. Like, retro, you know?"

Yoonhee wanted things to be cute. She wanted a world of softness, pastel colors, clean lines, which I can understand to an extent. It makes sense to want to be able to make things beautiful in a world that so often isn't. She would tell me about how she'd make over everything in Hattie's if it was up to her, from the scarred wooden tables to the pool table in the back with its smelly field of green felt. We took turns ordering seasonal beers or novelty cocktails, spending our paychecks on sugary alcohol that made us feel momentarily like we were the stars of a TV show or a movie about our lives, in which everything that happened, even the boring or bad stuff, was all part of the story.

"You have to romanticize your life," Yoonhee would say to me. "Otherwise, what else is there?"

When we were twelve, Yoonhee told me about her first kiss. It was during a trip to Seoul, the first she'd taken without her family. She was staying with relatives for the summer when Minho, her older male cousin Jimin's friend, who was sleeping over that night, came into her bedroom. The way she told me about it, it was like one second she was fast asleep, and the next she was wide awake and he was sitting at the foot of her bed, staring at her. The moonlight from outside filtered in through the curtains, lighting up her room in pale blue and white, and when she sat up, he leaned in, closing up the distance between them, and kissed her. He was sixteen. His lips felt like nothing, she said, but she had felt the tickle of his fledgling mustache across her upper lip. She drew back just as he was beginning to kiss her more roughly, insistently. Then he got up and left, as though nothing had happened between them at all. She didn't tell anyone but me about it, and the next morning she wondered if it had even happened at all.

I knew something was wrong by the way I felt inside when she told me about the kiss, and the way she looked as though she was going to throw up, but I was young enough to think that maybe it was special to have a boy like you that way, especially an older boy. That maybe she had wanted it. "Did you know he liked you?" I asked.

She wrinkled her nose. "Not really. He bought me an ice cream once. But I didn't think he, like, wanted to kiss me. It was kind of gross."

"Did you tell anyone?" I asked.

"It's not a big deal, people kiss people all the time," she said, getting angry, which surprised me. "I wouldn't have told you if you were going to be weird about it."

"I'm not being weird," I said. "He was the one being weird."

"Whatever," she said. "Don't be jealous. It only happened, like, once." She looked away from me then, and we never spoke about it again. She made me swear not to tell anyone else.

But as time went on, Yoonhee began to tell the story to the other girls at school. Only this time the details had changed. This time, he was not only Minho, the distant friend of her cousin, but Minho Oppa, a term of endearment reserved for older brothers or boyfriends. Minho Oppa had bought her ice cream almost every week that summer, and they shared their first kiss outside, on a shaded bench in the park. He told her that he loved her and bought her a necklace, and at this point in the story she would always show off the star-shaped charm that dangled off her neck, nestled between the hollows of her collarbones. I knew for a fact that her aunt had bought her the necklace, that it was a cheap trinket from one of the outdoor markets in Seoul, but now that it was from Minho Oppa, it seemed to shine brighter, as though it were made of sterling silver and not nickel.

The girls at school sighed. "Wow, I can't believe you went to Korea and got to have a summer romance with an older boy," Valerie Park said. "The only people I see when I go are my grandparents."

Yoonhee smiled, tossing her hair back so everyone else could see the necklace. "He's so cute," she said. "He's thinking of moving here so we can be together."

I could have asked Yoonhee why she was lying, why she was making up a story about a Minho Oppa who had never existed. But by then I knew that this was Yoonhee's way of making the truth, what had really happened, into something more beautiful, softer, easier to understand. And the more she told the story, the more she believed it, until gradually I almost came to believe it, too.

I play with my phone while drinking. I stare at the Europa app but don't open it. I think about deleting it like Rachel told me to, of not being able to contact Tae anymore. I feel dizzy at the thought, and for a second I consider doing it. Instead, I order another drink.

I'm on my third margarita when I hear someone call my name, snapping me out of my stupor. I look up at the neon cactus clock, which tells me that it's eight o'clock. I've been here drinking alone for two hours.

I turn to see Yoonhee standing by my booth, wearing a checkered charcoal dress. If I wore it, the dress would make me look middle-aged, boring, but on her it looks chic, fresh. "Mind if I join you?"

"What are you doing here?" I say as she slides into the seat across from me. Her hair swishes around her face and fills the air between us, and I smell freesia.

"I had a feeling I'd find you here," she said. "I'm waiting for James to pick me up." Her nails are like mint-colored ovals on the surface of the table. They gleam at me in the dim light of the bar. Someone starts playing an old bass-heavy pop song, the kind of dance-floor anthem that feels more suited to a spinning class or a club than Hattie's. The singer barks like a seal over the beat, repeating the syllables of the chorus over and over again until they sound like nonsense.

"Remember when we used to pregame to this song?" Yoonhee says. "You always hated it."

"Did I?" I say, making my voice light and casual like hers. I try to remember who I was back in college, the catalogue of my likes and dislikes from then as unfamiliar to me now as if they belonged to another person entirely. "I remember you always took forever to get ready. We'd have to tell you the party started an hour earlier just to get you to leave on time."

During our junior and senior years at Rutgers, Yoonhee and I had lived with another girl, whom we didn't see much of because she got a boyfriend in the fall of our junior year. We were far from the center of campus, but close enough to the frat houses, where we would wobble to parties on heels that slipped and slid on the sidewalks in winter, and we'd lean against each other for stability, shrieking when the wind blew up our skirts and the shots we'd done weren't enough to keep us warm.

Yoonhee laughs. "Some things don't change," she says. "It drives James crazy." She orders a gin and tonic, takes a sip, and makes a face. "Gosh, I forgot how strong they make these here."

We watch the ice melt into her drink as she searches for what to say next. "How have you been?" she says. "I know we haven't had much of a chance to talk these days. It's just been so busy with wedding stuff. You know."

I can't tell if there is an apology somewhere in what she's said. "I'm getting by," I say. "Guess I haven't been laid off yet."

Yoonhee sighs. "You don't have to tell me. The whole department is under stress right now. There's a lot of pressure to bring in money."

"I guess the sale from Dolores will help," I say.

"It will," she says, her voice agreeable, her eyes not meeting mine.

"What's going on, Yoonhee?" I ask. She's playing with a paper coaster, shredding it slowly to pieces, and I want to scream at her to stop. A new song starts playing, an acoustic pop melody about waking up late on a Sunday morning and making banana pancakes. Of all the stupid things to write a song about. "I don't know why you bothered to come find me here when you don't even want to talk to me about what's going on with your wedding."

She looks at me and takes another sip of her drink before responding. "I asked you to lunch today," she finally says. "You didn't respond, so I figured you were ignoring me. And I don't know, I guess I felt like trying to find you. To talk."

"What do you want to talk about?" I say in as calm a voice as I can muster.

She catches my hands in hers, the cool lavender scent of her hand lotion wafting toward my nose. "I'm worried about you."

I shake her off and fumble for my wallet.

"Wait," she says. "Don't go. I don't mean it like that."

"Worry about yourself," I say.

Her perfectly plucked eyebrows arch, and she looks hurt. But the only thing she says is, "Let me know if you want to talk like adults sometime."

In the end, she's the one who gets up first, leaving her drink half-finished.

It's ten o'clock by the time I leave Hattie's, wandering the parking lot and trying to remember where I parked my car. My phone buzzes and I ignore it, but it keeps ringing. My heart leaps when I see that it's an unknown number.

"Hello?" I say, my voice raspy. There is silence on the other end, silence and then the sound of water. Static. I close my eyes. I picture walls of water, waves of red and green and blue and violet, water that shouldn't be so warm that far up north. Dolores's eyes swim into my mind.

"Apa?" I whisper. I imagine the rush of waves, the roar of ocean. A place where the sky and the water meet, where creatures of the deep grow to mythic proportions and the waters shine so bright with pollutants that they light up the skies at night.

"Come home, Apa," I say. "Please come home." A click, and then there's nothing more. Just me, standing alone against the violet-gray of a light-polluted New Jersey sky, beneath the orange floodlights of an almost-empty parking lot.

CHAPTER 6

Fifteen years earlier

"Put some white on the corners," Yoonhee said. I obeyed. My fingertips were shiny with luminescent dust. When I blinked, the room spangled itself into streaks of light, refracted by the glittery eye shadow.

"I think I got some in my eyes," I said.

"Shush," she commanded. Using one finger, she gently smudged the shadow on the corner of my left eye. "Now you have to put gold highlights onto your ssangapeul." Yoonhee and her sisters, Yoonkyung and Yoojin, all had ssangapeul, or double-creased eyelids, that thin fold of skin that almost all the girls and women we knew paid to get if they didn't have one. Umma once offered to buy me a special kind of tape from the Korean supermarket that you could use to tape your eyelids back overnight, with the promise that it would help to form a natural crease over time. "I don't understand why you don't have ssangapeul when your father and I both do," she had said, as though it was my fault.

"You know I don't have them," I said. I would have rolled my eyes, but now Yoonhee was attacking me with the brush, studying me with exasperated concentration, like I was a difficult crossword puzzle. "Don't talk," she said. "If you make me poke you in the eye, it's on you."

We were fifteen and in Yoonhee's bedroom, putting on makeup from the samples that her mother brought home from the cosmetics shop in Palisades Park she worked at. Between us was a bottle of soju that Yoonhee had stolen from under her sister Yoonkyung's bed. Each sip of it made us feel more light-headed, the sweet, slippery taste of it making us giggle. We were going to our first real party that night, the kind with boys and alcohol.

"Are you sure Yoonkyung won't notice?" I said.

Yoonhee snorted. "Who, her? She's too busy making out with her boyfriend all the time to care."

Yoonkyung was one of the most beautiful girls I had ever seen. The second oldest of the Lee girls, Yoonkyung had long, naturally light brown hair and big, long-lashed eyes, like a K-pop idol's. People often asked Yoonhee if Yoonkyung was half-white, which drove Yoonhee crazy.

Yoonkyung was dating a white boy named Jason, a secret that no one else was supposed to know. Yoonhee swore me to secrecy, making me swear on the leather-bound gilt-edged Bible she had received for her confirmation. "Yoonkyung will actually kill me if anyone finds out," she said. Yoonkyung was known for making dramatic pronouncements, knowing that her beauty meant she could get away with bad behavior, and apparently she had held a pair of scissors to Yoonhee's long, well-brushed hair and threatened to cut it all off in her sleep if she told anyone else about her and Jason.

It was about a month after Apa had left, for what would be the last time. He wasn't due home for another couple of months, a fact that normally would have perturbed Umma, but oddly, she didn't seem to be at all bothered by his absence from our lives. In fact, she seemed almost happy, rising early in the mornings to make me breakfast and actually talking to me, asking me how my day had been, instead of just telling me what I could or couldn't do. She seemed younger, brighter, and much more apt to say yes whenever I asked her if I could go to Yoonhee's.

"It's really weird," I told Yoonhee. "It's like someone replaced her with a lobotomized version of herself or a robot or something. I've never seen her smile so much before."

"Maybe she feels like she can be herself more without your dad around," Yoonhee said. "Yoonkyung says that about Jason, to her friends. She's always like, 'Wow, I can't believe I have to put on makeup just to go to McDonald's and obsess about what his ex-girlfriends are wearing.'" Now she was smudging a chalky-looking brown shadow over my eyes, along with eyeliner, which was supposed to give me the perfect metallic smoky eye.

"Ta-da," she said, handing me the mirror. I gasped. "I look like I have a black eye," I said.

"You look glamorous," she said, ignoring me. She was wearing an ungodly amount of blush, her cheeks almost fluorescent pink in the light of her bedroom. She had even brushed it across the tip of her nose and then topped it off with magenta eye shadow that was only a few shades brighter than the blush. Her lips she had left bare, swiping nothing but lip gloss across them. "Now we have to decide what you're going to wear."

She pulled me to the closet, which was filled with items of clothing she had stolen over the years from her sisters. A few of the shirts still had tags on them. "How are you getting away with this?" I said.

Yoonhee shrugged. "Yoojin's not here, and Yoonkyung doesn't keep track," she said.

"You take Yoojin's clothes, too?" Yoojin was completely unlike her younger sisters—studious and serious and never without her nose in a book, though she was quick with a retort or a smack on the head if Yoonhee or Yoonkyung ever got out of line or interrupted her studying. She was away at college that fall, doing her freshman year at Brown. She mostly dressed like an old man, wearing sweaters and polos and button-down shirts, although she managed to make them look good. I was in awe of both of Yoonhee's sisters, who, despite being only two and four years older than us, seemed like adults already, full of a self-possession and polish that, at fifteen, I didn't think would ever come naturally to me.

Yoonhee, being the baby of the family, had a knack for getting what she wanted. It helped that her parents worked most of the time, her dad at an import/export business based all the way out in Queens and her mother at the cosmetics store. And while it seemed that money was sometimes tight for them, as it was for almost every family I knew, including ours, they lived in a big house in a shady cul-de-sac on the nicer side of town, and Yoonhee's mother carried luxurious-looking handbags and wore clothes that looked as though they'd been made for her. Even Umma, who could be snooty about the Lees because they were "showy" in a way she didn't like, admitted that Yoonhee's mother dressed well, and once I saw her, when she came to pick me up and stopped in to have tea, gently stroking one of Mrs. Lee's soft handbags with the back of her hand like it was a baby's cheek.

Yoonhee picked out a lacy black off-the-shoulder top for

me. "I think this would look really good on you," she said firmly. I shucked off my T-shirt and tugged it on, fidgeting uncomfortably in the mirror. I pushed back my shoulders and cocked one hip, like I'd seen movie stars do on the red carpet. Yoonhee laughed. "Look at you," she said. She slithered into a sheer pink blouse, which shimmered around her body like a cloud. We looked, respectively, like a bruise and the shiny skin around it.

Yoonhee had finagled an invite to the party tonight from Tara Yang, her lab partner, because Tara's best friend was Ash Kim, who lived in the big house on Sycamore that was rumored to have not only a heated pool but also a hot tub. It was early October and finally starting to get chilly out, but Yoonhee insisted that we go, because when else were we going to get a chance to hang out with boys in a hot tub?

As usual, Yoonhee had planned everything, and all I had to do was show up. She decided that I would tell Umma I was going to work on a group project with her and spend the night, and she told her own parents that we were going to a church event and would be home late. Yoonhee's parents were even more religious than Umma was, and anytime she invoked church, they capitulated, figuring we were safe as long as we were around other Koreans, not knowing that some of the same church kids who smiled and bowed respectfully to them on Sunday mornings were also sneaking out of their parents' houses and puking on neighbors' lawns on Friday nights.

If Apa had been home, Umma probably wouldn't have let me go. She would say she didn't like for me to spend the night at other people's houses when I had a perfectly good bed at home. "When I was your age," she often said, "I wouldn't have dreamed of spending the night away from my family. I was always afraid a war would break out in the middle of the night, and then I'd be separated from them for good." Umma was always saying intense things like that that made me feel guilty, guilty for my spoiled American life and for my need to do whatever Yoonhee wanted me to do.

"Don't ever forget how special you are," Apa always said. "Ever since you were little, I knew you were destined for great things. You can do anything you want to. You've certainly got the genes for it, coming from such a smart umma and apa." At this, Umma would tell him to hush and stop his hutsori, but I knew she thought he was right—that the least I could do to thank my parents for everything they'd done, for uprooting their lives to come to another country and have me, was to be extraordinary. I didn't know how to tell them that I didn't want to be special at all—that all I wanted was to be just like everyone else.

Once we were glammed up to Yoonhee's satisfaction, she threw a large gray sweatshirt at me and instructed me to put it on, while she did the same. We snuck out of her house in the sweatshirts, but we needn't have, because Mr. Lee was napping on the couch, snoring in front of the nightly news, while Mrs. Lee was still in the kitchen washing dishes. "Be careful," she called absent-mindedly.

As soon as the door closed behind us, the night turned electric. The moon was rising, and there was a snap in the air that made me grateful for the sweatshirt, beyond the subterfuge it had enabled. Yoonhee promptly threw hers off and hid it underneath a bush. "C'mon," she said. We half ran, half walked the ten blocks it took to get to Ash Kim's house, shivering in the cold and laughing at ourselves. Suddenly my eye shadow didn't seem too dark or my outfit too daring. In the shadows of the dark branches overhead, we felt like covert secret agents or incognito royalty on our way to rub elbows with commoners for one night. The moonlight turned the sheer fabric of Yoonhee's blouse filmy and gauzy, and when she turned impatiently to tell me to hurry up, she looked like a beautiful pink ghost.

The party was in full swing by the time we arrived. Yellow rectangles of light stretched themselves across the Kims' yard, and the house was thumping with music. We knocked on the door, expecting someone to come answer it, but after a few seconds of our standing out there awkwardly while the walls of the house seemed to pulse with the thrum of people inside, Yoonhee opened the door herself, and we stepped into what felt and smelled like a beery greenhouse. She grabbed two frosty cans from a cooler and thrust one into my hand. "Looks like we came at the right time," she yelled into my ear.

The Kims' giant flat-screen TV was tuned to a football game, and a crowd of boys was gathered around it. In the center of the kitchen, people were already playing pong, their cheers or boos crescendoing throughout the rooms of the house whenever someone scored or failed to. Ash Kim was standing on the staircase talking to people, her back to us, but you could tell from her waist-length, bleached-blond hair (Umma, seeing her in the parking lot one day when she came to pick me up from school, had been aghast) and the way she was leaning back into a boy's chest to laugh at something someone said, that it was her.

"Tara!" Yoonhee called across the room. A tall girl with her hair tied up into a slicked-back ponytail turned to see us, and squeals ensued. They ran to hug each other like they were old friends who hadn't seen each other in forever, as opposed to lab partners who had probably seen each other just that morning. "Love the eye makeup, Ro. It feels different for you," Tara said. I couldn't tell if she was being sarcastic or not, but Yoonhee immediately linked arms with me and beamed proudly. "Doesn't it look good? I did it myself." Yoonhee never seemed to analyze other people's words for hidden meanings, for a sign that they meant something else instead.

Yoonhee and Tara began talking about the boys present at the party, comparing notes on who was dating whom and who was planning to make a move on whom that night. I tried to follow along, nodding vigorously and making sympathetic noises when Tara began complaining about her boyfriend, Andy, who was supposed to be there but hadn't been able to sneak out, but I soon lost interest in the conversation. Still clutching my beer, I drifted toward the side of the living room, where it was a little less crowded.

I saw Brian Fitch, a kid I knew from gym class, walking toward me. "Hey," I said, and he nodded at me. Brian was an inordinately tall, pale string bean of a boy with a blue streak in his hair who wore bright red Doc Martens almost every day and rarely smiled, which made him just weird enough and cool enough that most people left him alone. We both hated gym class and refused to run after errant balls during the endless games of volleyball we were forced to play, a fact that had bonded us.

" 'Sup, Ro," he said. His streak was a slightly different shade of blue today, almost green.

"I like your hair," I said, uncertain of what else to talk about with him now that we didn't have the common enemy of our gym teacher, Mr. Bailey, to avoid.

"Thanks. I gotta redo it soon," he said, touching it as though he'd forgotten it was there. "My stepdad's gonna kill me," he said, as though he relished the prospect.

"You here with anyone?" I said. I wasn't sure what he was doing here—it didn't seem like his usual scene—but he looked much more at ease than I did.

"Just stopping by," he said. "Going to a show later at the Rub if you wanna come." My eyebrows rose of their own accord. The Rub was hardly fancy—it was a glorified coffeehouse, open late on weekend nights—but it was the closest thing we had to a live music venue. Local bands played there, and sometimes bigger ones stopped by during more regional legs of their tours. Only older kids went there, and while Brian fit the profile, I didn't think he was cool enough to get in, especially without ID, since they served beer and wine during shows.

"Yoonhee would kill me if I left her here," I said.

"Oh, right, y'all are friends," he said, in an amused voice. I didn't ask him what he meant by that, since it made sense. Yoonhee was a highly visible presence at school, always volunteering for committees and running for things, and I was not.

"Yep, since we were kids," I said with an enthusiasm I didn't feel.

"Cool," he said, already losing interest in our conversation. "I'm gonna go outside for a smoke. I'll catch you later." I could tell that he would have asked me if I'd wanted to come, too, had I said yes to coming to the Rub, or had I made more of an effort, or if whatever had gone wrong with our conversation hadn't.

"Cool," I said. I felt a small sting that I tried to ignore by gulping my beer.

My attention shifted to a small blue fish tank on a side table. The interior was nothing special—just your standard castle, with a few leafy algae plants and one snail, but the two goldfish inside it were beautiful. They had black and white spots on their fins, and their tails were long and gossamer thin, streaming behind them like wedding veils as they swam around the tank. I watched them move, their bodies like small gold streaks in the water, and began to feel my excitement about the evening seep out of me.

Yoonhee had made a big deal about the party, saying it would be our chance to meet new people at our high school, branch out, finally get popular and snag boyfriends, and I had gotten caught up in her excitement, too, mostly because it was something new to look forward to. Time always seemed to unmoor itself whenever Apa wasn't home, our evenings going by unpunctuated by his cheery greeting whenever he walked through the front door, and lately, despite Umma's odd light-heartedness in his absence, a thick silence had settled between us like snow. It was like we had nothing to talk about when Apa wasn't around.

But if I was being honest with myself, I had hoped that Yoonhee was right, that this night would turn out to be special. I wasn't like Yoonhee—I didn't care about being popular—but I did want things to be different, even though I didn't know what that meant. Mostly I didn't want her to leave me behind in whatever social ascent she was planning. But it was clear, judging from the way no one really turned to look at me, the way their eyes slid past me to Yoonhee, the fact that even Brian Fitch thought I was too weird to talk to, that nothing was really going to change for me tonight. I wanted to go home.

Yoonhee found me staring into the fish tank. "I'm going outside," she said. "Want to come?"

"I'm okay here," I said.

"Are you serious?" Yoonhee said. The smooth nonchalance of her voice was now spiky with disapproval and annoyance. "Why are you being a drag?"

"I'm just not really in the mood, I guess," I said.

"It wasn't easy to get us into this party," Yoonhee said. The corners of her mouth always turned down into a pout whenever she was upset. "It's kind of a big deal we're here."

"It's not exactly a club," I said. "We just walked in."

"I wanted us to have fun and meet new people for once," she said. "Can you just be cool? Tara's nice once you get to know her. Ash, too."

"I'm sure they're fine people. They're just not my people," I said.

"Look," she said, lowering her voice, "if you want to continue being a loner weirdo in high school, that's fine by me. But don't expect me to be okay with it, too, because I actually want to try making friends this year."

"Why are you being a bitch?" I said. Yoonhee drew back, and I was instantly sorry I'd said it, but now I was annoyed. She was making way too big a deal out of this stupid party. "All I said was that I didn't want to go outside."

"You always do this," she said. "You get so weird whenever I try and get us to hang out with other people. It's not normal. I'm doing you a favor, bringing you along here with me."

I felt my neck burn. "How generous," I heard myself say. "That's super cool of you to think of me."

She sighed. "Fine, suit yourself," she said. She grabbed another beer and left.

I went back to studying the goldfish, watching them dance slowly around each other, when a small voice piped up at my elbow. "Do you want to help me feed them?"

I looked down to see two eyes, magnified behind thick

glasses. It was a little kid, clutching a box of fish flakes. She pushed her glasses up on the bridge of her nose and cleared her throat. She seemed annoyed. "Well, if you're not going to help me feed them, at least get out of my way."

"Sorry," I said. "Are you—are these your fish?"

She rolled her eyes at me. "Duh," she said. "I live here."

"You must be Ash's sister," I said. I never knew what to do or say around little kids. They made me nervous, with all their crying and running and carrying on. But this one seemed like an impatient adult in the body of a tiny girl. She was wearing red corduroy pants and a T-shirt that had a picture of a crab on it. "Don't be shellfish," read the speech bubble coming out of the crab's mouth. "Help clean up our oceans!"

"Who are *you*?" she said. "You don't look like one of my sister's friends."

I felt briefly insulted. The way she said it indicated that she'd noticed my obvious uncoolness, my lack of ease around everyone else in the room, the way kids can just sense things. Then I realized there was no point in feeling insulted by a child, especially one who was right. "I'm not," I said. "I'm here with my friend. I don't really know Ash, actually."

"Ash's friends are stupid, like her," she said. She fed the fish carefully, tapping the flakes into the water and trying her best to make the distribution as equal as possible. We watched the fish rise to meet the falling flakes.

"I'm Audrey," she said.

"Like Hepburn? My mom really likes that movie *Roman Holiday*."

She looked at me like I'd said something unbelievably stupid. "I have other fish upstairs if you want to see them," she said.

I followed her through the crowds, past the increasingly

packed room filled with clouds of pot smoke and fumes. Someone was passing around a bottle of tequila, which everyone
was eagerly taking swigs from. Another song began to play,
this time an acoustic rock track that almost all the guys in the
room seemed to know. They burst out into song, holding on
to one another and swaying sentimentally like they were at a
concert. One of them pulled out his phone and began shining
its light up at the ceiling, which of course became a cue for
everyone else to do the same thing. The girls all rolled their
eyes, but they seemed amused by it, and one of them began
recording it on her phone.

The beer was beginning to make me feel a little sleepy. It
tasted disappointingly sour and earthy, especially after the
sweet, candy-like flavors of the soju that Yoonhee and I had split
in her bedroom. Audrey stepped daintily around the crowds,
making her way to the stairs. "Are you coming or not?" she
said.

Her room was the largest child's bedroom I had ever seen,
much larger than mine, and it was a symphony in shades of
purple. Everything, from the walls to the sheets to the pillows
to even the light fixtures, was done in varying shades of mauve,
lavender, and deep violet. And lined up against the walls were
a series of tanks, much bigger than the one downstairs, filled
with fish—minnows, guppies, goldfish, and one stunning betta,
its blue and scarlet fins rippling in the water like the folds of
an evening gown. I could feel Audrey watching my reaction as
I bent down to get a closer look. "This is awesome," I said. "Do
you have names for them?"

She nodded. "That one's October," she said pointing to the
betta. "And the rest of them are April, May, June, and August."

"What happened to July and September?" I asked.

"October ate July," she said solemnly. "And September

jumped out of the tank." October seemed to puff itself up at the mention of its name, as though it were preening.

"That sucks," I said. "Did you know that betta fish are also called fighting fish?"

"Yeah, everyone knows that," Audrey said, bored. She showed me the notebooks where she logged the fishes' habits and behaviors, how much they were fed each day, what the water pH levels were like.

"Cool," I said. I was beginning to like her, this strange little kid with a home aquarium and an attitude, who knew more about fish than I did at her age. She did not seem like she could be related to Ash, whose high-pitched shrieks and laughter I could hear all the way from upstairs. "My dad works at the Fountain Aquarium, at the mall," I said. "You should ask your parents to take you there sometime if you want to see even more fish."

She seemed impressed. "Do you go a lot?"

"Oh, sure," I said. "I go all the time. I basically grew up there."

"I asked Ash to take me once, but she said it'd be boring," Audrey said. For the first time, she sounded like her age, which I guessed was around eight or nine. "I'm going to be an ichthyologist when I grow up," she said.

"I bet you are," I said.

From downstairs, we heard more shrieking as people got drunker and rowdier. "Where are your parents?" I said.

"They're on vacation," she said. "They didn't want to take me and Ash because we would've had to miss school, so she's supposed to be watching me." Her voice sounded wistful.

"Do you miss them?" I asked.

"Yeah," she said. "Ash doesn't really like me to be around when she has friends over, so she told me to stay up here till the party was done." She tapped the wall of a tank, and we watched as one of the guppies, a small electric blue thing with speckles and a shock of red on its tail, zipped by, following her finger.

"That's kind of shitty," I said. "It's your house, too."

A look of skepticism and mild glee passed over her face at the sound of someone older using a bad word. "I guess so," she said. "She says I'm a weirdo and that I'm annoying."

"That may be the case," I said. "I mean, I certainly don't know you well enough to say." She smirked at this. "But like, who cares, right? If she thinks you're weird just because you like stuff that's different from the stuff she likes, it doesn't matter. It's just who you are."

"Why are your eyes like that?" she said, interrupting me. I had been working my way up into a rant about how no one seemed to understand girls who wanted to be on their own to think about and explore stuff, how girls like us were just trying to learn more about the world as we saw it, and how if we had been boys no one would have cared about whatever "phases" of interests we'd gone through.

"Like what?" I said.

"Like you got punched in the face," she said.

"Oh, that," I said. "My friend did it. She thinks it looks good."

"It doesn't," she said.

I was about to say something snappy in return, to say no one had asked her, but then I caught a glimpse of myself in the reflection of her bedroom mirror and began to laugh. She was right—I looked ridiculous. I went into the bathroom down the hallway and splashed cold water on my face until I'd rubbed all the color and glitter off. When I was done, my face felt lighter, freer.

I went back into Audrey's room, where we discussed the fish and their habits, when she'd gotten each of them, and which were her favorites. "I try not to be obvious about it, though," she said. "They get jealous."

I told her about Dolores, about how my father was on a trip to Dolores's birthplace in an effort to gather more data and samples from the Bering Vortex, to determine what it was in the waters that was giving the organisms there not only renewed longevity but also new evolutionary traits, like octopuses being able to change into colors they wouldn't have been able to master previously. How my father's work, while he insisted it had far-reaching implications beyond the lives and mating cycles of sea creatures, had failed to bring in the full amount of funding necessary for the trip, so while he had managed to finagle a trip this year, this would probably be the last time he could go out there for a while.

Of course, I didn't tell her that the real reason I thought he had left was that things had gotten worse between him and Umma. Their relationship was never the same after she found out about him and Laura. If she had something she needed to say to him, she'd relay it through me, making sure she was never in the room alone with him.

And yet they didn't seem to want to leave each other. "Why don't you just get divorced already?" I'd asked Umma once.

She looked at me like I'd suggested she sprout wings and fly away. "It doesn't concern you," she said. "Don't talk about things you don't understand." She was right—I didn't understand at all. *What was the point,* I thought, *in voluntarily submitting to so much unhappiness?*

When I got older, I would realize that what she had wanted was for him to ask for her forgiveness. To beg her to love him again, to swear that he would never again betray her. But she must have known that asking Apa, a man who came and went and did as he pleased, to do such a thing would just be asking for more heartbreak, and this time, it would be the kind of heartbreak that would mean she'd have to leave.

My phone went off, interrupting my conversation with Audrey. It was Tara. "Come get your girl," she said, slurring her words.

"What? Who?"

"Yoonhee's, like, unconscious."

"Oh, Jesus," I said. I walked quickly downstairs, with Audrey following me. "What happened? What's going on?" she said, excited. I ignored her.

Outside, I found Yoonhee asleep in a deck chair by the pool, the expression on her face oddly angelic despite the puddle of vomit on her shirt. "What did you do to her?" I said to Tara, my voice high with anxiety.

"She's fine," Tara said. "We were just doing shots and she got dizzy and said she had to lie down."

"Fuck," I muttered. "Fuck, fuck, fuck." Yoonhee and I had gotten drunk on our own before, but getting wasted tonight had not been part of the plan. Her parents thought we were at an evening Bible study class.

"Yoonhee, wake up," I said, shaking her. She opened one eye and yawned.

"Where'd you go, Ro?" she said. "I'm tired." She sighed and tried to roll over to go back to sleep, nestling herself deeper into the vomit on her filmy shirt. I swore again and tried to get her to sit up. A crowd had gathered around us, many of them laughing like it was no big deal that my best friend was lying passed out on a deck chair at a party we weren't supposed to be at in the first place.

"Back off," I told them.

"Throw her in the pool! That'll wake her up," said one boy whose name I didn't know. "Skinny-dipping party!" another said, to cheers and shouts.

"I want to go in the hot tub," she said. Her breath smelled rancid.

"No more partying for you," I said.

"God, you just hate seeing me have fun, don't you," she said, and for a second, I considered leaving her there and heading home alone, letting her deal with the fallout on her own. But then she slumped forward onto my chest. "I feel sick," she said, her nose pressed into my sternum. I sighed, accepting that my fate this night was to deal with this. Behind the crowds, Audrey watched us, her eyes big with shock and fear.

I peeled off Yoonhee's delicate pink shirt and threw it onto the dewy grass, where it lay like a dead jellyfish. I grabbed someone's sweatshirt from another deck chair and forced her head and arms through it, like she was a child. Her eyes flew open, and she squinted at me. "Where'd your makeup go?" she said.

"It wasn't really working for me," I said.

"But I did such a good job on it," she whined.

"I know you did. But it's time to go home now."

"If you say so," she said, sighing.

I led her home, pushing past the gawkers and onlookers, half carrying and half frog-marching her back to her house. The streets were quiet, with only the occasional car passing by us. Yoonhee threw up two more times along the way, doing it almost gracefully—once off the sidewalk straight into the gutter, and another time right into someone's potted pansies. "Good girl," I said, holding her hair back and rubbing her back.

At her front door, I made up some excuse to her mother, telling her that Yoonhee wasn't feeling well. I hauled her upstairs, tucking her into bed and leaving a wastepaper basket next to her head. As I was leaving to go brush my teeth, she called my name.

"Ro," she said, "I don't want to be mad at you anymore."

"Don't worry about it," I said. "Go to sleep."

"You're just so fucking annoying sometimes."

I laughed. "Yeah, you too," I said. But she was already fast asleep.

CHAPTER 7

I take only back roads on the way home from Hattie's, praying to get home in one piece. But despite how careful I am trying to be, I run a red light and almost hit what looks like a raccoon. It stares at me for a moment, its beady eyes glowing in the dark, before it scuttles away.

I think about how one time, right after Tae left for Arizona, I almost hit some teens on my way home from Hattie's, three skinny girls dressed in dark hoodies and jeans. I swerved away, almost crashing my car into a lamppost to avoid them, and they looked at me just like that raccoon had, their eyes alien and contemptuous, their faces bright in my headlights. I thought, for one wild moment, that I had actually hit them, and I imagined what my life would be like if one or more of them were hurt, or worse, dead.

The fear that ratcheted through my body in that moment scared me sober for two weeks. I stayed away from Hattie's, didn't even want to crack open a beer at home. *I am turning down a series of paths that could wind up becoming very bad for me,* I remember thinking right after the girls ran past my car into the night, as graceful as young deer. *No one is going to fix you for you,* I thought when I got home, giving myself a good hard stare in my bathroom mirror. But like all revelations, it didn't last long.

It's not like I have some kind of inherited problem. Umma never touches alcohol, and Apa, while he enjoyed the odd beer or two with dinner, was never a heavy drinker. It's just that sometimes life feels like one long series of events that range from boring to bad, and the fastest way to realign it all in my brain is to drink.

Tae never came right out and said he thought I might have a problem. But he did say that I was different when I drank—meaner, more likely to pick fights. I didn't know what to say to that, so I made a joke about how that wasn't true, since I was mean all the time. He laughed at that, but he didn't disagree. I told him not to worry, that I could stop whenever I wanted, but the truth is that I enjoy feeling like I'm playing chicken with myself, seeing how far I can go without doing irreparable damage to myself or someone else.

On the way up to my apartment on the third floor, I see a gold earring lying on the stairs. It shines in the dim light of the hallway, like a small spilled sun. I pick it up and consider what to do with it. I wonder if it's being looked for, if someone is frantically searching their place right now in the hopes of finding it. The metal is light, cheap, but maybe it was a gift, something with sentimental value.

I consider getting a pen and paper and leaving a note by the mailboxes. I imagine taking the earring around from door to door tomorrow morning, asking people in the other units if they've lost any jewelry recently. I imagine a whole alternate

universe in which my life is reoriented around being the kind
of person who bothers to track down the owners of lost things,
who takes action and initiative when items go missing and
doesn't give up until they're back in their rightful place. Maybe
the earring belongs to the girl who lives below me, who has a
cute dog and never says hi when I run into her in the laundry
room. Maybe the earring belongs to the preteen daughter of
the recently divorced man who lives on the ground floor, who
does a lot of conspicuous stretching in the hallways in his bik-
ing gear.

In the end, I don't do any of that. I leave the earring on
the stairs where I found it. I throw my clothes into a heap on
the floor and toss myself into bed, and fall asleep with all the
lights on, listening to a Van Morrison song that Tae used to
play on the guitar. I never understood what the song meant,
but it reminded me of him, especially that one line about
walking in "gardens all wet with rain."

I dream of fiery suns drowning in dark oceans, and when
I wake up, it's morning. Light is pouring in through the windows, and someone's knocking on the door, the sound of the
pounding syncing up almost perfectly with the throbbing of
my head.

"Jesus," I say, and I don't know if it's a curse or a prayer.
The room stops spinning when I put one foot on the floor and
then the other. I close my eyes and hope that by the time I
open them the knocking will go away, but it just gets louder
and more insistent.

I stumble down the hallway and catch a glimpse of my
reflection in the small mirror by the front door. I look about
how I expect, somewhere between unwell and undead.

"Who is it?" I croak, pressing my eye to the peephole. All I
see is someone's forehead.

"Open up," says Rachel. "It's me."

"And me!" says Hailie.

"Were you supposed to come over?" I say.

"You forgot, didn't you." I can practically feel the force of Rachel's sigh against the door. "Will you open up already?"

I undo the locks and stand there, swaying, while my cousin and her daughter regard me. "What happened to you?" Rachel says.

"Long night," I say. I make my way over to the kitchen table, which is really just a card table with two folding chairs in front of it, and sit down gingerly.

"Are you sick, Auntie Ro?" Hailie asks.

"No," I say, at the same time that Rachel says, "Yes." Rachel gives Hailie a look, the kind of look that Umma would give me whenever she wanted me to leave her and Apa alone to talk about Grown-Up Things. "Go do your homework in the living room," Rachel says.

Once Hailie is out of the kitchen, I notice Rachel's eyes darting around the apartment. The last time she came to visit, Yoonhee and I were still living together, and the place is noticeably starker without her decorating sensibilities. The floor is dirty, covered with balls of hair and dust in the corners, and there are books and sweaters and other detritus stacked all over the kitchen, spilling into the living room. A stack of dishes teeters in the sink, and I'm sure the smell of something that soured in the fridge a few weeks ago is still lingering in the air. An old mannequin that Yoonhee and I rescued off the street stands crookedly in a corner. We named her Minnie and dressed her up sometimes, but these days she mostly makes do with a Santa hat on her head, left over from some long-ago holiday party.

"Sorry, I would have cleaned up if I'd known you were coming," I say, gesturing vaguely. The pain of my hangover has now spread, somehow, to my shoulders, and it hurts to move.

"I called you, remember? We talked about this," Rachel says. "I just need you to watch Hailie for me while I take care of some stuff. You have the day off, right?"

I start to protest or think of an excuse. The last thing I want today is to be responsible for a child. All I want to do is sleep on and off until five o'clock, and then peel myself out of bed, order in, and watch TV for twelve more hours until I pass out at dawn. The thought of having to keep a kid entertained while I'm hungover fills me with dread.

"It'll be just for a few hours," says Rachel. "I wouldn't ask if it weren't important. Please, Ro."

"Where are you going?" Hailie calls from the living room, not even bothering to hide the fact that she's been eavesdropping.

"I have to run some errands," Rachel says. "This girl," she adds in an undertone just to me.

"Why can't I come?" she says. "I don't want to stay here. It smells."

"Don't be rude, Hailie," Rachel says. "Look," she says to me in a quieter voice, "I have to go see Simon."

My skin prickles at the mention of Rachel's ex-husband.

"We're just going to talk, so don't give me that face," Rachel says, even though I haven't moved a muscle. Simon was never rude to me or anything, but something about him never felt right to me, even back when Rachel had introduced me to him. He was much too deferential, too slick. When I asked him polite questions about himself, he would always manage to answer in a way that showed off how devoted he was to Rachel and what a supposedly good guy he was. It made me feel vaguely nauseous.

"Aren't the lawyers handling that?" I say. I don't really understand the ins and outs of their ongoing divorce proceedings, other than that things are getting nasty—especially the custody question—and it's mostly Simon's fault.

"If I can just talk to him directly, I think it could help," Rachel says. "I don't think he gets that it's our daughter he's talking about—he just thinks every conflict is some kind of competition."

"That sounds like an incredibly bad idea," I say.

"I know how he is," she says, an edge in her voice now. "We were together for ten years, remember?"

"Sure, but he was an asshole for most of them. *Is* an asshole." I think of all the times Rachel would call me after their fights. How she was one of the first people I called when Tae left. After dropping Hailie off at school, she picked me up from work with a bag full of greasy fries and took me to her place, where she didn't ask me any questions and we watched episode after episode of *The Golden Girls*. I think about how most of the time, she's a total Dorothy, tough as nails and world-weary, but when it comes to Simon, she's Rose, making the same mistakes over and over again and perpetually confused when things don't work out.

"I think he's sick of all this fighting, too. I just want it to be done, and so does he. I don't think it's a bad idea," she says. "Sometimes it's better to talk things out face-to-face."

Before Rachel dropped out of her master's program to get married and have Hailie, she had been studying to be a social worker. During that time, she read a lot of books with titles like *Connecting Through Conflict* and *Discover Your Inner Child*.

"Here's money for lunch—maybe you can take her to the movies or something? Or the park. We haven't gotten in much outdoor time this week," Rachel says, sliding a crisp fifty-dollar bill across the table, like we're doing some kind of deal.

"Okay," I say. Rachel leans across the table and hugs me, and I feel a rush of guilt. It's so easy to make people happy sometimes. I don't know why I don't do it more often.

"You're the best," she says, collecting her things and moving toward the door. She's wearing a full face of makeup, I realize, which she hasn't done in a while, maybe not since she left Simon. "Bye, Hailie," she calls to the living room, where a stony silence is the only reply.

"Oh, and maybe it wouldn't hurt to do a little vacuuming in here?" she says before she pops out, leaving me alone with the dust bunnies and her daughter.

A few years ago, I saw a clip online of a lone gray dolphin circling its enclosure in an abandoned aquarium in Japan. The aquarium had gradually run out of funding, and all the staff had been laid off and some of the animals sold elsewhere. But sea animals, particularly large ones, are often difficult to care for, and there was not enough room in the neighboring aquariums or zoos for all the animals. And so some of them were left to fend for themselves as the aquarium's daily operations came to a grinding, shuddering halt. The building was closed down, and despite some public curiosity about the fate of the animals, they were largely forgotten, until a group of animal activists broke into the aquarium.

They found moss and algae growing in the tanks; water that had turned a sickening gray-green from lack of cleaning and filtration; dead fish by the hundreds, floating belly-up in the water like wilted flowers. Some of the larger animals had tried to escape, battering themselves against the thick plexiglass of their tanks until tiny cracks appeared, and they were wounded, dazed. Many of them had turned on one another, the lack of daily feedings turning almost every tank into a kind of battle royale.

But worst of all was the lone gray dolphin, a twenty-year-old female named Eriko. She had a lopsided dorsal fin and had calved twice during her time at the aquarium. While most of her companions had been shipped off to other facilities—dolphins, being intelligent and bright-eyed, with their perpetual open-mouthed grins, are often in high demand—Eriko had been left behind, probably because of her dorsal fin and the fact that, while lively and playful, she was known for being stubborn and untrainable, not pliable enough to be taught tricks.

The video of Eriko was shaky, clearly filmed on someone's phone, and the camera quality was substandard. Narration from one of the animal activists, with accompanying subtitles in English, informed viewers that Eriko has been left alone for at least two weeks, with little to no food, and was showing signs of intense distress. Her skin had turned a pallid, sickly green, and her eyes were dull and lifeless, barely bothering to track the movements of the camera. Worst of all, she kept on circling the full circumference of her enclosure, speeding through the water despite the fact that she must have been exhausted, as though she thought that by swimming fast enough, she could find a way out.

In the end, the video had gone viral, as it was meant to, and the activist group was able to raise enough money to get Eriko and the other abandoned animals to a sanctuary in Beijing. Eriko became an international celebrity, making the evening news and even inspiring a children's book called *Eriko's Journey*. We have copies of it in our gift shop. In the book, they added that Eriko went on to be reunited with her two calves, Fumiko and Mariko, at the sanctuary, but that was just a pretty fabrication that the author and publisher had decided to tack on, to make the story more palatable to families.

Eriko's Journey is the only book for kids I have at home, so when Hailie announces that she's bored, I read it out loud to her. Her eyes get wide when I read the parts about how lonely Eriko was when the aquarium first shut down, and while she doesn't cry, she breathes a huge sigh of relief at the end, when Eriko is reunited with her daughters. "So everything was okay in the end," she says, satisfied.

It occurs to me that maybe this book wasn't the best choice to read aloud to a kid whose parents are going through a vitriolic divorce. "Totally," I lie.

I don't tell her that the real Eriko did live for two more years in Beijing, but that she had to be kept away from the other dolphins, because her time alone had made her aggressive and anxious, apt to turn on them or her handlers with little provocation. And that despite the aquarium staff's best efforts to train Eriko out of these behaviors, she continued to circle her enclosure multiple times a day, always in the same rapid concentric circles, as though she wasn't convinced that whatever was chasing her could ever be left behind.

"Do you want to go do something?" I ask. Hailie just looks at me, as if to say, *I have no idea why my mom thought it'd be a good idea to leave you in charge.* I'm inclined to agree. "Just give me a sec to change," I tell her.

I throw on a pair of jeans and one of the few clean shirts I have left and run my hands through my hair, which has gotten so long I can practically sit on it. Umma hates it when I grow my hair out. She tells me it makes me look like a water ghost. I tie it up into an unruly knot, where it sits on the crown of my head, tilting a little to the side, like a small nest. Tae used to laugh at me whenever I had my hair up like this, telling me I looked ridiculous, but sometimes he'd pull me in close and kiss the knot of my hair affectionately. It was one of the many inspired things he did that I didn't even remember to miss until I felt their absence.

As an afterthought, I trace some eyeliner onto my lids, and instantly I look more awake, though not by much. I go back into the living room and collect Hailie, who presents me with a drawing. "That's you," she says. My head is the size of a balloon and my hair is a witch's nest, and I'm holding a cup of coffee in my hand. On my chest are two small darts, pointing downward.

"Cool!" I say a little too enthusiastically.

"Those are your BREASTS," she tells me seriously, pointing at my chest in the drawing.

"Yep, noted." I look for my keys, not really sure how else to respond. I'm too hungover for this. Are kids supposed to go through a stage in which they avidly point out things on other people's bodies?

"Mommy says I'm going to get breasts, too, someday, and then I'll have to wear a BRA," she says.

"How old are you again?" I ask her.

"Five," she says, holding up her fingers.

"So you have a ways to go. Don't worry too much about breasts and all that other stuff. Just focus on being a kid and enjoying that," I tell her.

She looks at me like I'm being the weird one now. "Okay. Can we go already?"

I decide to take us for pizza. We get one large cheese pie with extra pepperoni, and then we both eat way too much and immediately regret it. For one alarming moment, I think I'm going to puke in the parking lot in front of her, but I get it together, gulping down some Diet Coke, and the bubbles help settle my stomach. "Do you want to go to the park?" I ask her, and she nods vigorously.

There's a small green park not far away from the pizza place. It's mostly empty today, except for a few joggers and a couple of teens who are huddled in a car, laughing loudly and playing music. I can smell their weed from here and I kind of wish I could ask them for some, even though the smell makes my head hurt.

I steer Hailie toward the playground, which is designed to look like a Viking ship, with one long plastic boat in the center and a whole bunch of slides and monkey bars spiking out of it. There's even a spyglass attached to the boat, and plastic oars that you can wiggle around. Hailie squeals and runs toward the boat when she sees it. I pretend to chase her for a while but give up when I get winded, so I watch her play instead, checking my phone intermittently for any texts from Rachel. Nothing so far.

A woman, her hair in loose ringlets cascading down her shoulders, approaches us, a little blond boy in tow. "Hi there," she says, smiling. "Mind if we join you? This is Trevor." Trevor tries to shrink behind his mother. He's holding some kind of action figure that he's hiding behind his back.

"Sure," I say, not sure why she's asking me. It's public property, after all. "That's Hailie," I say. Hailie sees us and gives a sly little wave, which freaks Trevor out even more.

"Go ahead, honey," his mother says, practically pulling him off her. But the moment she's out of his field of vision he goes wild, running all over the boat and shaking the oars in their sockets, going up and down the slides. Hailie watches, bemused, until they somehow figure out how to integrate each other into their play, the way little kids do.

"I'm Beth," the mom says, shining her toothpaste grin at me again. "We just moved to the neighborhood."

"Cool," I say, forgetting to introduce myself. I don't know why my vocabulary immediately deteriorates to that of a high school boy's whenever I'm confronted with someone who seems intensely more adult than me. But upon further examination, Beth doesn't seem that much older, after all. I usually have trouble guessing white people's ages, but something about the way she looks at me, then looks away nervously, while smiling the whole time, and the way she keeps playing with the charm bracelet on her wrist makes her seem younger than I'd thought.

"Your little girl is so precious," she says, trying again.

"Oh, she's not mine," I say. I stumble to correct myself before Beth can call an Amber Alert on me for stealing someone else's kid. "I mean, she's my cousin's. I'm just watching her for the day."

The smile on Beth's face falters just a little. "That's nice of you," she says. Then, unexpectedly: "We used to live near my sister. She would take Trevor sometimes during the day, when things got to be too much, or if I had to run out unexpectedly. It can be a lot, you know?" She says this wistfully, like I know exactly what "it" she's talking about, and even though I don't, I nod anyway. She tells me they moved here from Boston for her husband's job, and that while she's relieved they didn't have to go any farther than New Jersey, it feels like everything they've left behind is worlds away. I make sympathetic noises until she runs out of things to say. We lapse into silence when we realize that we don't have anything in common beyond being at the same playground at the same time.

I wonder, for a second, if she'd had visions of us becoming young-mom friends, arranging play dates between Trevor and Hailie, exchanging cookie recipes, complaining about our husbands. And honestly, all of that doesn't sound so bad. In another life, if Tae and I had stayed together, maybe we would have had something like that. I used to think, maybe because of the way Umma had been with me, that being a mom meant the end of being or having a self, that the only way to sustain another person's life was to completely give up your own. But when I consider the way Beth looks at Trevor, or the way Rachel looks at Hailie sometimes, maybe giving up part of yourself isn't such a bad thing, especially if it means you get to be part of something bigger—something that will last, hopefully, long after you're gone.

There's a high-pitched wail, the sound of a scuffle, and another cry. "Trevor!" Beth says, alarm in her voice. She darts onto the playground, and I follow her.

We find Trevor crying and crumpled on the ground, under the monkey bars. Hailie is standing on the platform looking down at him, her hands on her hips, and I give her a quick glance. "What happened?" I demand. She shrugs.

"She pushed me!" he says. Beth scoops him up, brushing the dirt off him and inspecting him frantically, and he starts crying even harder. Trevor's action figure, a robot, is lying facedown in the dirt. I reach to pick it up.

"He started it!" she says. "He was mean to me."

"So you pushed him?" I say, incredulous. Hailie looks away, off into the middle distance, as though she's bored by all of this.

"I'm so, so sorry—" I start to say to Beth. I try to hand Trevor the robot and she snatches it away from me.

"Get away from him," she says, her voice all dark and cold. I could swear it's gotten an octave deeper. "Lucky for you he doesn't seem to have broken anything," she adds. Trevor's crying in earnest now, his tears mingling with his snot and dripping down his shirt front, but he's able to stand and follows his mother as they leave the playground and get into their car and drive away.

"Fuck!" I say, not caring that Hailie can hear me. "Jesus, Hailie." She looks at me then. "What did that kid say to you? Don't they teach you not to push people at school?"

"Mommy always told me I have to stand up for myself," she said. Her lower lip starts to tremble. "He started it."

This is all way more than I bargained for. I wish I hadn't answered the door when Rachel knocked. I wish I hadn't drunk so much last night. I wish I didn't have to deal with any of this, that I could be back at home with the covers over my head. The pizza roils in my stomach. "Can you just tell me what happened?"

"He asked me where I lived, so I said I lived with Mommy and he asked if you were my mommy, and I said no and he asked me where my daddy was and I said Daddy doesn't live with us anymore, and he said, 'That means your parents are getting a divorce,' and I said no they're not and he said yes they are, and he said his mommy says only problem children's parents get divorced, so I pushed him," she says, all in one breathless rush.

I close my eyes. "Okay," I say. I hoist myself up onto the platform next to her. "So, you know you can't do that, right? You can't just push people around, even if you don't like the things they're saying."

"Yeah, but he was being bad. He started it."

"You keep saying that like it means something, but I'm telling you it doesn't."

Hailie starts to cry then, in deep, shuddering gasps. "Mommy said if anyone is being mean to me, I have to stand up for myself and not let them push me around ever," she says. "That's why she sent Daddy away, because he was being mean." Hot tears roll down her face. What kills me the most is that unlike most kids, she doesn't hold her arms out to be held or hold her hands up to her face when she cries. Instead, she just stands there, her hands balled into fists and arms rigid, wailing, so in the end, I'm the one who has to reach for her first. I wrap my arms around her until she collapses into me like a little rag doll, and I pat her shoulders awkwardly and tell her that everything is going to be okay, even though neither of us really believes it.

One of my parents' recurring fights was that Apa, according to Umma, never thought about the things he said. He could be mean, irascible. One moment he could be the nicest, most charming person at the party, and the next he'd be arguing with someone over some minor disagreement, so sure he was in the right that he didn't care what anyone else thought. One time I saw him argue with another man over a parking spot, both of them raising their voices. "You want to fight me?" he said, getting out of the car. "Go ahead. Come out and hit me." I watched Umma's face in the rearview mirror, an expression on her face I couldn't quite read. Her face was a dark shade of red, and her eyes glittered with angry tears. Years later, I would realize that look was shame.

"What kind of example are you setting?" Umma hissed when he finally got back in the car, after the other man had driven away. "What is wrong with you?"

I braced myself for another fight. But Apa seemed not to hear her, simply turning the radio back on and sliding the car into the contested spot with ease. He always seemed invigorated by his own displays of temper, afterward acting as energetic and cheerful as he'd ever been, like nothing had happened.

It didn't occur to me until I was older that perhaps this was something I'd inherited from him, too, in addition to my nose, which has a tendency to flare out when I smile for pictures, and my eyebrows, which grow into one long bushy line when I don't take the time to pluck them. Umma has naturally arched eyebrows that never seem to require grooming, whereas I looked like a tiny Korean Frida Kahlo for most of my early life, until Yoonhee got fed up with it and took a razor to the stubborn patch of wiry hair between my eyes. When Apa found out what we'd done, he'd just laughed, despite Umma's distress. "I guess we're not eyebrow twins anymore," he said.

But I worried, as time went on, that perhaps I had also inherited his impatience, his tendency to double down when challenged, or the bouts of depression that sometimes left him incapacitated for days, lying in the dark in his study at home.

I'd gone to see a psychiatrist once, a few years after Apa went missing. I kept waking up in the middle of the night, soaked with sweat and shaking, from dreams about drowning. "I just need a prescription for something," I told her. "To help me sleep."

"I'm not sure that not being able to sleep is your only problem," the psychiatrist said. "Have you ever talked to anyone about your father's disappearance? A counselor or a therapist?"

"Look, I already know the ways in which I'm screwed up," I said. "I just need something to help me manage it."

"It doesn't really work that way," she said gently. "First, we have to talk about what you're going through, in order to understand the problem here. Honesty is the key to overcoming your fears and anxieties."

I didn't go back after that.

Hailie falls asleep in the car on the way home, and Rachel texts that she's on her way back, too. There's no mention of how the meeting was or how Simon seemed, but I imagine, from the fact that she doesn't mention it, things probably went sideways. I sigh, bracing myself to tell her about how our afternoon went.

I carry Hailie, still sleeping, upstairs to my apartment. I swear, kids get ten pounds heavier when they fall asleep. On the way up, I notice that the earring is still there where I first saw it last night. It stares at me like a small golden eye as I struggle up the stairs.

When Rachel arrives, she seems fine, if distracted. "How's Hailie?" she asks me.

"Asleep," I say. "I put her down in the bedroom."

"Great," she says. She sits down on the yellow couch. A cloud of dust goes up around her, which she chooses to ignore. "Did you all have fun?"

"Well, she pushed a kid off the monkey bars on the playground and made him cry, so that wasn't the best."

"She what?" Rachel's face goes white.

"He was fine. Mostly. Apparently he told Hailie that only

'problem kids' have parents who get divorced. His mom was a real bitch about it."

"Oh god," Rachel says. "He could have gotten really hurt." She massages her temples. "I can't go through this again," she says.

"What do you mean, again? Has she been doing this with other kids?"

Rachel tells me that it started earlier this year. The pushing, the name-calling, stealing other kids' things. Hailie never had any behavioral problems before, and she's always liked preschool and had plenty of friends. But ever since the separation, Rachel's been getting calls home from the teachers regularly, telling her that Hailie has been acting out.

"I don't know what to do anymore," she says. "I've tried punishing her, taking away stuff, yelling. Nothing seems to work."

"Does she know you guys are separated for good?"

Rachel looks down at her knees. "I've been telling her it's a trial," she says softly. "That it's something we're just trying out for now, because Daddy needs to fix his behavior before we can move back in with him."

"Rach, you have to tell her that isn't happening. I mean—it's not happening, right?"

She doesn't answer me, but I can tell from the way she shrinks into the couch that the answer she'd like to give me has nothing to do with what she actually wants. That she wants nothing more than to go back to the way things used to be, to be able to go home to her big beautiful house in Tenafly, where her handsome doctor husband will greet her at the door and send her expensive flowers every anniversary. That she's tired of trying so hard and getting stuff wrong on her own.

"I just can't get used to the idea of life without him," she says. "We've been together for so long. I know it sounds stupid, but I miss him."

"Hailie said you told her to never let anyone push her around. Granted, she shouldn't be pushing other kids on the playground, but Simon pushes you around a lot. It's been happening for a while now."

"He was really sweet today," she says. "No, don't roll your eyes, Ro. I know you don't like him, but he's still important to me. He'll always be Hailie's dad."

"He tried to knock you down the *stairs*. In front of your *child*. Don't tell me he didn't mean it or that he didn't realize how close you were to the edge. He wanted to hurt you, and Hailie saw it." My heart is racing. I see the look on Rachel's face and tell myself I should shut up already, but I can't seem to stop. "I don't care how sweet he was to you today during your lunch date or whatever, you can't go back to that guy. That's exactly what he wants, to reel you back in so he can treat you even worse next time."

She shakes her head, not looking at me and biting her lip. "You don't know what you're talking about. You've never been married. It's not easy to turn your back on a whole life just like that. I have a fucking kid, okay?"

As if on cue, Hailie stirs and calls out, before either of us can say things we'll regret, and Rachel gets up and goes to her. I listen to them talking in my bedroom. Rachel's voice is gentle and warm, and I hear Hailie giggle at something. The indignation I felt, the righteous certainty that coursed through me just a few minutes ago ebbs away, leaving a vast weariness.

After they leave, I'm opening a beer that I'm telling myself is just to take the edge off my headache when I get a text from Umma. It's just one sentence: "Ro, I haven't heard from you . . ."

Do all parents of a certain age get crash courses on how to send the most ominous texts possible? I wonder. Then my annoyance is followed by a wave of guilt. I respond, telling her I'll come for dinner Monday next week, and ask what I can bring. "Nothing," she says. "Just yourself." Which is blatantly untrue. If I show up without anything, I'll never hear the end of it. I make a mental note to stop by the Korean supermarket on the way to see her, to get a box of golden pears. My mouth waters at the thought of the crisp white fruit.

I eat the leftover pizza standing up at the counter, and then take a shower, bringing the can of beer with me. The hot water feels good against my chest and shoulders, especially with the cold beer against my lips.

I think about the look in Rachel's eyes when she said she missed Simon. I think about Eriko the dolphin, swimming around and around in her tank, all alone till the end. I think about Hailie pushing that boy off the platform, watching him fall down into a pile of wood chips, thinking that that would stop her from feeling the pain of her parents no longer being together. I watch the water circle the drain, thinking about all the ways you can go crazy from loneliness or pain, the things you'll do or settle for when you get desperate enough.

CHAPTER 8

Six years earlier

Strings of paper flowers festooned the ceiling in graceful parabolas. They had been haphazardly taped up in spots, and the overall effect was one of confused beauty. I watched one of the strings slowly emancipate itself from its Scotch tape anchor as I ate my breakfast, wondering how late Yoonhee had stayed up decorating.

It had been Yoonhee's idea to throw a harvest moon party. She was going through an astrology phase. She claimed that the moon had the power to influence our actions and thoughts, and that this one was going to have a particularly intense effect on our careers and relationships. "'It's time to ask for what you want,'" she read aloud to me from her horoscope app as I dutifully helped her blow up silver balloons with the helium tank she'd gotten from somewhere. The special party cocktail of the night was something she called moon punch, which I suspected was just Sprite mixed with vodka and prosecco.

"I think it's a sign," she said excitedly, gesturing to her phone. "It means I should ask for a promotion."

"You don't need a horoscope app to tell you that," I said. "You're basically single-handedly running that department."

Yoonhee had started out as an assistant to Joy, the director of development at the aquarium, who was notorious for being unable to keep an assistant for longer than three months. She was a former development officer for some art museum up in New England and knew almost nothing about aquariums, a fact she often brought up in meetings. "Well, I'm no marine biologist," she'd say before launching into some completely unrelated point about a random expensive item that was "absolutely a must" for an upcoming donor event. Joy had five pairs of glasses that she rotated out throughout the week, and she loved Yoonhee despite being completely threatened by her. Yoonhee had learned to tell how Joy was feeling based on what pair of glasses she was wearing that day. For instance, if she was wearing the oversize tortoiseshell pair, it meant she was feeling approachable and casual; if she was wearing the dark green harlequin glasses, it meant steer clear.

Yoonhee had applied for and landed the job soon after I'd started working full-time at the Fountain. "It'll be so great to work together," she said, so genuinely excited that I couldn't tell her that it made me feel strange to know that she'd be working at the aquarium, a place that still felt like it belonged to only Apa and me.

Joy soon came to rely on Yoonhee for the cheerful calm she exuded and her visual design skills, immediately glomming on to the fact that Yoonhee knew how to use Photoshop. Over the years, Yoonhee had slowly managed to win more and more of Joy's confidence, until eventually she was the one making calls to high-profile donors and coordinating events like our annual gala. It turned out that Yoonhee was good at her job and that she liked doing it. She was good at saying yes and no to important people without actually promising them anything, and she liked setting goals and exceeding them.

"What about you?" she said. "You deserve a raise at least, after all the covering you've done for Carl and Francine."

"I'm happy where I am," I said in the same tone that I used whenever Umma asked me when I was going to leave my job. "There's no future in it," Umma told me the last time she tried to bring it up. "You're twenty-four years old, and your father wouldn't want to see you stuck in the same dead-end situation he got into with that place."

I was too scared to tell anyone, even Yoonhee, that I didn't really know what was next for me. Everyone always seemed to be climbing upward and striving for more all the time: more money and responsibility, a better title, greater prestige. And it wasn't like I didn't want any of those things for myself; it was more like I wouldn't have had any idea what to do with them had they come to me. I wanted, if I was being honest, to slow down, just for a little while. Everything felt like a race for which there wasn't even a definitive prize, and that didn't seem to end until you died.

"When you were little," Umma told me once, "you learned how to walk at such a young age that we were all astonished. But the faster you learned how to go and the easier it became for you, the less you wanted to walk anywhere. It was like you were becoming an infant again. You would sit down in the middle of the sidewalk or in the supermarket and refuse to move until either your father or I picked you up." She thinks this is a story about what she sees as my lack of ambition manifesting itself early on; I think this is a story about how almost anything, even something as basic as walking, can become less enjoyable when it's constantly being monitored for progress.

Yoonhee's plan for the party was that, at the end of the night, we would write our wishes for the full moon onto tiny slips of paper and then set them on fire, per something her horoscope app had recommended. "Where will we put the ashes?" I asked her. "What if we set off the smoke detector?" She waved me away, telling me to let our guests in.

Soon our tiny apartment was filled with people, most of them Yoonhee's friends or people I'd known in passing in college but lost touch with after we graduated. The playlist I'd crafted, one of the few party preparations that Yoonhee had entrusted me with managing, boomed through the speakers that one of James's friends had brought.

Yoonhee was wearing sparkly eye shadow and a gray dress with sheer sleeves and a full tulle skirt. She matched the balloons, which danced overhead as people laughed and drank and talked. Our apartment soon grew warm, and the smell of moon punch was thick in the air. "What's in this?" James said, pretending to choke on his while Yoonhee swatted at him playfully. But soon the punch was gone, as was most of the alcohol. "Crack open a window," came a cry, so somebody wrestled open our rusty windows, letting in a rush of cool night air.

I was drinking gin and tonics and had stationed myself halfway between the kitchen and our couch, where piles of Yoonhee and James's friends were lounging. I was wearing a maroon jumpsuit that had once been Yoonhee's. She'd given it to me after it shrank in the wash, making it ankle-length on her. I tugged at the bodice, wishing I'd worn something a little cooler. My underarms were starting to sweat, and I worried that they'd leave dark marks on the jumpsuit.

I had just managed to wrest myself away from a conversation with a guy in a shirt that had wolves airbrushed on it, who was appalled that I had never listened to *The Dark Side of the Moon*. He kept telling me to put it on, insisting that it was perfect for a moon-themed party. "It's not that kind of party," I said, meaning it was not the kind of party where we would all be silently listening to old British guys play synthesizers for forty minutes.

"Are you serious?" he said. "That album literally changed my life."

"You touch that aux, you die," I said finally, and I stared him down to let him know I meant business until he slunk away, annoyed.

James pulled out a joint, which was passed from person to person. I didn't really like smoking then—I didn't trust it the way I trusted alcohol, which I knew and understood. Smoking usually made me feel like part of me had escaped through a hatch at the top of my head and slid upward to the ceiling, a sensation I didn't always enjoy. But since I didn't know many of the people at the party—the few friends I'd kept up with from college couldn't make it that night—and the guy who had handed me the joint was cute, I took it. I inhaled slowly, holding the smoke in my lungs for a little too long before I released it. It burned the back of my throat, and I resisted the urge to cough.

Almost instantly the light in the room turned to a warm gold, and the party started to get fun. A dumb pop song that had been dominating the airwaves that fall came on, a song with an exceedingly catchy drum-snared chorus that almost everyone knew the words to, and at some point, everyone started dancing, even climbing on top of the couch and our few folding chairs to really get into it. Yoonhee pulled me in and twirled me, bending me backward like we were ballroom dancing. We shimmied our shoulders and swiveled our hips. I always liked dancing with Yoonhee. Neither of us were very good dancers, but she had a way of throwing herself into the music confidently that made me feel like I could, too.

Then the party shifted into what I thought of as phase 3, which is when a party has pushed past its fever pitch but is still going: the energy is good, no one seems to be in a rush to go, and there's still a chance that someone might open another bottle of wine. Phase 3 is the best part of any party, made up of small moments in which it feels like almost anything can happen.

I removed myself from the dance circle and headed into the kitchen to get another drink. I was rattling around with some ice cube trays when I looked up to find the guy who had handed me the joint standing in the doorway. "Need any help?" he said.

He was taller than I'd thought. His face—deep-set eyes behind his gold-rimmed glasses, a determined chin, his mouth curved up in a half-smile when one of the ice cubes I was try-ing to remove skittered across the kitchen floor—looked so familiar that I blinked twice before remembering to respond. I couldn't think of where I'd seen him before. Time slowed down, and even the music and chatter from the party seemed to subside. "Do I know you?" I asked. *Real smooth,* I thought to myself.

"I don't think so, other than from just now in the living room. I'm Tae," he said, extending a hand toward me. I took it, noticing how sure his grip was, as well as the calluses on his palm and fingers.

"I'm Ro," I said.

"Like, row your boat?" he teased, but not in an annoying way.

"It's short for Aurora," I said, rolling my eyes slightly to show him I wasn't exactly amused by the joke but that I wasn't going to dismiss him completely because of it. "But no one calls me that."

We stared at each other a moment as I tried to remember what I had been doing before he'd walked in. "Sorry, I'm a little high," I said, laughing way too hard in spite of myself. *Get it together,* I thought. "Want a drink?"

I made him the world's sloppiest gin and tonic and sloshed part of my own on the floor, waving him away when he offered to help clean it up. I tore a few paper towels off the thin roll on the counter and threw them on top of the fizzing puddle. I watched the liquid weep through the sheets. "So, what brings you here?" I asked, trying to lean casually against the kitchen counter.

"One of my friends knows James," he said. "What about you?"

"Oh, I'm here all the time," I said. "I mean, I live here. With Yoonhee."

We knocked our cups together in a silent toast.

"Cool party," he said. "I like the playlist." I felt warmth course through my cheeks and chest.

He was a science teacher at a middle school in Teaneck, but he also played bass in a local indie band with one of James's friends. They called themselves Jigsaw, after the guy from the *Saw* movies, which I'd never seen. He grimaced when I asked him why. "It was Kyle's idea, and the other guys like it. We don't sound anything like that. I voted against it, but it was three against one," he said.

"What would you have named the band if it were up to you?"

"I suck at naming things," he said. "But I've always wanted

to name something after my dog. She died when I was twelve."
He showed me an old photo on his phone of the two of them,
a tiny Tae in yellow shorts and a baseball cap hugging a shaggy
white Great Pyrenees.

"She looks like a polar bear next to you," I said, laughing
at the look of mingled confusion and happiness on the dog's
face. I hadn't grown up with any pets. Umma and Apa always
claimed that dogs and cats were more trouble than they were
worth. "What was her name?"

"Frankie. Well, Frank. I insisted on naming her," he said,
and then we were both laughing, at the absurdity of a dog
named Frank, the unstudied weirdness of little kids, the guile-
lessness of dogs. It felt good to laugh with him, like we'd been
doing it forever.

"I guess Frankie's kind of a dumb name for a band," he said.

"I'd listen to a band called Frankie," I said.

"Yeah?" he said. "Well, if you want to listen to a band called
Jigsaw, you should come to one of our shows sometime. You
can just say you're with me and they'll let you in for free. Save
you five bucks cover."

Then it hit me—I had seen him somewhere before. A few
months ago, when Yoonhee and I had gone downtown to a
bar called Rumors and a band had come on, three skinny
white guys and one Asian guy. I hadn't paid much attention
at the time and we didn't stay for the whole set, because I was
too focused on trying to follow Yoonhee's complicated story
about why she was upset with James for not texting her back
fast enough earlier that week, but it came back to me that I
had actually enjoyed the music they'd played. I remembered it
being kind of shoegaze-y, the drone of the guitars offset by one
high wailing guitar line, with a rolling bass that I could feel in
my gut.

"I think I saw you guys down at Rumors a few months back," I said. "I thought you looked familiar."

"No way," he said. There was that smile again. *Oh no,* I thought when I realized that the fizzing I felt inside my stomach wasn't just from the tonic in the gin and tonics. "You should have said hi."

"I get nervous in crowds," I said. My palms itched, and I wiped them against the jumpsuit. I was about to ask him if he wanted to get out for a bit and walk around when Yoonhee yelled my name. "It's time for wishes," she said.

We went back out. It wasn't much cooler in the living room than it had been when we left it, despite all the windows being open. Yoonhee was handing out strips of paper and pens. "Okay, shut up, everyone," she said, slurring a little. "Be quiet." I stifled a laugh. Yoonhee went into Kindergarten Teacher mode sometimes when she was drunk.

She pointed out the window, where the moon shone like a bright yellow coin in the sky. It looked almost frighteningly close to us, like it was about to bump its big face into the earth. "The moon tonight is closer to us than it's ever been," she said. "That's pretty fucking cool. Don't you think that's fucking cool?" Everyone laughed, but they nodded, as if they all totally got it.

"We're going to write down our wishes for the moon," she announced. "It can be anything. It can be really big or really small, but it has to be something you want, and you have to be serious about it. Then we're going to fold them up and put them in this bowl here," she said, indicating a metal bowl that she'd put on the floor.

"So normally, we'd burn them to make them come true, but Ro doesn't want me to set our apartment on fire, which I guess is reasonable," she said. I felt ten pairs of eyes swivel toward me, including Tae's. "So instead of doing that, we're just going to mix them all up in this bowl and then each person is going to pick one of the wishes and read it out loud to the group, and then we'll all clap. And we'll release it into the universe that way."

"And no making fun," she added, glaring at James, who clearly wanted to laugh. "This is a circle of safety."

Despite the jostling and joking around that ensued, within a few minutes we were all quietly hunched over our pieces of paper, puzzling over our wishes. Yoonhee wrote hers down right away and tossed it into the bowl with confidence, as though that alone would ensure that her wish came true. I watched Tae as he bit his lip, thought, and then scrawled something down. I stared at my own slip of paper, its blankness taunting me. What did I want? What would I wish for if I knew it would come true?

It occurred to me that there was only one thing that I really wanted. And there was no way the moon or anyone else could ever give it to me.

"Time's up!" Yoonhee said. "Ro, you're the only one who hasn't put your wish in the bowl."

"Okay, okay," I said. I wrote my wish down, folded it up, and Hail Mary'd it in from across the room.

Yoonhee mixed up the slips of paper with both hands, like she was tossing leaves for a salad. "Remember, we have to be respectful of the wish, once it's been spoken," she said to everyone. This time there was no laughing or cracking jokes. Having to think about their wishes, what they really wanted, had made everyone go quiet.

"I'll go first, and then we can go around the circle," Yoonhee said. She reached a hand into the wish bowl, pulled one out, and read it out loud to us. "I wish to win the lottery," she read out loud. She rolled her eyes. "Very cool, James," she said.

"What?" he said, looking around and grinning. "You said no making fun, right?"

"Fine," she said, sighing and clapping. The rest of us joined in. It felt weird at first, clapping in a circle like that, like we were all in an AA meeting or something, but as more and more people took turns reading aloud other people's wishes, it started to feel like we weren't just releasing the wishes into the universe—we were cheering them on, releasing them on their cosmic journey out and up to the moon.

Most of the wishes were pretty straightforward. "I wish to lose ten pounds this year." "I wish for a new car." "I wish for my younger brother to get into his dream school." "I wish for a raise." But some of them were surprising in their honesty, and they made my throat catch. "I wish my sister and I were closer." "I wish for a job that will help me pay off my parents' debt." "I wish I had the power to do something to change the world." We clapped after each one, until my hands began to sting. A night breeze blew in, shifting the curtains and bringing with it a strain of reggae music that was playing somewhere down the street.

Tae passed the bowl to me. I picked a slip of paper from the bowl and read aloud, "I wish to always be in love with the same person." I looked up and saw Yoonhee smiling at James, who looked embarrassed but pleased. I felt a prickle of annoyance. *What a thing to wish for,* I thought. As if being in love was a static condition, as if love was a state one could choose to leave or stay in.

When the bowl got to Tae, he hesitated a little before he reached in and pulled out one of the few remaining slips of paper. He unfurled it and read aloud, "I wish I could talk to my dad." This time, the claps were a little more uncertain, as though people weren't sure how much they could applaud something as nakedly sad as that. My cheeks felt warm, and I focused on watching the balloons gently collide into one another around the room.

I could feel Yoonhee watching me from across the room, but I didn't lift my eyes to hers. *I'm fine,* I tried to tell her telepathically. I didn't want to feel her apology, her guilt over something that wasn't hers to feel guilty or sorry about. After a while you get tired of hearing it.

I was fifteen when Apa went missing, somewhere in the approximately fifty-square-mile zone that made up the Bering Vortex. All I heard, day in and day out, were other people's condolences. *I'm so sorry for your loss. I'm sorry that this happened. I'm so sorry.* It made me angry, how people reacted to it, so ready to believe the worst. Instead, I wanted them to tell me that everything was going to be all right; that boats went missing and came back all the time in far-flung, treacherous locations like the Bering Vortex; that they were sure my father would turn up soon. Or even better, that there had been some kind of mistake, and that actually my father was alive and well and coming home after all.

I remembered thinking, the day Umma got the news via a phone call from the Fountain, that it wasn't true. I didn't believe it, even when Umma began crying and screaming from the kitchen. The noise she was making seemed to me all out of proportion with how she'd treated him when he was around, as though he was an inconvenience that she wanted gone from her life. But the wail that emerged from her mouth was almost inhuman, animal in its pain, and I had to help her onto our couch. "I knew I shouldn't have let him go again," she kept saying. She stayed in bed for three days while I ignored all the incoming phone calls and drew the shades and went to school and came back home again.

When I told Yoonhee, she was shocked that I was in school at all and told me to go home, but I didn't know what to do. I didn't want to be stuck at home with Umma, who seemed to have sunk into a sea of grief so deep neither of us could see the bottom of it. She barely ate the rice and banchan I scrounged together from the dregs of the refrigerator for her. "Umma," I said, "you have to eat." She would turn away from me, saying she just needed to sleep. At night, I sometimes heard her rouse herself and shuffle to the bathroom, and I would listen to the sound of her urinating and wonder how she had held it in all day, since as far as I knew, she never left the bed during the day. It was as if grief had somehow leached her body of fluids, turned her blood into salt.

I scoured headlines and news articles for signs that I was right, that all of this fuss was for nothing. The papers covered the disappearance of Apa's boat for about two days before the newest sex scandal involving some politician was exposed and that dominated the news cycle. I called the aquarium, the foundation that had given Apa the research grant, even the company that manufactured the boat every day, just to see if anything had changed, if any of their search-and-rescue teams had found even the slightest trace of the boat and its passengers. I made charts, maps, diagrams of all the possible places the boat could have gone missing, or perhaps run aground on something and sunk.

When I couldn't find any leads among the logical sources, I

turned to the illogical ones, sinking deeper and deeper into an internet black hole about other mysterious deaths and disappearances. The Roanoke Colony. The Dyatlov Pass incident. The Bermuda Triangle. Malaysia Airlines Flight 370. I became obsessed, turning to Reddit conspiracy theories about how lizard people were running the world and how numerology could explain almost every single one of these disappearances. I even stumbled on a thread about Apa's boat and read the whole thing, all eighty-five replies to the original post, which had been made by someone named riley248, even though every comment made me feel sick.

"If you ask me," riley248 said, "the Vortex got them. It's called that for a reason. Humans, living things—we're not meant to exist in places like that. In old days they'd mark those spots on the maps. 'Here be dragons' and shit. Well, the jury's still out on dragons, but you sure as shit don't go messing around in the ocean, especially in a zone that polluted."

"Do you think they planned it?" MrBlackHat wondered. "Maybe they all went crazy Jonestown-style, sank the ship. Some kind of ritualistic thing. This reminds me a lot of the Akron chemtrails cover-ups, back in '06. Ecoterrorists??"

"One of the researchers was doing research at an aquarium out east, working with cephalopods," said derp_tastic_dino. "Looks like Cthulhu called."

Every new comment suggested an alternate reason or circumstance for Apa and the crew's disappearance. One person even wondered if it was a publicity stunt. Several people had pointers to offer in terms of other cases that it reminded them of. By the end of the thread, my head was spinning.

Only one person in the thread, umbrellahuntress, seemed to think that the crew was still alive, but not in our world. "I've read about how other dimensions can just well up out of nowhere," they wrote. "They call them 'thin places' in Ireland. Zones where you can feel the presence of other worlds. I've been researching the Bering Vortex for some time, and it sounds to me like a thin place." Their comment had been downvoted by several users, with replies about how this wasn't a place for speculation about things that we didn't have scientific proof for. The thread ended in the usual back-and-forth superiority squabbles that all internet arguments do.

But I liked the idea of thin places. To me, it seemed easier and more palatable to think that a pocket of air had simply opened up over the ocean and swallowed him up than it was to think he was dead. So despite the fact that we held a memorial for him and that his desk was cleared out at work and Umma eventually started using his study as a separate storage room, I continued to believe that Apa wasn't really gone. He was just missing, and it wouldn't be long before he came back through the front door, whistling the way he always did, his hair maybe longer or grayer than it had been. He'd say, "How's my Acorn?" the way he used to, before opening the refrigerator to stare into it, like an errant teenager, until Umma yelled at him for wasting electricity.

It was partly why I'd started working at the Fountain. I thought that if I could at least be where Apa had spent most of his waking hours, I would be closer to him, and it would be easier to wish him back home. Mostly, though, I just didn't know what to do next with my life.

I spent summers volunteering at the aquarium at first, leading tour groups and helping out with minor administrative tasks, and then when I graduated, I applied for an entry-level opening in the animal husbandry department, even though I hadn't taken very many biology or math classes in college, which the application said "was not required but strongly encouraged." Umma was upset when I told her. After I got the job, she didn't speak to me for a week, but I didn't care. It brought me a kind of peace to walk around the quiet blue-green halls of filtered light, watching the silvery bodies of these animals that were so different from us, busily living their lives. Fish, sea mammals, crustaceans, cephalopods, mollusks, penguins—all of them were so much less demanding, easier to understand, than the shifting currents and tides of other people and of my own mind.

Every once in a while I went back to my Reddit holes about the Bering Vortex Vanishing, as people started calling it, but eventually I stopped feeling the need. There was never any new information anyway, nothing to be gleaned from the endless forums and message boards and YouTube videos that people uploaded from the darkness of their bedrooms, filled with grainy footage of my father and the other crew members, along with the boat itself. I had seen and read almost everything there was to know about the Vortex.

Eventually Apa's disappearance turned into just another hole that Umma and I tiptoed around, ignoring it unless it was absolutely necessary. As soon as she'd recovered from her initial bout of grief, Umma went through all of our family photos featuring him and moved them, frames and all, into his study. New white spaces appeared on our walls and side tables, as though the house was growing bald spots. Gradually Umma stopped talking about him at all, though she continued to wear her wedding ring and sleep on her side of the bed. "I can't get used to taking up the center of it," she said to me when I asked her why.

I thought I saw him a few times. Once in the crowds at my college graduation, sitting on the bleachers with a camera, aiming it at me. Another time at the grocery store, when I saw an Asian man of his exact height and build and hair length testing the ripeness of a melon and I almost dropped the grocery basket I was carrying. And another time down the Jersey Shore, when I went to the beach with Yoonhee and our friends and thought I saw, walking along the waves by himself, a figure in orange swim trunks that looked like him. But it was always someone else or just a trick of the light, my eyes seeing things that weren't there. And every time it happened, when my heart leaped and I thought wildly that he'd come back after all, only to realize that I was wrong, I believed in him a little less, until one day that small flicker of belief died, too.

It was two in the morning by the time the party broke up. Things had gotten awkward after the bowl game, and people were calling cars and saying their goodbyes. When almost everyone had gone, Yoonhee found me in the kitchen. "Are you okay?" she asked, touching my shoulder.

I didn't look up, just kept searching for a garbage bag to throw all the orphaned beer bottles and plastic cups into. "I'm fine."

Yoonhee gave me the look that meant she knew I was lying, but she leaned in and gave me a crooked hug. "I'm going to bed," she said. "Don't stay up too late."

I came out into the living room to find that Tae was standing by the door, the last to leave. The light from our hallway illuminated the lenses of his glasses. He was wearing a dark blue oversize coat with a turned-up corduroy collar, and he had his hands in the pockets. His eyes were slightly bloodshot from the weed, and I wondered if mine were as well. I resisted the urge to reach out and touch the stubble on his chin and upper lip, the wiry black hairs interspersed with a few strands of silver. "So our next show is in a few weeks," he said. "If you give me your number, I can text you the details."

My stomach fluttered as I put my number into his phone. He placed his phone to his ear and called me. "Well, aren't you going to answer it?" he said with mock seriousness.

I picked up, the phone warm against my ear. "Hello?"

"Hey," he said. "How did you get this number?"

"Oh, some weird dude at this party gave it to me." It was strange, I thought, how I could both see and feel him smiling through the phone.

"Same thing happened to me," he said. "This girl just walked up to me and insisted on giving me her number. She was really pushy about it."

"Maybe they meant to get in touch with each other, and they got us by mistake," I said.

"If that's the case," he said, "I'm glad that happened."

Neither of us moved. From the living room, where my playlist was still going, Neil Young's thin voice quavered through "Harvest Moon."

"Well, I'll see you around," Tae said. Then to my surprise, he leaned forward and kissed me, somewhere between the corner of my mouth and my ear, right where my phone had been. When the door swung shut, I sat down on our couch alone, both exhilarated and incredibly sad, for reasons that felt as tangled as the garlands of paper flowers that Yoonhee had painstakingly hung up. And as I began to drift off to sleep, still surrounded by the silver balloons bobbing around the ceiling, I wondered what Tae had wished for.

CHAPTER 9

On Monday, I wake up early. The sun's not even up yet and the traffic outside my window is at a low hum, the dull roar of the highway not yet at its full power. My sheets are soaked with sweat, and I realize it's because the heating in my building has come on, although it's 65 degrees outside. The radiator thumps and bangs furiously, like there's a tiny man inside hell-bent on hammering his way out.

I decide it's no use trying to get back to sleep and brew a pot of coffee. I sip it as I watch the sun come up, an anemic orange line that gradually thickens, until I decide, just for the hell of it, to go in early to work.

The Fountain Plaza doesn't open till eleven, but the lot where employees usually park is almost full by the time I get to the mall at eight a.m. My shadow stretches across the cement as I walk up to the entrance and swipe my ID card. Rick, the morning security guard, nods at me. "Early for you today," he says. He's folding tiny cranes out of squares of patterned paper, and they stand on the edge of his station, lined up like little centurions.

"Morning, Rick," I say. "How many are you up to?"

"Six hundred and forty-three," he says, putting the final touches on the crane he's folding out of floral pink paper. It joins the others, all of whom stare back at me, a paper family. I've never asked what he's folding them for, but he's been doing it ever since he started at the Fountain, about six months ago. His fingers are quick and sure, like he's folded so many that he doesn't need to look down at the paper anymore. I imagine his house must be filled with paper cranes, spilling out onto every counter and surface, crowded into jars and boxes and bookshelves.

He catches me staring. "Passes the time," he says. "I used to smoke. Ever since I was sixteen. I couldn't even get out of bed if I didn't have at least one cigarette. Couldn't climb a flight of stairs without wheezing, either, by the time I was forty."

"So what happened?"

"My girlfriend got pregnant and said she'd kill me if I didn't quit. So I did. But my hands got shaky, so I got into origami. Gotta replace one habit with another, right?" A smile breaks across his face as he reaches into his pocket and shows me a picture of the sonogram, which looks like a shimmering half-moon, rippling out onto a field of black. A curve of white outlines the shape of what looks like a tiny skull.

I pass the photo back and congratulate him, and he hands me the pink crane. I turn it over in my hands, feeling its sharp folds and the prick of its beak.

"Trying to get to a thousand before the baby comes. Crystal

says if you make a thousand cranes it's good luck or something. She's thinking we can hang them up in the nursery."

"What'll you do then?" I ask.

"I'll figure out how to make something else," he says. "Maybe I'll move on to frogs. I've always liked frogs."

I cup the crane inside my right hand, where it nestles into my palm like a secret.

The inside of the mall is cold and quiet. I take the long way to work, listening to my sneakers squeak against the white tiles. Sunlight filters in through the windows near the ceilings, although not much natural light is allowed in. If it weren't for the sound of Muzak, the fake potted trees leaning gracefully into one another overhead and the sound of water gushing in the coin fountain that gives the Plaza its name might fool you into thinking you're in some kind of park or oasis.

I pass the fountain on my way to the aquarium, which is on the other end of the building. It comforts me to see the carpet of copper and silver at its bottom, the reefs of nickels and dimes and pennies beached there. When I was little, the mall used to have a contest, where kids would try to guess how much money had been thrown into the fountain. At the end of the week, after they'd collected all the coins (which they claimed went to charity), whoever guessed closest to the actual amount would receive a $50 gift certificate that could be redeemed at any store or restaurant in the mall, and got to have their picture in the paper and hung in a hall of fame near the entrance of the mall. I entered the contest each year and lost wildly every time, guessing either much too high or too low. The winner was almost always this boy named Adam Whitaker, a kid who didn't even live in town but whose father was a math professor at Princeton. "You'd think they would have taken him out of the running by now," Umma always said disgustedly when she saw his picture in the hall of fame.

I walk past the luxury stores, which are all grouped together in one corridor of the mall. It's hard not to feel at least a little seduced by the slick sheen of their glass windows, showing off the slim, headless mannequins wearing soft knits and printed scarves and the symmetrical displays of handbags that cost more than two months' rent. Yoonhee used to drag me into those stores when we were teens, ignoring the pointed looks of the salespeople as they followed us around and watched us squeal over the rich fabrics and embossed logos.

Then there are the kiosks filled with novelty products no one needs, like CBD-infused candles, beveled crystals etched with holographic photos that make their subjects look like pale ghosts, resin pendants with real flower petals encased inside them, leather bracelets that you can get your name engraved on. None of them are open yet, but some of the vendors are setting up, and we nod in the way of people who recognize one another but don't know one another well enough to breach that initial acknowledgment.

At the entrance of the aquarium, there's a large placard featuring a cartoon sea otter wearing a T-shirt with our logo on it. "You otter come on in!" the speech bubble coming out of his mouth says. On the back of the placard, he's waving goodbye, saying, "Hope to sea you again soon. Thanks for stopping by!"

Carl's corny ass is definitely responsible for this. I swipe my card and walk inside, sighing as I steel myself for another day.

Dolores sails down from the rock she's been sitting on when I walk into her exhibit room. She's strawberry-colored today, her arms and legs a frill of pink and white.

"How was your weekend, Lo?" I say, placing my hand against the glass as she displays her white suckers. Her eyes seem merry, amused. I open the hatch at the top of her tank and lower her bucket of food into the water. She plays with her food all the time, first eyeing it like it's a living thing that can escape her before pouncing on it, as if to say, "Gotcha!" Then she'll ignore the rest of the pieces floating around her until she gets bored again and hunts them down. I never get tired of watching her.

There's a theory (highly unscientific, of course) that octopuses are actually alien life-forms, remnants of extraterrestrial life that once came to our planet and either died out or left. Octopuses can fold themselves into the tiniest of spaces, as long as their sharp beaks, the only hard parts of their bodies, can fit into them, and sometimes when Dolores doesn't feel like being gawked at by the visitors, I've seen her wedge herself into crannies of her tank, just one eye peering out. We've gotten complaints about it before from visitors, claiming that they didn't pay for a ticket to come see an empty tank, and we always have to point out that she's there—she's just hiding. I don't think she's shy or scared. I think it's because she knows that there's more to see and notice if you stay hidden. If she could, she'd extend one or more arms toward each of the visitors, taste their arms and faces just to see what they're like.

I can't bear to think about her being somewhere else, no

matter how big or nice her new tank might be. Would they know how to keep her entertained, or how to chop up her seafood into chunks of various sizes, so that she can take her time eating it, wherever she was going? Would they even bother talking to her, wishing her good morning, playing her music?

This can't be real, I think. Maybe Yoonhee is wrong or the deal will fall through. Moving an animal as big and complicated as Dolores would be a huge undertaking, even for a billionaire. As if on cue, Dolores rolls one of her eyes, like she's agreeing with me.

We can't help anthropomorphizing the animals. Any researcher or biologist who spends enough time with them and tells you that they don't is lying. We wouldn't be human if we didn't see some reflection of ourselves in everything.

I don't really know if Dolores gets lonely or bored. I'm just projecting, mapping my own preoccupations and concerns onto her, the way humans have been doing to animals for eons. But whatever she feels, she's alive, and when I'm around her, I feel alive, too.

By the time I'm done prepping the animals' food for the day, it's nine. I sit down in the staff kitchenette and check my email while my coworkers file in. We greet one another with small smiles or nods, and everyone gets their favorite mug and lines up patiently to use the coffee machine. I sometimes reflect on these learned behaviors that we've all managed to acquire over our years as working professionals, and how if anyone wanted to get a good sense of how humans behave, the workplace would be one of the best ways to observe us.

I imagine Werner Herzog narrating it all in my head. *"See them line up in neat, orderly patterns in order to receive their morning refreshment. It is fascinating that no one tells them to do it, and yet they know, as if by instinct."*

Carl walks into the room. "Morning, team!" he says. "Bright and early for you, huh, Ro?"

I'm instantly irritated, but then I remember that I have a tiny Werner Herzog in my brain and try to focus on that instead. *"Notice how the self-proclaimed leader of the colony seeks to establish his authority immediately with a greeting, and how the response of each member of the colony is reflective of their social status,"* Werner says.

"Figured I'd catch up on some work," I tell Carl.

"That's the spirit!" he says. "Come see me in my office in a few—need to discuss the prep for Dolores's big move with you." *Dolores's big move.* As if she's switching careers or something.

Francine darts a look at me, her antennae going up. "Anything I can help with, Carl?" she asks in a syrupy voice.

"Nothing that implicates you directly, Francine. But I appreciate that team spirit," he says, beaming at us. "Unless you think you need the help, Ro."

"Notice the young female, how she hunches protectively over herself at the communal table but refuses to join the others," Werner hisses in my ear. *"She has received an invitation to be part of the colony's activities."*

"Nope," I say. "Thanks, though." I give Carl a look that I hope translates to chipper competence.

"The lone female seems reluctant to be part of the daily hub-bub," says Werner as everyone else takes their time getting their coffee, chatting with one another about their weekends. *Okay, that's enough,* I think to myself, putting a stop to my mental narration. I can be called "the lone female" only so

many times in one morning before I snap, even if it's by a voice in my own head.

The meeting in Carl's office is short, just ten minutes. To my surprise, Yoonhee's there, too, when I walk in, wearing a mauve dress with fluttery sleeves that looks more suited to a tea party than to work. I mumble *hey* to her and stare at the tiny globe on Carl's desk while he talks about bottom lines, budgets, and cuts.

"Yoonhee's going to be our point in Dev on this," he says, his voice practically vibrating with delight over the unnecessary abbreviations he loves to use. "We're going to need you to develop a list of items needed for the transition, as well as a memo on Dolores's care and feeding that we can pass along."

Yoonhee addresses all her questions to Carl. She doesn't once call Dolores by her name, instead referring to her, hilariously, as "the asset," like we're in a spy movie. "The buyer is eager to know if she's in good health, so getting some vitals on the asset, to start, would be great. He'll be coming by later this month to take a look himself, so if there's anything you could do in the meantime to ensure that the asset is ready for perusal, we'll be in good shape."

"Wait," I say, trying to stifle my laughter. "You want me to tell Dolores that her new dad is coming by to take a look at her and that she should get ready? Do you want me to book her a hair appointment, too?"

There's an uncomfortable silence. Carl clears his throat. "If this is difficult in any way, Ro, we understand. Just say the word and we'll have someone else oversee the transition."

"I'm just trying to get some clarity around my directives," I say, and I see one of Yoonhee's eyebrows go up. It's the kind of thing one of us would have said to make fun of other people, once upon a time. "But you do realize that she's an animal, right? Like, she is going to behave how she's going to behave. We don't have any control over that." A note of desperation enters my voice, against my will. I want to punch myself for how sad I sound. "Isn't there anything else we could do? We can't lose Dolores."

Yoonhee sounds annoyed. "Believe me, we tried to think of every possible way to avoid this happening. Dolores, in addition to being an incredible asset for the Fountain, is a significant revenue draw for us, and it's a loss for all of us, not just you." There's no trace of the Yoonhee I've known since I was six years old, my old partner in crime, my former roommate. There's only her stupid mauve dress and perfectly manicured nails tap-tapping away at her phone. I don't know why I ever thought I could get through to her.

"Maybe the two of you can chat offline about this," Carl says nervously. "In the meantime, let's make sure everything's ready for the eventual handover, and that Dolores will be as comfortable as possible during the move."

"When is it happening?" I ask.

Yoonhee looks away. It's the only sign of her obvious discomfort. "The client is coming by in about a week. From there, depending on how quickly we can get everything together, we can transport her as soon as the end of the month."

"By the end of the month." My hands seem to have acquired a life of their own. They're twitching and fluttering in my lap, and I stare at them, as though they don't belong to me anymore. "Pretty soon, huh."

"We're bringing in a moving crew. They're specialists," Yoonhee says.

"Sounds like you've thought of everything," I say.

"Someone's got to, right?" Yoonhee says with a fake cheerfulness.

Carl shifts in his seat and clears his throat as we glare at each other. "Great," he says. "Thanks, both. I think we've really gotten somewhere today."

Yoonhee doesn't even try to catch up with me after the meeting. It's as though whatever talk we had at Hattie's on Friday never even happened. I can feel her eyes on me as we walk out of Carl's office together, but I don't turn around.

The rest of the day passes in a haze as I move from room to room, enclosure to enclosure. The penguins are fighting, their lives as filled with drama as usual, and one of the nurse sharks is sick, meaning I have to call our veterinary staff in and help hold him in the small, shallow tank that we coax him into, his skin rubbery and cold underneath my hands. By noon, I'm exhausted.

I check my phone at lunch and see that Umma has texted, reminding me about dinner tonight. "Don't be late," she says.

I wonder how Umma will react when I tell her about Dolores being sold to a private buyer. She never understood why Apa was so obsessed with her, even after he explained that Dolores's unique genetic makeup was part of his research. Umma didn't like animals that she deemed untrustworthy, a group that included sharks and cephalopods. She preferred the fluffy otters and the bright-eyed dolphins, or the seals.

I think Umma wanted, above all, for Apa to be a normal husband. Someone who had a nine-to-five job, one that didn't take him away to far-flung places where she couldn't follow; someone whose day-to-day tasks she could understand or at least pretend to take an interest in. Someone who would go with her on Sundays to church, instead of scoffing at it, and bring her flowers on her birthday and remember anniversaries and other special occasions.

It occurs to me now that Umma must have been perennially disappointed with her marriage to a man who didn't see her, who was always chasing something she couldn't understand or provide, whether it was in the arms of another woman or in the far corners of the ocean. It was why she was always so angry when I was a child, so ready to boil over with years of resentment and grief. And it was probably why, when Tae left, none of it felt new, like I'd been rehearsing for his departure since the day we met. Because I was used to people leaving, and in my heart of hearts, I never thought someone like Tae would stay for someone like me.

I wonder if Umma had hated having to leave Korea, if she missed home. If the United States even feels like home to her now. "If we had stayed in Korea . . ." was a common refrain of hers. If we had stayed in Korea, we would have been there when Halmoni, my mother's mother, died. If we had stayed in Korea, she would have remained close with all her brothers and sisters, and I would have had more cousins to play with and grow up with. Most of all, if we had stayed in Korea, she wouldn't have been entirely dependent on Apa for everything.

There was always a sense, when I was growing up, that our family was a self-contained unit, and that if anything happened to us, we wouldn't have anyone we could call or lean on. My parents were never very good at asking for help, which I suppose is one way I'm like them.

By the time I leave work, I'm bone-tired and I smell like fish guts. I have enough time before heading to Umma's to stop at home and take a quick shower. I run a comb through my wet hair and rifle through my closet in search of something suitable to wear, suddenly nervous, as though I'm headed to a blind date. I settle on a dress that I haven't worn in months, a floral-patterned yellow sundress. It's a little short on me, but it's the only clean, presentable thing I own that Umma won't immediately make some kind of comment about.

Umma tends to give me things I'd never buy for myself, things that she thinks fit into the trappings of the life she wanted for me. On my birthdays, she gets me cashmere sweaters or Swarovski pendants, sterling silver necklaces ending in hearts or stars—gifts for the little princess she wishes I could have been. They're all stacked in the back of my closet, like ghosts relegated to one corner of my life. I hesitate before putting on one of them, a glittery crescent moon on a delicate silver chain. The rhinestones on the moon seem to tremble when the light hits them.

Apa used to tell me that Umma's criticisms were rooted in care, as though I didn't know that. "She wants you to look your best because she loves you," he said.

"But why does she have to make me feel so bad about it?" I asked.

He considered this for a while. "Well, I guess it's because she doesn't know how to express it any other way."

I drive to the Korean supermarket on the other side of town, where I stand in line for ten minutes to buy a box of Umma's favorite Korean pears. The pale golden orbs are packed inside white plastic nets that look a little like scandalous sweaters or fishnet stockings, their tender skins peeking out from the weave of the netting. Umma used to peel Korean pears in the kitchen whenever guests came over, people from church or colleagues of Apa's. She would cut the skin away with surgical precision and swiftness. "When your father first brought me to his house to meet his parents, I had to help his mother cut and peel pears after dinner," she told me when I was little. My own hands were clumsy with the paring knife, and when I tried to peel the pears the way Umma did, in one long thick peel, all I did was cut myself or hack away at the pear until most of the crispy white flesh was gone in addition to the skin.

Ahead of me in line is a young mom with a toddler in the shopping cart. The kid keeps looking over at me, her eyes agog. I give her a wink and she smiles, a line of drool falling from the corner of her mouth, and her mother makes a small, soft exclamation and wipes it off with her bib. She murmurs something to her in Korean that I can't make out over the ambient noise of the supermarket, and the little girl crows, throwing up her chubby hands in the air. When the mother moves up to pay the cashier, I see that she is pregnant. She is buying, among other things, packs of dried seaweed, and I wonder if she is planning on making herself seaweed soup.

Umma used to make seaweed soup for me every year on my birthday. She told me that in Korea, it was common for expectant mothers and mothers who had just given birth to be served seaweed soup, which is why people also have it on their birthdays. The nutrients in seaweed are supposed to help replenish the woman's body and aid with the production of breast milk. "When you have a baby, I'll make seaweed soup for you then, too," she said.

I haven't had seaweed soup in what feels like years, and I find myself craving the golden, oily liquid, the taste and textures of the seaweed and beef in the soup bursting across my tongue. In middle school, there was a period when I stopped liking seaweed soup, after I brought it to school for lunch one day and someone asked me why I was having "swamp stuff" for lunch. All of a sudden, the thick seaweed turned to slimy ropes in my mouth and the taste of the liquid felt slippery, like a too-long ribbon in my throat.

The toddler waves goodbye at me before they leave, and I raise my hand to wave back. "You were the sweetest, happiest little thing when you were little," Umma always said about me whenever she reminisced about my childhood, a strange note in her voice that I never knew how to read. "You were the best baby in the world."

When I went to college, Umma sold the two-story yellow house that I had spent most of my life in and moved into an apartment complex a few towns away. By then, she was doing part-time admin work at church in addition to conducting, and she was also giving voice lessons to kids.

Despite the fact that I've been to her building before, my visits are infrequent enough that I still like to keep my phone's GPS on whenever I go over there. She lives in a neighborhood that seems to be populated mostly by young commuter couples. It's close to the train station, and sometimes in the middle of the night you can hear the whistle of the train.

The sun is low in the sky by the time I arrive and pull into a spot on the street in front of her building, behind a dark blue Volvo. I kill the engine and check my watch. I'm three minutes early. To kill time, I adjust my hair in the rearview mirror and remind myself that I am an adult woman, not a child who can be cowed or intimidated by her mother, and then I steer myself out of the car and up the stone pathway into the well-lit lobby.

When the door to Umma's apartment opens, I notice it smells like a candle is burning, which is unusual, since she doesn't usually like strong fragrances. "Hi, Umma," I say, holding out the box of pears.

It always startles me how petite Umma is. She's small-boned, fragile almost, with a bob of perfectly shaped hair that sits like a polished helmet on her head. It's gone grayer with time, but she still looks almost exactly the same.

"Arim, you're here," she says. She hugs me, and we pat each other awkwardly on the back.

"I brought pears," I say unnecessarily, since she has already whisked the box out of my hands and taken it away to the kitchen. "You didn't have to bring anything," she calls, but I can tell she is pleased. I smile at my reflection in the mirror of her foyer. Maybe tonight will be fine, and she won't ask me any weird questions about dating or Tae or my job, and we'll just have a nice dinner and get to act like a normal mother and daughter.

But when I move to take my shoes off, I notice something. There's a pair of men's loafers in the foyer lined up next to Umma's flats, and a distinctly masculine-sounding humming coming from the kitchen. "Umma?" I call. "Is someone here?"

She pops back out of the kitchen, but this time she's followed by a Korean man about her age. He has a paunch and thinning hair and is, perhaps most shockingly, wearing an apron, and appears to have been cooking, which is how I know I must be hallucinating because the idea that my mother would let anyone else help out in her kitchen, let alone a man, is truly insane. "Uhm, hello?" I say, so confused that I say it in English.

"Arim," she says, a smile on her face. I realize she's nervous. "I want you to meet Mr. Cho. Mr. Cho, this is my daughter."

"It's nice to finally meet you," he says in English. I stand in front of the two of them, and for a second, I see the image of my father standing there instead next to her, and it's like he never left at all. But of course, the moment I blink, Apa is gone and it's just me and Umma and whoever this is.

"I've forgotten the kimchi jjigae," Umma says, standing up almost as soon as we sit down to dinner.

"I'll get it," Mr. Cho says. He motions for her to sit down, and while he's away from the table, I give Umma a look that she ignores. Apa would never have volunteered to get something from the kitchen for her, and the fact that she's allowing Mr. Cho to go into her kitchen unsupervised tells me that this is far from his first time here.

Dinner is, of course, weird. It's a typical meal, the kind that Umma always cooked when I was growing up, with rice and banchan and a whole fish, its yellow eye staring up at us. Mr. Cho does most of the talking and pours us wine, which even Umma takes sips of throughout the meal. He asks me polite, friendly questions and spoons extra helpings of food onto Umma's plate.

"Your mother tells me how hard you work. And at an aquarium, too. It sounds very interesting and important."

"It's not, really. I just feed and clean up after fish."

He tries again. "Anyone special in your life? A boyfriend?"

My chest tightens. "No, not anymore."

"I'm sure it won't be long before you find someone new," he says. "It's not good to be alone for too long, you know."

"It's not so bad being single," I say. "I don't have to deal with anyone else's problems that way."

I can feel Umma's eyes on me, her half-pleading, half-commanding glare as Mr. Cho continues to try with me and I continue to dodge his questions. I down two glasses of wine that I don't feel until I stand up and excuse myself to go to the bathroom.

I splash some cold water on my face and try to assess what the hell is going on. It hits me then that Umma has gotten herself a boyfriend. I laugh out loud into my hands, dizzy from the wine. *And why shouldn't she?* I think to myself. *My mother is an adult woman who can make her own decisions, and she deserves to be happy.* But there is a part of me that cannot compute this information at all, that cannot reconcile the mother I've known all my life with the image of a woman newly in love and coupled up. Not that she and Mr. Cho were being lovey-dovey or anything over dinner, but there had been something in the small glances and smiles they had given each other that had felt mildly shocking to witness.

A phrase that Umma herself used to say whenever she came across behavior that she disapproved of comes to mind: *That kind of thing is for Americans.* It's what she said when I asked if I could attend slumber parties or if we could get a pool, or why she and Apa never kissed or held hands in public. The underlying message, as I understood it, was that any kind of excessive or gratuitous behavior was a luxury, and that we—despite the fact that we were Americans ourselves, even if my parents were not so by birth—could not and should not expect such things from life.

When I emerge from the bathroom, Mr. Cho is helping Umma clear the table. "No, no, please," he says, motioning for me to sit when I move to try and help. "You're the guest of honor tonight." I drop a spoon and it splatters onto Umma's carpet, leaving a stain, and I brace myself for a disappointed sigh. But instead, Umma cheerfully comes over with a wet paper towel and blots away at the stain, proclaiming that no harm has been done. She scolds Mr. Cho playfully for trying to do the dishes, saying he'll break all her nice things. Her tone is warm, almost flirtatious, in a way that it never was with Apa. I see the way Mr. Cho looks at her when she's not looking, like he can't believe his luck, like she's the best thing he's ever seen, and it makes me angry. *Who gave him the right to look at her like that?* I think.

I wander into the living room, looking around Umma's apartment for physical signs of the disturbance I feel, as though the proof that I am not going crazy will be found in some clue on her beige walls. But everything in Umma's apartment is as it has always been, at least as far as I can tell. The few plants she keeps by the window look green and healthy. Her cream-colored couch—the one luxury she'd allowed herself to purchase when she moved—is still spotless. The small gilded clock that she's always had is still ticking away, and her shelves are lined, as they've always been, with music books and note-books and a few Korean novels, as well as some cookbooks.

When Umma moved out of our house, she put most of the framed photos she'd moved into Apa's study in storage, but she'd chosen a few from their wedding day, as well as some from my childhood and before I was born, to display on the side tables and walls of the apartment. I always wondered why some photos had made the cut and others hadn't, if she'd chosen them at random or deliberately. I stare at a photo of her that was taken when she was a few months pregnant with me, her stomach just beginning to show through her sweater, Apa standing next to her. It looks like they are at a party, and Umma's hair is bigger, fuller, held in place with a bow of some kind, while Apa's hair is long and shaggy. Apa looks as though he is talking to someone on the side—perhaps this was at a university party, back when he was a PhD student—but Umma is looking straight at the camera, her eyes dusky with eye shadow and her lips lined with lipstick. They are so young and effortlessly slim-hipped and beautiful and happy in the photo that I wish I could leap into the frame and tell them to stay as long as they can in this memory, even if it means I would never have been born.

Umma brings out a tray of the sliced pears, while Mr. Cho brings out a pot of coffee and cups. They set everything down on the coffee table, working deftly around each other, like they've been doing this for a long time. "I'm so glad you were able to come for dinner tonight, Arim," Umma says. "I know you've been very busy with work."

I take a slice of pear with my fingers, instead of using a fork, which I know will bother Umma. The cool white flesh explodes inside my mouth, and I take my time chewing it before I respond, inanely, "Well, you know what they say, when you do what you love, you never have to work a day in your life."

"That's true," Mr. Cho says earnestly. "My daughter is a doctor. It's incredibly high stress, but she loves being able to make a difference."

Of course his daughter is a doctor, I think. "And what do you do?" I ask.

There is a pause before he responds. "I'm an acupuncturist," he says. He shows me a small diagram that he pulls out from his wallet, of the different pressure points on a foot, a back, a hand. He explains all the different places in the body that correspond to other places, the way that everything is connected—how the ball of the foot connects to the liver and the lungs, how the heel connects to the pelvis.

"Is that how you met?" I say. "Through acupuncture?"

He nods excitedly. "Your umma and I were introduced through a friend at church, who mentioned that she was having some headaches and intestinal issues. We met for a session and hit it off right away. You see, I'm a widower, too," he says.

I feel my stomach twist. "You should have gone to a real doctor," I say to Umma in English, not caring that I'm being rude. "What if it was something serious?"

"I'm fine," she says defensively. "Mr. Cho's acupuncture helped me a lot."

"Don't worry, Arim," Mr. Cho says. "Your umma was just experiencing some common stress symptoms. I've put her on a strict regimen of ginseng teas and acupuncture twice a month, and she looks better already."

"Are you paying for all of this out of pocket?" I ask Umma, ignoring him. "Insurance doesn't cover acupuncture, does it?"

"Arim," Umma says, "Mr. Cho is a good friend of mine."

"I'm sorry," I say. "But I didn't realize you'd be here, Mr. Cho. Umma's never mentioned anything about you before." It's suddenly too hot in the living room, and I'm sweating in my silly dress. I feel very young and very old at the same time. I want to lie down across Umma's cream-colored couch and take a long nap, and when I wake up, have all of this be a distant memory. But instead, I turn my attention toward studying Umma's face, which looks pinched and worried now.

"No, no, it's me who should apologize," Mr. Cho says gallantly. "I was so excited at the thought of meeting you that I invited myself over for dinner. I should have known better than to intrude."

"Don't be silly," Umma says, her voice tight. "I invited you both here to be my guests for dinner, and Arim is just being dramatic, as usual."

Mr. Cho turns to me. "I know how hard it is to lose a parent," he says in a voice so gentle that I want to scream. "It is a psychic wound that will never heal. I myself went into deep mourning when my own mother passed away, and that was over twenty years ago. Your mother has shared with me how difficult your father's passing was for both of you."

She's talked about Apa with him, I realize. Umma and I were never able to talk about Apa's disappearance, not in the days leading up to the small memorial service we held for him, and never in the years since. When I did try to bring it up with Umma, she shut down completely. Maybe it was easier for her to pretend that he hadn't meant anything to her at all, even when all I wanted was to know that someone else felt what I was feeling, which was like a part of the earth that I'd been standing on had been ripped away from under me. And yet here she was, telling this complete stranger—her new boy-friend, of all people—all about our family's business, when she couldn't even bring herself to say my father's name to me.

"My father's not dead," I say to Mr. Cho. "If that's what she told you, she's wrong."

"Arim," Umma says, "he's not coming back."

"You don't know that," I say. "What if he is? What if he's still out there?"

"It's been years," she says. "If he was alive and if he wanted to come back, he would be here by now."

"What do you mean, 'if he wanted to come back'?" I say, my voice breaking a little. "You're the one who wanted him gone. And it looks like you've moved on just fine without him."

"What is wrong with you?" she says, like I've thrown up on her carpet. I can't bring myself to look at her. "Stop being rude. I didn't raise you to be like this."

I didn't raise you to be like this. As if she could absolve her-self of all responsibility for the way I'd turned out. As if she could determine, just from looking at me, where I ended and where she began, and decide which parts of me were worth loving and which weren't. "I should probably go home," I say, standing up. "I'm not feeling so good."

"Don't be ridiculous. Sit down and finish your fruit."

"Don't mind me," I say, rummaging for my purse and throwing my sweater on, despite the fact that I am drenched with sweat. "It was nice meeting you, Mr. Cho."

"Sit down," Umma says, in a voice that would have stopped me dead in my tracks when I was a child and that still, if I'm being honest, strikes fear deep inside me. But I'm already heading for the door, flapping one arm into a sleeve of my cardigan that has somehow managed to turn itself inside out, like a great ungainly bird.

I catch a glimpse of a small ceramic box that sits by the foyer, near where Umma put her keys, that I painted for her years ago at one of those "paint your own pottery" studios. It's shaped like a star and has the words *Love you to the moon and back* painted carefully on it in almost illegible blue squiggles. I remember having to explain what the phrase meant to her. "But why the moon?" she had asked. "The moon is very close to the earth. Why not the sun?"

I'm down the hallway and waiting for the elevator when I hear Umma's voice at my back. "Arim, please." She's standing there barefoot, and it registers dimly in my mind that she has run outside after me without first putting her shoes on, something she would never do normally. Her bare feet look very pale and small on the carpeting of the hallway, and there is something so sad about them that I have to look away. "Come back inside," she says, her voice a plea. "Stay. I just want to—"

But then the elevator opens with a ding, and I shake her off, and I hate myself and her and everything, and I watch her watch me as the doors close between us, cutting off whatever it was she was going to say next.

CHAPTER 10

The way Umma tells it, if it hadn't been for my grandmother and the fact that my mother, in her early twenties, bore a strong resemblance to a notable pop star of the time, a woman with a reputation for her angelic looks, sweet singing voice, and surprisingly suggestive song lyrics—it was not uncommon, she told me, for grown men to chase her down sidewalks to get an autograph, only to find that she wasn't the famed singer after all, and then ask her out anyway, all offers she declined, being a well-heeled Seoul girl of the upper middle class—my parents might never have met at all.

Umma told me that they met on a city bus, headed to the same university campus, where he was a biology major and she was studying voice. Apa, skinny and bespectacled, with all the kinetic energy of a coiled spring, followed her off the bus and, when she turned around to tell him, in the politest of terms, to shove off, he stuttered out a question: Would she like to attend a chamber music concert with him that night, in the music hall? She replied that she was already planning on attending the performance. "Then I'll see you there," he replied, and instead of telling him that she was going to be there with friends and had no intention of indulging his awkward advances, she said, "I thought you were going to ask me if I was Kim Sung-hee."

Apa had just been released from his two years of mandatory military service, where he hadn't had much access to the usual conduits of pop culture. In pictures of him from back then, his hair is buzzed close to his head, a souvenir from his time in the army. Sometimes I wonder if that's why he took so much pride in his hair and the fact that he still had a full head of it well into his forties and fifties.

"Who's Kim Sung-hee?" he asked.

Umma found his lack of knowledge about her putative doppelgänger refreshing, and she agreed to meet him on the steps of the recital hall at seven o'clock that evening, where instead of being deterred by the presence of her giggling friends, Apa proceeded to charm everyone, including my mother. "I thought he was so strange," she told me. "I'd never met anyone like him, with that odd mix of shyness and arrogance."

"Confidence," Apa would correct her, if he happened to be within earshot.

"Arrogance," she would say again, but she'd smile at me when he wasn't looking. I wished, in those moments, that they could always be just like this, like two parents who loved each other.

After the concert ended, he took her out for jajangmyeon and hot tea. "I hadn't had dinner, and I was so hungry I almost spilled the noodles down my shirt," Umma said. "Your father thought that was hilarious." When I imagine this, their first date, I picture Umma, forgetting her manners and slurping down her bowl of noodles instead of daintily eating only a portion of them as she normally would have, and Apa enjoying the contrast between her well-bred Seoul manners and the hunger with which she attacked the food.

He told her that he planned to attend graduate school in the United States as soon as he finished his undergraduate degree at Seoul University, where he was already slated to graduate with top honors. She found that she liked his ambition and casual brilliance, as well as his evident besottedness with her.

But a few months later, she grew increasingly uncomfortable with the occasional glimmers of impatience she saw in him—he was easily frustrated by small inconveniences like late buses or wrinkles in his shirt, she told me—as well as his tacit assumption that she would, sooner or later, marry him and agree to move to the United States. She broke things off with him in the very same jajangmyeon restaurant where they had first eaten together, under the cheap fluorescent lighting and watchful circumspect gazes of the old waiters. She had not meant to be cruel; it was just that she was growing nervous at the prospect of being carried along in the current of my father's plans for the future, with little to no say about how she fit into them. "I wanted to be independent," she told me when I got older, with a trace of sadness in her voice. "I didn't want to just be someone's wife."

Like many women of her generation, Umma was not expected to have a job in the same way that her eventual husband would; her main responsibility was to maintain her looks until she married and had children, at which point, the task of raising and rearing those children would become the sole focal point of her life. And yet she found that being around Apa's ambition and hopes for the future was contagious in a way that he had probably not intended. She told me that she began dreaming, too, for a life that didn't exactly preclude marriage and children but that could encompass all that a woman was supposed to be content with and more—perhaps even a career. She was a talented enough singer, but talent was not enough to make it as a performer, and she decided that she would settle for becoming a teacher.

And then two months after the breakup, on the first really warm spring day of the year, a truck carrying a shipment of radishes ran a red light while Umma was crossing a busy street, careened onto the traffic island that she was just stepping onto, and wrapped itself around a streetlight, hitting her in the process. Umma told me that to this day she still can't remember how it happened. One minute she was walking along the street, and the next she felt a white star of pain eclipse her whole body, and when she woke up, she was in the hospital, lying under a mass of tubes and wondering if she had died.

My halmoni, who had always liked Apa, called him and told him to come quickly. "I told him to bring flowers," she said to Umma, who was too weak and dazed with pain to protest.

I have been told this story so many times that I can picture the scene in the hospital as if I had been there myself. I can see Apa bursting in, his face round with youth and worry. I can see Umma, broken and bruised but still capable of being mortified by her mother's meddling. I see Halmoni, praying fervently for my mother's recovery and later pleased by how successful her meddling turned out to be. "I always knew he'd be a good husband for your mother," Halmoni often said. I don't have many memories of her—only the smell of tiger balm and mothballs, plus the feeling of my hand in hers whenever we had to cross the street in Seoul, during that summer when I was five and Umma left Apa for a month and took me with her. Halmoni wouldn't speak to Umma the whole time we were there, addressing her complaints about my mother only to me. She passed away when I was six.

They were married later that fall, and they moved to Indiana, where Apa had gotten a scholarship, and any lingering dreams Umma had about becoming more than just another wife—she was taking English lessons, hoping to eventually get her teaching certificate to teach music in schools—were dashed when, one morning on her way to class, she suddenly felt nauseous and had to pull her car over to the side of the road. At the time, she thought it was a reaction to the flatness of the landscape, which she found disorienting after the view of distant mountains she was accustomed to seeing on the horizon in Seoul. "Ugh, it was so brown everywhere," Umma always said about Indiana. "Like an ugly carpet." There, by the tall stalks of wheat, she vomited the contents of her breakfast and realized, with a rapidly sinking heart, that she was pregnant.

While waiting for me to arrive, Umma grew lonely in Indiana, with only her busy, beleaguered husband for company. Although she had not been much of a churchgoer during her girlhood in Korea, she began attending the church on Main Street not far from their apartment building, where she connected with the other international doctoral students. She began coming back, not only for the company and the free gingersnaps they served after services, but to sing the hymns along with the rest of the congregation. "Singing was the only thing that brought me joy in those days," Umma said. She joined the choir, where she was praised for her crystalline soprano (she did not tell anyone at the church that she had studied voice formally at one of the top universities in Seoul) and made some new friends. Apa, busy with his studies, was happy that she was taking an interest in something, though he continued to remain skeptical of the church and the hold it had over Umma. "Your mother had her English classes," he said. "She could have made some friends there, if she'd bothered trying."

When they moved to New Jersey, where Apa would complete his PhD in marine biology, Umma was overjoyed to find Korean supermarkets, restaurants, and churches among the more densely clustered suburbs they had moved to. She began taking me to church with her at an early age, and although Apa again disapproved, there was, at this point, enough of a strain in their marriage that it was understood, without either of them having to say anything, that he would allow her this.

Some of my earliest memories are of being separated from Umma, who attended the adults-only service at the church, to sit on a scratchy felt carpet in the basement, which smelled like mildew and peanut butter, and watch my Sunday school teachers waggle around finger puppets of Jesus, Mary, Joseph, and the rest of the gang. Along with the other children, I learned how to say the Lord's Prayer and the Apostles' Creed and was confirmed by the age of thirteen. But unlike the other children, I liked Sunday school, the way there was always an explanation for everything (the answer to almost all the questions the teachers posed to us, I soon learned, was that God could do anything and knew everything) and the idea that unlike my actual father, God was available at all times. My favorite Bible story was the one about Noah and the ark, because the idea of God sending a rainbow at the end of the great flood to say sorry for destroying the earth and its creatures was, I thought at the time, beautiful.

Yoonhee and I met in first grade, when her family moved to town and, like my mother, joined the church to seek out a Korean community. Unlike me, she was bored by Sunday school and kept her eyes open wide during the prayers. I stole looks at her even though we were all supposed to keep our eyes shut, because I was fascinated by the sequined pink scrunchie in her hair. We became friends when I asked her about it and she brought me a purple one that looked similar to hers the very next Sunday, saying her mother sold them at her cosmetics store, and I was so happy I could barely sleep that night. I refused to take it out to go to bed.

Umma soon took on the responsibilities of conducting the church choir, as they were in need of someone who could read music. She took to the job with relish, and although the salary was next to nothing, she took great enjoyment in depositing her meager checks into the family bank account every two weeks. "You know, yeobo, you don't really need to work. I make enough money for all of us now," Apa pointed out. By then he had left the university, where, while working a low-paying research job, he had applied and been turned down for several tenure-track positions, and had begun working at the aquarium.

But it wasn't about the money. Her visits to church increased in their frequency, as she joined Bible study groups, volunteer trips to soup kitchens, and even Wednesday-night prayer sessions. Apa couldn't understand it. "They're all a bunch of con artists," he railed whenever she brought up something that the pastor had said in the sermon that week. "Claiming they can talk to God when they're just like you and me."

In Sunday school, they told us that anyone who was a non-believer or denier of the Lord would go to hell, and I burst into tears at dinner over this. "I don't want Apa to go to hell," I said, and then he and Umma really had it out, with him threatening to pull her out of the choir if she didn't stop indoctrinating me with what he called lies and hoaxes, and her threatening to leave him and take me with her.

Soon Umma and Apa were fighting almost every week, and their shouting grew so frequent that I learned to stop reacting to it, instead going quietly into my room and shutting the door to watch *The Little Mermaid*. We owned an anime version of the story that hewed more closely to the original Hans Christian Andersen fairy tale, in which the little mermaid turns into sea-foam at the end of the story, sacrificing herself for the prince who doesn't even love her. I found the mermaid's readiness to die for the prince a bit silly, but the final scene, in which her fish friends watch helplessly from the ocean as she turns into bubbles and then into a spirit of the air, always made me cry until I fell asleep.

When we were teenagers, Yoonhee and I started cutting Sunday school to go to the Wendy's next door to the church, where we split a Frosty with fries and lingered for hours in one of the sticky booths, talking about boys and the things we had heard they liked to do. I was horrified by the idea of sex and vowed that I would remain chaste until marriage, as we had promised to do in Sunday school. "You'll see," she said, giggling and licking Frosty off the back of her plastic spoon. "One day you're going to like a guy and he'll like you back and then you'll want to do it."

"No, I won't," I said. "Boys don't like me anyway."

"That's because you don't like them," she retorted. "They're really not that complicated." At thirteen, Yoonhee had already had two boyfriends, one of whom had given her a heart locket that she wore every day, even after they broke up, and whom she had let feel her up under her bra. "Just for a few minutes," she said defensively when I looked askance at her. I wanted to ask her what it had felt like, but she changed the subject.

Puberty was what first made me doubt God's existence. Following Umma's example, I prayed twice a day—once in the morning and once at night—and each time, I prayed for the following items: (1) breasts, (2) my parents to stop hating one another, and (3) a boyfriend. When God provided no satisfaction on any of these, I stopped believing in Him, and it was easy, like a habit I had been waiting to break. Instead of the reassuring sense that my prayers had at least reached some kind of celestial message board where, I was sure, they would be ferried up the phone tree to the Lord himself, I felt as though I had been speaking into a hole in the wall for all these years.

But as my faith waned, Umma's continued to grow, as fervently and secretly as though she was having an affair, which in a way, since this was probably all happening at the same time as Apa's actual extramarital activities, she was. At the height of Umma's covert relationship with God, she would wake up every morning at five a.m.; crawl out of bed while Apa was still snoring, his head strapped into the sleep apnea machine that made his sleeping form look like something out of science fiction; and drive to church, where along with a handful of other devout Christians, many of them also middle-aged Korean immigrants, she'd get on her knees and pray for anywhere from an hour to an hour and a half. She would return home just in time to wake me up for school, a strange light in her eyes that offset the shape that her hair always took on whenever she didn't have the time to style it. I have the same cowlick in my own hair, a ripple that veers my part to the right and defeats the most tenacious of styling gels and the hottest of straightening irons.

One Sunday, when I was seven—still small enough to think that the Bible was real and that God was a kindly old white man with a beard made of clouds—Apa came with us to church. I wasn't sure why or how Umma had managed to get him to agree to attend, but he was meek and acquiescent that day, even agreeing to change out of his usual uniform of khaki pants and a stained button-down into a dark blue suit that he looked incredibly uncomfortable in. Perhaps it had something to do with the fact that he and Umma seemed to like each other more at that juncture. She hummed while she was cooking breakfast, and he whistled while he was shaving, as if they were a couple from a TV show.

"Why is Apa coming with us?" I asked in the car.

"Today's a special day," Umma said, smiling at me in the rearview mirror.

Instead of being sent downstairs to the basement like I usually was, I was ushered into a pew near the front with Apa, while Umma disappeared downstairs to change into her choral robes. We were wedged between two families that Umma was friendly with. I fidgeted with the program and stared at the Korean letters, puzzling out the few words I understood. "You know that word," Apa said, pointing out phrases in the brochure. I managed to decipher that the scriptural reading of the day was from the book of Mark, that there would be a soup kitchen trip this coming Wednesday, and that donations were being collected for overseas mission trips in Turkey. "There's a country called Turkey?" I asked.

Apa drew a map for me on the program with one of the golf pencils supplied by the church, explaining where the Mediterranean was. He drew routes, borders, and lines intersecting with other lines, and then told me about the ocean currents in that part of the world, until we were shushed by a glare from one of the older women sitting near us in the pew. Apa gave me an amused faux-stern look, as though I was the one to blame for talking, and I stifled a giggle.

The organ began to play, and the choir, dressed in purple robes, with Umma at the head, filed out. She took her place by the conductor stand at the front and raised her hand. It was like a magic trick, watching her summon forth sound and harmony from the mouths of the choir, and even when the sopranos went sharp and I saw her wince, she seemed graceful and fluid in her movements in a way that I had never seen before.

After a few hymns and the long ritual of standing up, then sitting down, then standing up again for various recitations of the Bible, the pastor gave a mercifully brief sermon on the story of the prodigal son. Because this was my least favorite story of the Bible and also because the sermon was in Korean, I tuned out, barely listening as I drew whales and dolphins in the sea that Apa had drawn. It didn't make sense to me that the child who had left home and disobeyed his parents was more important than the one who had stayed behind, who had tended the fields and listened to his father even if he had wanted to go out into the world just like his younger brother. My main takeaway from the story was that God was capricious and cared about you only if you were hell-bent on making trouble and running away from Him.

Then the sermon was over, and we were standing again, this time singing along with the choir to a song that spoke of a world without end, amen, amen, and then we were sitting, and this time the pastor was calling the names of various people, including Apa, asking them to come down to the front. I watched in astonishment as Apa, looking as uncomfortable as a child charged with spelling a word he doesn't know, walked to the front of the sanctuary. Umma, now seated on the side, looked on, and although I couldn't see her face, I felt the warmth of her pride and approbation as he knelt in front of the pastor to receive a palmful of water on his head, and the pastor pronounced that in the name of the Father, the Son, and the Holy Ghost, he was now baptized and born again in the eyes of the Lord and His church. "Amen," came the murmurs of the congregation around me, and I repeated the word, more confused than ever.

Umma had taken me to be baptized as soon as I could be let out into the world, and there were photos of my baptism at home, me a mass of frilly white skirt in Umma's arms, the frame of the photo a little crooked. Umma said that I had been a very good baby, holding still while the pastor dipped his hand into the holy water and blessed me with it, not even crying when the other children began to wail.

Apa stood back up, and I could tell that he was resisting the impulse to toss his head back and shake off the water. He stood and smiled uncertainly along with the other children and their parents who had been baptized that day, as the congregation prayed for their spiritual well-being and promised to look out for them as fellow children of God. I looked over at Umma once or twice and found, to my astonishment, that she was crying with what seemed like joy.

Afterward, we went out to a diner not far from the church,

where Umma let me order a stack of pancakes and drench the whole thing in maple syrup and whipped cream, even though she normally would have been appalled by the whole sugary mess. I spooned forkfuls of doughy pancake into my mouth and watched as Umma declined coffee, ordered an omelet, and ate it delicately while Apa had a burger with fries. He had always liked fast food, claimed that eating anything that paired meat with cheese made him feel like a real American.

I didn't know how to ask what had changed, but it was clear that something had. There was an air of quiet happiness about the two of them, and a solicitousness in Apa that I almost never saw, as he pulled Umma's chair out for her and flagged a waiter down to make sure she could order the herbal tea that they had forgotten to bring out.

"Arim," Umma said when we had finished eating, "we have something to tell you."

I felt much older than my seven years as she told me, in the hushed, excited tones that she usually reserved for phone calls home to Korea, that I was going to be an older sister to a baby boy. A silly grin spread across Apa's face. "A son," he said, taking her hand and squeezing it. "You're going to be a noona, Arim. What do you think of that?"

I studied my parents as they turned toward me, their faces so open and eager that it hurt my heart to look at them. "Is he in there?" I said, eyeing Umma's stomach suspiciously. She didn't look at all like the pregnant women I had seen, though there did seem to be, now that I was looking more closely, the smallest slope there, above the waistband of her church skirt.

"Yes," she said, "I can feel him moving around now. He must hear your voice. Say hi to your noona, Acorn," she said to the baby.

"That's my nickname," I told her, but I stopped when Apa

gave me a look. A look that said, *You're not going to be a baby anymore. You're the older sister now.*

I was old enough to know that sons were better than daughters, and that no matter how much a girl was loved, a son would be loved three times as much. Whenever Yoonhee's mother told people at church that she had three daughters, they responded with pity, as though she'd said something terrible. "Only daughters?" they said, as though she must be neglecting to mention a son or two.

"It's because boys have penises," Yoonhee said when I had first raised this issue of sons versus daughters with her. "Penises are good because they can make babies."

"But they can't make babies by themselves," I said doubtfully. I was still scarred by what Yoonhee had told me about sex. She had received the talk early on from her older sisters and explained to me, using Barbie dolls and stick figures drawn on construction paper, how it all worked.

"Yeah, but the penis is where the baby comes from," she said impatiently. "The penis is where the baby is hiding, and then when the man puts his penis inside the woman, the baby slips inside and that's how he or she grows."

I imagined that this boy child growing inside my mother, who was the reason for my parents' sudden happiness and my father's willingness to not only attend church but get baptized, would bring even more happiness once he was born, with his magical penis and round baby face that all the adults would coo over. "We can't afford it," I said firmly to my parents, crossing my arms. "A baby is too expensive."

Umma and Apa laughed, as though I had said something enormously funny. "I think we'll manage," Apa said, while Umma wiped the tears of mirth from her eyes. Her eyeliner smeared a little, and I decided not to tell her.

"What if I don't want him to be born?" I said, and immediately I knew that I had said the wrong thing. The air around our booth had gone dark and cold, and while I knew it was the sun just passing behind a cloud outside, it felt as though the sun of my parents' brief warmth and approval had also disappeared.

"That's enough, Arim," Umma said.

I looked to Apa, my usual ally when it came to disagreements with Umma, but he only looked away from me, disappointed. "We thought you'd be excited," he said. "You're always complaining about how bored you are at home. You'll be able to play with your brother, teach him new things. Wouldn't you like that?"

"No," I said, and my parents gave each other a look. Their sudden unity, this easy conspiracy with each other, enraged me. I began to cry, big wet embarrassing tears and heaving sobs that made everyone else in the diner turn to stare at us, until Apa paid and we left.

The months afterward were a blur. The spare bedroom next to mine at the end of the hall that had become a repository for Apa's tennis gear and papers was cleaned out, repainted a bright, cheery blue and stenciled with a pattern of elephants around the top. Furniture was bought, and tiny, mysterious clothes arrived in shiny packages. Umma's stomach grew, and I imagined that the baby was building a house for himself inside her, which worried me. When Umma began experiencing cramping and headaches, I grew to hate my baby brother in addition to resenting him, upset that he was hurting her.

To humor Umma, I sometimes went through the ritual of placing my hand against her belly to feel the baby kick. Despite my lack of enthusiasm for the baby, I had to admit it was still an astonishing thing, to feel the wall of her stomach bend to accommodate the movements inside it, to know that inside, something the size of a grape, then a shrimp, then a fist, then a banana, was hell-bent on getting larger and larger until it had destroyed my life. "Go away," I whispered to the baby sometimes when I felt its ghost visit me at night. "We don't want you here."

"I like babies," Yoonhee said when I told her. "They smell nice. One time I saw a baby, and its fingernails were the tiniest things I've ever seen."

"You can have this one when he comes out," I said.

"Maybe you'll like him," she said.

"No, I won't," I said. At this point, this was my automatic rejoinder to almost everything my parents tried to tell me that the baby and I could do when he got big enough. "You can take him to the park. You can teach him how to go down the slide. You can take him to school and show him where all the classrooms are," they said, as if these were things that any normal girl would die for a chance to do. "You'll fall in love with him instantly, just you see."

"No, I won't," I said, until they finally gave up.

But in the end, we never found out what having a baby around would be like. I was home from school one afternoon a few months later when I walked into the upstairs bathroom to find Umma sitting in the tub, fully clothed. "Umma?" I said. Dark red stained the porcelain and the front of her pants. At first I thought she had cut herself on something or slipped in the shower, though that didn't explain why she was still in all her clothes.

"Go call your father," she said in a voice so calm it frightened me. I raced out of the bathroom and dialed his office number, and then, when he didn't pick up, his cell, which went straight to voice mail, I called 911, where I told the woman on the other end in a voice as flat as Umma's that my mother was dying.

The sound of sirens still reminds me of the way Umma looked as the medics helped her onto a gurney and she was lifted into the ambulance. How pale and small her face seemed, like she was a little girl; the grimace of pain that flashed across it as she struggled not to cry out. My tears turned everything into a wash of blue and red. "Umma, Umma," I called.

"The kid," I heard one of the medics say. She turned to me. "Is your dad home, sweetheart?"

"No," I said, my voice thick with the sound of snot escaping my nose. "He's at work."

"Do you have someone you can stay with while we take your mom to the doctor?"

Yoonhee's mother pulled up a few minutes later, with Yoonhee in the front seat. They took me to their house, where I was given a bowl of red Jell-O that I couldn't eat because the color and consistency of it reminded me too much of the thick, clotted blood that had stained my mother's clothes and the bathtub. Yoonhee taught me how to do a French braid, and for a while, as I closed my eyes and allowed myself to feel soothed by the feeling of her fingers in my hair, I was able to pretend that everything was fine, that Umma was coming to pick me up soon.

When it was dark outside, Apa finally called Yoonhee's house to say that he was on his way to pick me up and that Umma was okay, she had finally stabilized, and they had managed to stop the bleeding. "And the baby?" I heard Yoonhee's mother say on the phone, as Yoonhee and I held our breath and listened in on the line.

There was an unfamiliar sound, like a cat being strangled

or an accordion being thrown down a flight of stairs. Apa was crying. Yoonhee's mother made soothing noises on the phone, as though he were a child, while he pulled himself together.

Yoonhee hugged me, and then, before I could fully pull away, I felt something soft slip itself around my wrist. It was the pink scrunchie that I had admired when I first saw Yoonhee, the light catching on every trembling sequin. "You keep it," she said.

I took out the braid she had put into my hair and watched as it loosened itself around my face in her bedroom mirror, wavy and wild where it was usually lank and straight. I pulled the scrunchie through it and tugged at the strands on the end of my ponytail until it sat high and tight at the top of my head. "Fountain hair," Umma called it.

When I got home, I saw that the tub had been scrubbed and bleached clean, and I knew Apa must have done it, though I couldn't imagine him getting down on his hands and knees to scrub anything. I studied the bathroom intently, like a murderer revisiting the scene of a crime, to look for any telltale traces of blood, but it had all been wiped away, the only proof that I had ever had a brother now gone.

That night, in bed, I prayed to God and asked Him for forgiveness, and to help my mom get better. I promised that I would be good forever if He would only let her come back home and if He would also give the baby back. I even prayed to the ghost of my baby brother, which I imagined I could feel at the edges of my consciousness. *I'm sorry,* I told him. *I didn't mean it.*

I was just jealous because you made everyone happy, I told the ghost, and I felt him flicker with a kind of understanding before he disappeared for good.

CHAPTER 11

It takes about twenty minutes to get home from Umma's apartment building, but I decide to try doing it in fifteen. There's no one on the road anyway—after eight p.m. on the suburban roads of Paramus on a Monday night isn't exactly a peak traffic hour—so I let myself speed a little, watching the amber streetlights recede in the rearview mirror.

There's a fragment of pear wedged behind one of my molars, in the gap left behind from where I had a wisdom tooth taken out a few years ago. I remember when I took off work for the procedure, how Tae had to come pick me up at the dentist's office and drive me back home. According to him, I was so woozy from the medication that I spent ten minutes talking about the way a cloud in the sky was shaped. I woke up a few hours later to the most excruciating pain I'd ever experienced and had to fill my mouth with cotton balls to soak up the blood. I was worried that the hole in my mouth would never close up. Tae bought me six different kinds of ice cream, and we tried them all and ranked them over the course of my healing process, arguing over which one was better. I still can't look at ice cream without feeling a little nauseous or remembering how good it felt to let Tae take care of me. He made me juk and spooned sesame oil and soy sauce into the rice, the way his mom used to make for him whenever he got sick as a child.

When I tried to go to work the next day, despite the fact that my mouth was still bleeding, Tae stopped me and told me to call out sick, telling me that I needed to rest until the wound closed up.

"But I have to go to work," I said. "I have responsibilities."

He gave me a look and said, "Your only responsibility right now is to recover." I'd never thought about that before, that letting myself fully heal from something and taking care of myself could be just as important as work. And it's that memory, the memory of how it felt to be important to somebody, to see myself as someone worth taking care of, that makes me swing my car toward Hattie's, where I get completely blitzed on whiskey and sodas and then do shots with a group of Swedish tourists who have just taken the bus in from Times Square.

I ask them what they thought of New York City, and they tell me it's quite beautiful, though dirty. All tall and blond, they have dazzling white smiles and are bristling with cheer, like Vikings with universal healthcare. I have no idea why they're at Hattie's, but they seem happy to talk to me and, more important, to keep buying all of us drinks. By the third round of shots, the neon cactus over the bar is winking at me and everything feels warm and soft. They teach me how to play a Swedish drinking game that I can't quite follow, but it doesn't matter, and when one of them leans in a little too close to me and tells me I'm pretty, I flirt back with him.

"Are you Chinese?" he asks me, in the open, frank way of

white Europeans who think racism is an American problem. I pretend I don't hear him over the music, because if I act like I hear him, I'll have to react to it and adjust my behavior accordingly, and right now I don't feel like adjusting anything.

One of the reasons I like drinking is that it feels like a shortcut—to feeling funnier, prettier, more interesting, less inclined to dwell on the things I can't change. And then, sometimes, it lets me step outside myself, examine all the ways in which someone else might be seeing me for the first time. For instance, when Oskar tells me my English is very good, I'm able to step lightly outside my body—just like I'm taking off a sweater—and waft over to the jukebox, where someone is playing the same Queen song for the hundredth time, instead of obsessing over why white people the world over are all the same. Or why Umma would just spring the news on me that apparently she's had a boyfriend for some time and that she didn't think it was important enough to tell me beforehand.

None of that really gets to me when I'm drinking. I don't think about wisdom tooth surgery, or about how Tae made up a dumb but catchy song about my teeth in the days when I was still recovering that I pretended to get angry at, or how Oskar's hands are circling my waist now and how I want to bat them away but I also don't want him to stop paying attention to me, because I have this weird feeling that if he looks away and decides I'm no fun, I might die of loneliness.

Later, in the bathroom, I remind myself over and over again in the dirt-flecked mirror that I am carefree and breezy and alive. But all that falls away when I realize how badly I want to call Tae. I fumble with my bag, and it falls on the floor and my phone spills out, along with my keys. There are three missed calls—one from Umma, and two from a number I don't recognize. The hairs on the back of my neck stand up as I dial the mystery number, my heart in my mouth as the line rings. "The caller you are trying to reach is not available. Please try again," an automated message intones.

Then I'm a kid again, trying to call Apa while Umma bleeds in the bathtub, wondering why he won't pick up, why it has to be me who eventually calls 911 and hoists her out of the tub and half carries her into bed until the medics come. I remember how I later wondered if that was the year Apa first started seeing Laura, Laura of the Polaroids. It makes me sick to think that maybe their affair was happening while Umma was pregnant, but I can't help but imagine that that was why he didn't pick up, why his cell phone went straight to voice mail.

I go back to the bar and order another drink. I'll call in sick tomorrow, or maybe I won't call in at all. Let Carl fire me if he wants. The Swedes are still there, but this time I ignore them, sick of their heartiness and their questions. Finally they drift away, all except Oskar, who asks me if I want to go hang out somewhere else and then gets mad when I ignore him. And it's not even because of his question earlier or the fact that he's a stranger that I'm ignoring him. I haven't slept with anyone since Tae, and I know the sex would probably be fine and fast and easy—like a dollar slice, like falling asleep drunk without brushing my teeth or taking off my eyeliner—and that afterward I'd feel even worse than I do now, because if there's anything I know now after all the mistakes I've made with guys, it's that they always leave you a little worse off afterward.

"If you change your mind," Oskar says, sliding me his number.

"I won't," I say, even though I can already feel myself wondering if I should. After he leaves, I stare for a moment at the bar napkin where he's written his complicated-looking international number before placing my drink on top of it and letting the condensation from the glass blur it into an incoherent scrawl.

Now it's the hour when Hattie's gets a little scary and a little sad, like a Tom Waits song that won't end. The clock tells me it's one a.m., and my drink has long since evaporated. I'm thinking about ordering another when my phone rings. It's an unknown number. I consider hurling my phone across the bar and watching it skitter across the floor like a lost star before I pick up.

"Hello?" I say.

White noise crackles in my ear.

"I'm listening," I say. But there's no voice on the other end, nothing to indicate that anyone but me is on the line. And it's that silence, that lack of a response, that pushes me into a wild, desperate fury.

"Who the fuck are you?" I say. "Why do you keep calling me?"

I think I can hear someone breathing before the noise is drowned out by what sounds like rushing water. But it could just as easily be wind or static or nothing at all. Once when I proudly told Apa that one of my teachers had said you could hear the ocean when you held a seashell to your ear, he'd scoffed and told me this was just a myth. It was called seashell resonance, he said, and he'd cupped his hand around my ear to show me how it worked. He said it was just the reverberation of ambient noise around us, and that putting any kind of vessel to the ear, whether it was a shell, a cup, or a hand, would result in the amplification of that noise.

How long have I been imagining the sound of the ocean in phone static? How long have I been aching to hear my father's voice and looking for traces of him in the world? How long have I been waiting for him to come home, to be the father I have wanted all my life?

"I'm calling from your car insurance provider to let you know that you've qualified for a deal—" an automated voice says.

I hang up quickly. I feel a hot wave of embarrassment envelop me like a fever. Of course the calls were never Apa. Of course it was just spam. But realizing this makes me painfully aware of just how much I have wanted it to be him, calling to look for me, to say he's coming home. And telling myself the truth feels like losing him all over again. My chest starts to hurt, like someone is making a fist inside it, squeezing my lungs again and again. I can hardly breathe.

I close my eyes and try to imagine myself the way I was happiest, small and holding Apa's hand and listening to him tell me about the world and its wonders and perils. But I can't, because it feels as though the bar is tilting to one side. I'm convinced, for a second, that it is, that the floor is parting like water beneath my feet. I wait to be swallowed up. Instead, I come back to myself, and there I am, nearly gasping for air as I open my eyes to stare directly into the neon cactus clock over the bar. It's eighteen minutes past one, and except for the bartender, who is assiduously avoiding my gaze, I am all alone.

I finally pick myself up and wobble out to my car, which I find immediately for once. *I am getting a little ridiculous,* I think to myself, because the sight of my trusty car waiting for me all by itself, long overdue for a wash and a tune-up, is enough to make me feel sentimental.

I crawl into the driver's seat, where I try to think about driving. I should really call a cab, but I decide, fuck it. I've made this drive home before when I've been way more wasted, and I've been fine, every single time.

I turn the radio to a station that plays classic rock and start driving, going as slow as I dare. The sound of a beating heart and synths fills the car, and I feel the warm rush that comes from hearing a song you've listened to so often it feels like a second skin.

When Tae and I started dating, he would leave me little presents around my apartment, like mandarin oranges, left in a bowl on the counter when I wasn't looking, or one time, a small snow globe with a plastic palm tree on an island inside it, and when you shook the globe, instead of snowflakes, a storm of tiny iridescent flamingos showered down, like pink rain. He was always better at doing things like that than I was—remembering dates, giving little gifts.

He was into mixtapes, too, which I made fun of him for, saying he was single-handedly keeping the dying cassette tape industry alive. He had mixes for everything, all labeled in his careful, precise handwriting and categorized according to the titles he gave them. He told me he thought of them as diaries, almost, like small scrapbooks going all the way back to high school.

The first mixtape he ever made me included the song "I'm Not in Love" by 10cc, which I'd never heard before. After I'd listened to it, I rewound the tape and started it all over again, listening again and again until I worried the tape might break. The thing that haunted me most about the song was the way the voices in the backing track were layered over one another, how it sounded like what I imagined fog parting would sound like if it could sing, and the way the lyrics of the song were so obviously at odds with the emotions behind it. It felt like a feeling I'd known my whole life.

The song reminded me of one of those optical illusions where you think it's a fancy goblet or vase or chalice until you realize it's the silhouette of two people about to kiss. The picture is both those things at the same time, and yet it's only by squinting, letting your eyes get a little out of focus, that you can start to see them both simultaneously, the chalice and the kiss. As someone who'd spent her whole life being afraid of telling people I loved them—I could count on one hand the number of times I'd ever heard it said in our family—it made a perfect kind of sense to me that sometimes the best way to tell someone how much you need them is to tell them the exact opposite, defining your feelings for them the way you'd describe the shape of something by using the negative space around it.

I asked Apa once why they didn't get Dolores a friend. I worried she would be lonely all by herself in her tank. But he reassured me that octopuses were loners, and that they typically hunted and lived on their own in the wild, linking up only to mate.

"You should get her an octopus boyfriend, then," I said.

He laughed and made some joke about how Dolores was happy to be a single lady. But then he got serious and said that if Dolores were ever to mate, it was likely she'd die. It was miraculous she'd even survived for this long, he said. Most giant Pacific octopuses live no more than five years.

Octopuses spend their lives as active, clever hunters, their brains powering their muscled arms and killer instincts. But once a female octopus lays a clutch of eggs, she loses interest in almost everything but protecting them. After a few days, she even stops hunting and eating. In captivity, some octopuses slam themselves against the walls of their tanks after laying eggs. Worst of all, Apa told me, they start grooming themselves too much, until their arms get tangled up in one another and their glorious vibrant skin pales. They lose muscle definition, and their eyes get more and more pronounced until finally they fade away. Cephalopod researchers call it the death spiral.

Octopuses are some of the world's smartest animals, and Apa was haunted by the question of why breeding would lead them to eventually harm themselves to the point of death. "If Dolores mates, she'll eventually kill herself," he told me. "It's instinctual." He called the process a word I couldn't pronounce at first; he had to spell it out on paper for me—senescence, or the gradual decay of an organism's functions. It sounded like a magic spell, something beautiful rather than the nightmarish process he had outlined.

"So your octopus is a virgin who can't have sex or she'll die?" Tae said when I told him about all this. I agreed that it sounded pretty goth. I had taken him to see Dolores a few times, both during and after work hours. We discovered that she liked Jigsaw's music, the slow drone of the guitars and the thrumming bass. She would perk up whenever he played it. "I think she likes the vibrations," I said as she whooshed through the water in a blur of bubbles.

Tae liked how much I knew about the aquarium and the animals in it. He mentioned that he'd brought his students here on field trips, and yet we'd somehow never crossed paths before.

He bought me a T-shirt from the aquarium's gift shop that first day I took him to see Dolores. It had on it a cartoon drawing of an octopus holding a flower in one of its arms and a sign reading: YOU OCTOPI MY HEART. I still wear it to sleep. A few weeks ago, I discovered that there was a hole in the hem. Before I could stop myself, I'd enlarged the hole with my fingers, absent-mindedly watching it get larger and larger until the shirt was almost more hole than fabric and it was too late to stop myself from destroying it.

Over the next few weeks, I think about calling Umma back. She texts me a few times, too, telling me to call her. And it's not like I don't want to speak to her, or even that I begrudge her whatever happiness she can find with an aging acupuncturist. It's just that for the last few years all I've wanted to be able to do is talk to her, and now that she wants to talk to me, it feels like a badly scabbed-over wound that I'm not ready to reopen.

At work, I continue making preparations for Dolores's move. I type up my notes about her, what a typical weekly diet looks like for her, and submit them to Carl for approval. Yoonhee avoids me, acting like I've got a contagious disease when we see each other in the hallways. I get drunk almost every night once I get home from work, alone on my couch, scrolling through Yoonhee's Instagram page and keeping track of her wedding preparations. One day she's picked out a color scheme. Another day, flower arrangements. On another day, she asks her followers to vote in a poll about what style of wedding dress she should go for, telling us she's debating between strapless and off-the-shoulder. The winning dress is a color called porcelain and is so frothy it makes her look like a cake topper.

One day I wake up and decide to cut down on my drinking. I think about what Rick said, about replacing one habit with another, and I look up a YouTube tutorial for how to fold some basic origami shapes. I learn how to fold a crane and make a little family, poised for flight around my kitchen table. I tell Rick about it, and he gives me a copy of a book he's been using to learn how to make things. I teach myself how to make a giraffe, an elephant, a tiger. Soon I have a whole paper menagerie, and to celebrate I buy a case of wine and drink a bottle by myself.

I download a dating app—not the one Yoonhee met James on. At first it's fun, like a game where you have to swipe through as many people as possible before you get one who matches with you. I go on a succession of dates. I meet an engineer. I meet a poet. I meet a ceramics teacher. I meet a social media marketing guy. I meet a guy who doesn't work at all, whose entire life is bankrolled by a trust fund.

"What do you do?" they always ask me.

"I take care of fish," I say. Sometimes I take them home, but mostly I let them take me home.

The sex is exciting at first. I find myself becoming different people in bed with each guy, not exactly on purpose, just to try things out. The engineer likes doing it in the morning, the poet likes doing it high, the ceramics teacher likes me to talk dirty to him, the social media guy likes absolute silence. The trust fund kid is the most adventurous but also the most boring, somehow. I let him whisper in my ear all the things he wants to do to me before he eventually rolls off and falls asleep, and then I grab my things and leave. They always go crazy when you don't want to spend the night, and he blows up my phone the next day.

I play the 10cc song for them and none of them get it, even though they all make a big deal about their own music taste and practically quiz me about what bands I like. "It's a pretty cheesy song," they say, and I want to scream, "That's the point!"

One night, after none of my matches have texted me back, I drink a bottle and a half of wine and call Tae on the Europa app. I'm so drunk I'm not even nervous about what I'll say. When he finally picks up, his voice is so clear and familiar I want to crawl into the phone to curl up next to it.

"Ro? Did you mean to call me?"

"I've got a question for you," I say.

"I don't really have time for this," he says, but he's listening, as though he is afraid that I will do something drastic if he doesn't let me talk.

I ask him if he remembers the time we took a trip upstate to a brewery he liked, where he told me about all the different kinds of beer there were and we tried them all even though I didn't like any of them, and then later, tipsy as hell, we went to a contemporary art museum where one entire room was hung with canvases that were just pure plain white, like a field of snow. We thought we were hallucinating or that the exhibit was still under construction, but it turned out that was all there was to it.

"I just wanted to know if you remembered it. If you remembered that museum. All those canvases were white, right? There weren't any drawings or paintings on them? It wasn't just me not seeing them?"

He's quiet for a moment. "I remember," he says. "It wasn't just you. Is that what you wanted to ask me?"

"Yeah, you know. Just trying to make sure I didn't make it all up in my head."

He asks me how I am.

"I miss you," I say, and bite my lip so hard I taste blood.

I hear someone talking in the background, a low laugh that sounds like it belongs to a woman.

"Are you drunk?" he says.

"Fuck you," I say.

"I don't think you should be calling me like this," he says softly. I want him to get angry at me, to hang up abruptly. I'd even settle for him doing something like calling me a crazy bitch, just to see him hurt the way I hurt.

But instead, he tells me to remember to drink water and take an Advil before I go to sleep, otherwise I'll be hungover tomorrow. He tells me to take care. I want to ask him what that means, why people are always telling you to "take care" when what they really mean is "goodbye," but by then he has hung up.

In the days after Tae hangs up on me, I learn how to fold a frog, a camera, a flower, and a telephone. I make Rick a bright red frog to thank him for the pink crane, and he puts it on the edge of his desk where it sits like a benevolent watchful flower.

I start to fold a new frog for myself for every day I go without drinking. I line them up on my dresser. It starts out with just three frogs, a small family, and then it becomes five frogs. Seven frogs. It stays at seven for a while, until the eighth, ninth, then tenth frogs join them. I imagine to myself that they're watching over me. That they care.

The day Dolores's buyer comes to the aquarium, I'm playing her some deep cuts from My Bloody Valentine. Yoonhee comes into Dolores's exhibit room looking even crisper than usual, and I have to begrudgingly admit to myself that she is still the only person I know who can make off-the-shoulder dresses work in a professional setting.

"He's here," she says.

"I don't know what you're talking about," I tell her, and then he walks in, just like that, in a blue oxford shirt and dark jeans, looking not at all how I pictured. No fancy retinue or anything. He has a shock of red hair and a practiced smile on his face.

He sticks his hand out and shakes mine before I've had a chance to collect myself. "You must be Aurora," he says. "I've heard a lot about you." He has the kind of laser focus that the ultrarich have, the kind who meditate between meetings and fancy themselves to be connected to some kind of higher consciousness, and it is so intense that I forget to correct him and tell him that no one calls me that.

Yoonhee inserts herself, and I'm explained, as is Dolores, who immediately retreats behind a rock to study the newcomer. He introduces himself as Phil Houck, and I realize that the mysterious benefactor of the Fountain, Dolores's would-be owner, is related to Rob Houck, the CEO of Europa—the company funding Tae's mission to Mars. Yoonhee catches my eye, and a moment of our long-ago best-friend telepathy flashes between us when we both realize this fact at the same time. Money makes the world small. When I ask Phil about this, he says casually that he and Rob are cousins.

Phil nods along as Yoonhee explains everything, and his eyes light up when he sees Dolores, who is spying on him. "She's beautiful," he says reverently, and I almost like him for a second.

Octopuses aren't exactly social creatures, but their natural curiosity means that any reticence is easily overcome by the introduction of new phenomena or beings into their environment. So when Phil walks over to the tank and taps gently on the glass, Dolores unfurls herself, stretching as though she is showing off, which she might be. She turns mint green, then lavender, then a pale lemon color.

"I've never seen anything like this," Phil says. I notice he turns to me instead of Yoonhee.

"It means she's in a good mood," I say.

It turns out that Phil knows something about octopuses. Apparently marine biology is something of an extracurricular interest for him. He had a home aquarium as a child, in which he kept hermit crabs and sea urchins. He thanks me for my detailed notes about Dolores. "They've been incredibly useful," he says.

I open the lid of the tank for him, and Dolores swims up to the surface. I let him feed her, and we watch the silver fish from her bucket drift downward into the blue water while my speaker continues to play drony shoegaze. When I drop her daily puzzle into the water, she solves it in record time, and he marvels. "My four-year-old's got nothing on her," he says.

Yoonhee seems pleased at how well things are going, and I don't know what I am, because despite myself I'm having a hard time hating Phil.

He asks me for a tour. The three of us walk through the aquarium's main exhibits and I explain the animals, their names, their relationships with one another, the daily routine of care. I can feel Yoonhee's surprise at how much I know, and I would be annoyed if I wasn't surprised, too, at how good it feels to explain everything I know after all my years working at the Fountain and to calmly field Phil's endless questions.

"This is all amazing," he says, beaming at me. I keep waiting for him to interject with something stupid, and it happens only once, when we're looking at a school of rays and he incorrectly identifies one of them as a stingray. When I point out that it's actually a skate, he looks annoyed for a second before conceding that I'm right.

He asks me where Dolores got her name, and I tell her that she was named after someone's grandmother. Out of nowhere, he says, "You know, some people think that octopuses are aliens. Like, from outer space."

"I've heard that theory," I say.

"What do you think of it?" Phil asks me. It sounds like he genuinely wants to know. "You're the expert here."

It's flattering to be considered an expert on anything, especially when I spend most of my days haunted by the things I don't know and baffled by the things I do. "I don't know," I say truthfully. "It doesn't seem entirely impossible, if you think about it."

"Yeah," he says, nodding earnestly. "I don't think anything is entirely impossible. I mean, the things people would have thought impossible hundreds of years ago, we can accomplish now in seconds."

I remind myself, when I feel the irritation rising up inside me again, that of course he thinks this way. For a white man with money, a tech investor of all things, anything new feels like progress. "Sure," I say. "That makes sense to me."

"It's a shame how our public institutions have completely failed at protecting our planet and its wonders," he says with a total lack of irony, as though he has nothing to do with any of this. "But it's on us, those of us who do have the resources, to step up, right?"

I nod along, as though I am included in this "us."

He tells me about the home aquarium he's building now, in his home in Palo Alto, and about how Dolores's tank there will be even larger than ours. He plans to stock it full of underwater foliage native to the Bering Vortex. He shows me photos of the space where he's planning on installing everything, and I have to swallow hard, because it's true, the tank is much bigger than her current one. Eventually, he says, he wants to build a research lab, a privately funded venture with an aquarium open to the public attached to it. "The only way we're going to be able to save these magnificent creatures is if we can get people to care," he says, and even though I hate that he's the one saying it, I can't help but wonder if Dolores will actually be better off living with someone whose annual income is significantly more than the aquarium's revenue, which is shrinking every year.

Yoonhee asks Phil to come by her office to go over some final paperwork before he leaves for the day. He says he'd like to take a look at Dolores one last time before he does that, so we go into her exhibit hall. It seems she's asleep, which is unusual, and every so often her colors shift slightly, from coral to green to white to black.

"That's awesome," he declares, but this time his boyish excitement feels a little put-on. He's already checking his phone, like he's ready to move on to the next thing.

I don't tell him that I think this gradual shift in Dolores's coloration means she's dreaming. That what we're experiencing, right in front of us, is an intimate look into the consciousness of another being that is as unlike us as it is possible to be. Keeping this one last fact about her to myself feels, in a way, like I'll still get to hold on to a part of her, long after she's gone.

He asks if he can touch her (politely but expectantly, as though she's a dog in the park), and I want to say no but Yoonhee gives me this look—not like she'll kill me if I say no, but in this way that feels almost like she's pleading with me. She looks tired, and even her expertly applied makeup can't hide the dark circles under her eyes. I feel bad for her, all of a sudden, even though I don't want to. It's her job on the line, too, if this sale doesn't go through.

He puts his arm in the water and waves it around. Dolores opens one eye and shoots an arm up toward his hand, which probably looks like a sea anemone to her, and for a second, I feel his nervousness. "Whoa there," he says as she tastes his arm and tugs gently at it, like it is a plaything for her.

"She won't hurt you," I say neutrally, just the way Apa would have.

"I hope not," he says in a way that's meant to be funny but isn't, and there it is, the arrogance at the bottom of his curiosity and excitement, the sense that this creature he is not only buying but sinking so much money into better not be a faulty investment. The relief I feel at being able to dislike him again is so pure that I swear Dolores must be able to read minds, because the next thing I know, she is squirting water at him. He yelps with surprise and withdraws his arm forcefully, splashing even more water on the floor, and someone is laughing and for one unhinged moment I think it's Dolores, giggling at herself, and then I realize it's me.

"Oh my god," Yoonhee says. Our eyes meet and I think she might burst out laughing herself, but then she takes in the gravity of the situation, at just how utterly pissed Phil is that this octopus has managed to make him look stupid, and snaps to attention.

I'm laughing so hard I'm crying. Tears streak down my face, and Yoonhee and Phil just look at me like they think I'm going crazy. "I'm sorry," I say. "I just—I've never seen her do that before." Dolores looks at us triumphantly from her tank, turning a bright banana yellow and puffing herself up so that she's almost twice her usual size.

"You can't do that, sweetie," I say to her, once Yoonhee has led Phil out of the room with smooth apologies and a lot of glaring in my direction. But I give her an additional portion of food, just to let her know that she did good.

It's after hours when Yoonhee storms into the locker area, where I'm getting ready to go home. "What was that?" she says. "I had to spend an hour talking him down."

I shrug my jacket on. "This isn't SeaWorld. She doesn't do tricks. If he's buying her, he should know that she's a wild animal."

"You didn't have to laugh about it. He's a really big deal, okay? And so is this sale."

"You mean a really big deal for you," I say.

Her lips press themselves into a thin white line, in the way

I've seen so many times, when she's incredibly pissed but trying not to show it. "I'm going to have to tell Carl about this and ask him to assign the handover to someone else, because it's clear you're not taking it seriously."

The idea of Yoonhee's trying to get some kind of punitive administrative response from Carl, of all people, makes me see red. Not because I care about what he could do to me, but because this is exactly the kind of behavior I hate—when people go above you to get at you. I slam my locker door shut. "Go ahead. What are you going to say, that she acted out and you blame me for it?"

"I know you think I'm just doing this to get ahead, but this is bigger than you, okay?"

"Great. I'm going home now."

"I'm trying to help you!" Yoonhee yells, which is just about the worst thing she could have said. I turn around, and when I can focus on her again, it's almost as if I've never seen her before. Like she's a total stranger, like we've never held hands at night during sleepovers when we couldn't sleep or played endless rounds of Truth or Dare or MASH on oil-stained restaurant place mats or sneaked warm vodka shots and pulls of cigarettes at our parents' houses.

"What are you talking about? How is any of this helping me?" My voice shakes, and I clear my throat, as if that is going to help.

"Look," she says, "I didn't want to tell you this, but your job was up for elimination."

"They were going to fire me?"

"It wasn't specific to you. But the board was going to make cuts, and they thought they could do away with part of your department. You would have been on the chopping block."

"So, what, I'm supposed to be grateful to you? You're taking away the only thing I care about at this job."

Yoonhee breathes in deeply through her nose. "I'm sorry. This is all coming out wrong. I just, I want you to be okay, okay?"

"Well, I'm doing fine actually," I say. "Not that you'd know."

"I know you've been through a lot," she says carefully. Like she's been practicing this. "But at a certain point, you're going to have to take ownership of—well, your life."

"What does it look like I'm doing?"

"Can I be honest?" she says. And already I know that nothing she says after that is going to be something I want to hear, because no one ever, ever has anything good to say if they have to ask you if they can be honest before they say it. "It looks like you're hiding."

It doesn't feel like the kind of blowout fight they show in the movies, where both people start yelling and throwing things, which I'm sorry about, because that would probably feel better than whatever this is. Instead, it feels like when the credits of the movie roll and you're not entirely sure what you just saw but part of you feels cheated, like, *Is that all there is?* So when Yoonhee just watches me gather my things and lets me leave, it's not that I don't expect it. It's just that in spite of myself, I was still hoping for something more.

I find myself driving to Rachel's. I don't mean to, initially, but I know that if I go home, there will be nothing between me and finishing another bottle of wine or going through four beers like they're water. I don't know what feels worse—having my former best friend tell me she feels sorry for me or having to admit that she's right. That I've been hiding all this time, using Apa and Tae and Umma and Yoonhee and everyone else in my life to avoid looking at the ways I've disappointed myself.

I used to think that things would have been easier for both of my parents if I had never been born. If Umma had been able to wait before having a kid, if she'd been able to go to school the way she wanted to, if Apa had been able to get a better job instead of having to settle for something that would pay more. It's hard not to look at the chain of circumstances surrounding our family and imagine that, had it not been for me, they would have been happier, that Apa would still be around. When you grow up thinking that way, it gets easier and easier, with time, to fragment yourself. To reduce yourself to the parts that are most useful or valuable to other people.

Apa told me that each of an octopus's arms is operated by its own brain. "Imagine," he told me, "if each of your four limbs—your arms and your legs—had a mind of its own. Imagine the things you could do, all at the same time." According to Apa, if we were neurologically structured the way octopuses are, we'd be able to do things like playing the piano while also dribbling a soccer ball or mixing a cocktail, all while carrying on a relatively complex conversation on the phone or solving a math equation.

Even when an octopus's arms are removed from the rest of its body, they can still react to stimuli. In one study, when researchers pinched an octopus's severed arms, they jerked away, because they could still feel pain.

to me about anything that happened with her and Apa is just so typical."

"Think of it this way," Rachel says. "It's clear he's important to her. And she wanted to tell you about it, but she didn't know how."

"She could have told me at literally any point before I had to meet the guy. I'm just saying a bit of warning would have been appreciated."

"It's a muscle, you know," Rachel says. "It takes practice, talking about yourself and asking people for what you need or want or expect from them."

"Is that from one of your books?" I say.

"Nope," she says. "That is a bona fide original. Keep it if you want. I had to remind myself of it every day, with Simon. We were together for so long that I couldn't even begin to fathom it when I felt us falling apart. I don't know that talking about things would have helped. But it would have made our disintegrating less—"

"Painful?"

"Drawn out," Rachel says. "It was always going to be painful. But if I'd known then what I know now, I wouldn't have tried to go it alone for years or told myself for so long that it was just because of me, that *I* was the reason our marriage wasn't working.

"She wants to be closer to you," Rachel continues when I don't say anything back.

"So what do I do?" I ask while I nervously fold and refold the napkin she's given me into the shape of a star, a flower, a plane.

Rachel takes the napkin from me. "You let her in," she says.

CHAPTER 12

The first time I met Tae's mom, I had stayed over at his apartment the night before. I woke to him whispering insistently that I was to stay inside his bedroom until he gave me the all clear.

"Are you being robbed?" was my first question.

"No," he said, grimacing as though he wished that was what was happening instead. "It's my mom. Can you just stay in here till she's gone?"

I was too groggy and alarmed to be annoyed by this, and part of me got it. It's weird to talk about sex and dating with your immigrant Korean parents, even when they know, ostensibly, that chances are their unmarried, twentysomething children probably aren't saving it for marriage.

"Umma?" I heard his voice in the living room as I burrowed underneath the covers, as if that would help if she were to suddenly burst into his bedroom. I breathed in the scent of his laundry detergent, a bracingly clean scent that I could never replicate with my own laundry, no matter how much detergent I poured in or how many dryer sheets I stuffed inside.

I could hear Tae's mother bustling around in his kitchen, putting groceries away and asking him cheerily how he was, complaining that he never called her and that he was getting much too thin. I figured it would just be a few minutes or so until she left, that Tae would probably rush her out under one pretext or another, but I heard their laughter and his coffee machine percolating. I fell back asleep underneath the covers, and I dreamed that I was being parceled out and portioned into all the Tupperware and plastic bags that Tae's mom must have brought, labeled with a Sharpie and stored neatly away in his refrigerator and pantry.

When I woke up, the apartment was quiet. I peeked out from the bedroom to see that Tae was sitting alone at the kitchen table, working on his laptop. "What are you working on?" I said.

"This week's lesson plan," he said, taking a sip of his coffee. The stove clock said it was now noon. "You slept a lot."

"I thought you were going to wake me," I said, sliding into the chair across from him. "Sounded like your mom was here for a long time."

"Oh, she's still here," he said mildly, and I jumped up from the chair like I had been bitten by something. "She just ran out to the car to get something. I told her you were here. She wants to meet you and take us both to lunch."

"No, you didn't. Oh my god." We'd been together for nearly two years at that point, but I wasn't anxious to meet Tae's parents. He had been hinting at it, but I always skirted the issue by changing the subject. It wasn't that I didn't want to meet the people who were important to Tae; it was that I was worried what would happen when his mother, whom he was close with, decided I wasn't good enough for him.

"Don't worry about it. She'll love you," he said, giving me a kiss on the cheek. "Though you might want to brush your hair or something," he added before turning back to his computer.

I ran into Tae's bathroom and got ready in record time, splashing cold water on my face and doing my best to wipe away the black eyeliner that had gathered in the corners of my eyes, cursing all the while. The night before, we had gone out for dinner and I'd had most of the bottle of wine we'd ordered. My head was pounding. I had just managed to get my hair into a manageable shape on my head by patting it down with water and running my fingers through it quickly (Tae, for all his fastidiousness, was like most guys and had nothing but a flimsy plastic barbershop comb in his bathroom cabinet) when Tae's mother came back into the apartment, trilling, "Let's go, kids!"

Lunch, at a noodle place not far from Tae's apartment, was awkward but not horrific. Tae's mother was much nicer than I'd thought she'd be, her hair frizzled into the usual perm that almost all Korean ahjummas over a certain age seem to get at some point. She had nearly perfect eyebrows, which made me wonder if they were tattooed on, the way Umma's were. She laughed at everything Tae said and asked me kind, careful questions about myself, shooting worried glances at me when she thought Tae wasn't looking.

"Oh, an aquarium!" she said when I told her about my job in my halting Korean. "How interesting." I had forgotten the word for *aquarium* in Korean and had to describe it as "a zoo for fish."

She seemed, to my surprise, relieved about me, and I wondered if Tae's string of white girls had simply made her happy that he was finally dating a Korean girl.

I asked him about it later, when we were back at his place, and he laughed. "It doesn't really matter to me whether my parents are okay with whoever I'm dating. I just wanted her to meet you."

"Do you think she liked me?" I asked.

"I don't know," he said, which I appreciated, even though it stung. "It's hard to tell with her sometimes. But she knows how much you mean to me. I talk about you all the time."

This felt completely incomprehensible to me. Umma and I had primarily operated by a "don't ask, don't tell" policy. After Apa disappeared, all she seemed to require from me was that I not drop out of school, get pregnant, get arrested, or do anything else that would permanently embarrass her or, in her words, lead to "wasting my life." It never occurred to me to loop her into any of my life decisions, especially after I told her about getting the job at the aquarium and she gave me the silent treatment for a week.

When she met Tae, about a year and a half in, it was because he had insisted on it, saying he wanted to meet her, and against my usual instincts, I caved. We had dinner at Umma's place, and she approved of how well he ate, how polite he was, how much better his Korean was than mine. He even succeeded in making her laugh. "You should have dated someone like him years ago," Umma said to me afterward, and beneath the sting of her implied criticism, I felt a warm glow.

But Tae called his mother every week without fail, and his refrigerator and cupboards were always overflowing with groceries and dishes she'd dropped off. He didn't talk much about his dad, whom I never met. Judging from photos, he seemed like almost every other middle-aged Korean dad—bespectacled, a little balding, a little round around the middle. I gathered that he and Tae had clashed a lot when he was younger. "He's better now, but he used to drink," was all Tae ever said about it. It was why, even when we were out with friends or at one of his band's shows, the most Tae would ever drink was a few beers at a time, and why he got quiet whenever I drank whatever he thought was too much. He never said anything, just watched me carefully, didn't smile at my jokes, and reminded me to drink water before I went to sleep.

Apa would have liked Tae. They had a similar enjoyment of life and an upbeat resilience, a masculine certainty that no matter what happened, they would rise above it. It was very un-Korean, I often told Tae, for him to be so optimistic. It was why he was such a good teacher, even though he taught middle school, which even I knew was a notoriously difficult age.

"The kids can get rowdy, but they're all there because they just want to learn and be listened to," Tae said about his students. He had been teaching for only a few years, but he had already amassed a huge following among his students, and even the older ones who had gone on to high school came back to visit his classroom often, calling him "Mr. P" and jostling one another for his attention.

"Explain it to me like I'm one of your students," I said sometimes when he was stressed about some problem at work or with his friends. He could get like that, quiet and internal when he was upset about something. But I would sit him down and make him go through it with me one piece at a time—when the parent of one of his students was upset because he thought Tae was an overly harsh grader, even though Tae gave out extra-credit opportunities all the time; or when one student had stopped handing in his homework and kept falling asleep in class; or when Garrett, one of his bandmates, went on a bender and stopped showing up for practice.

"Thank you," he told me once.

"For what? I'm just listening," I said.

"You're good at helping me stay present," he said. "I'm used to trying to fix everything on my own. But you don't make me feel that way."

And for a while, maybe, that was enough for him.

Every year, Tae asked me what I wanted for my birthday, and I would insist that I wanted nothing, and every year he would surprise me with something small and utilitarian, yet thoughtful. It drove me crazy.

The first year we were together, he gave me a pale blue thermos that was guaranteed to never leak, because he knew I had a tendency to spill coffee on myself when I was rushing in the mornings, which I often was. The second year, he bought me a green water-resistant "forever" wristwatch that he claimed would never run out of batteries. He was like a dad that way, always excited about things on the internet that made claims to innovation. The third year, he bought me a set of ceramic mugs from a local artist that were all painted, he said, according to different colors of the ocean. Each mug had a name: Storm, Calm, Breaker, and Reef.

"Reef is not something an ocean can be," I said.

"You're really hard to shop for," he said.

Reef, which was a strange azure color with an underglaze of orange, broke during an argument we were having. Not because either of us were the type to throw things at each other, but because during our fight we weren't paying attention to the fact that it was teetering in the dish rack until it fell into the sink and shattered.

All our fights were really just the same fight over and over again. Tae wanted me to get my life together, but he would never say so directly. He would just pick at little things about me, like the fact that I didn't clean my apartment often enough, or that it seemed like I was never going to leave my job even though I didn't seem to enjoy it. "Why are you like this?" he would ask me, exasperated when he saw that I had yet again left my taxes till the last minute or had failed to schedule the doctor's appointment that I said I would.

It was cute in the beginning, because what girl doesn't like the idea that someone else can fix her, make her a little more competent and confident and generally better at life? I humored his suggestions for how I could manage to drink more water throughout the day, or when he woke me up early to take me jogging. Our sojourns through the park near my building were laughable—him striding ahead, his hair pulled back with a goofy sweatband, and me tagging along behind him. "One more lap and then we'll go in," he'd say, like I was a recalcitrant dog who did not want to be walked.

In retrospect, I think Tae found my sloppiness appealing. As the oldest of three boys, Tae took over running the house at a young age, while his parents ran the grocery store that they still managed. So making sure that he and his two younger brothers all had clean-enough clothes, did their homework, and didn't subsist entirely on cereal was second nature to him.

Before me, the white girls he had dated mostly had fancy educations and baked a lot and wore athletic gear to work out—girls who didn't need him, not in the way I did. His last three girlfriends were all girls he'd met in college or right afterward, and I made him tell me their names and stories in full: Claire Watson, Megan Spencer, Victoria Sayre. I looked them all up on the internet, studying their glossy hair and LinkedIn pages and carefully curated Instagram profiles. Claire was private on social media, but I gleaned that she was a mother of two now, in Boston, and working at some kind of marketing research firm. Megan had a dog, a chocolate Lab with a sizable social media presence, and was a yoga instructor in Miami. Victoria worked in consulting, and she had recently gotten engaged to a man twice Tae's size, a military vet who looked like he could bench-press her.

"Do you still keep in touch with them?" I asked, and he hesitated before responding.

"Is this one of those trick questions?" he said. "Like, where if I say no, that looks bad, and if I say yes, that also looks bad?"

"Just answer the question, Tae." We were sitting on the yellow couch, which he professed to hate even though it was the one thing about me that he didn't try to fix, I think because even he was exhausted at the idea of having to maneuver it out of my apartment.

"Not really. Every once in a while, we'll wish each other a happy birthday or something like that," he said, shrugging. "It's not a big deal. You're the one I'm with now."

Which of course made it the biggest deal in the world. It wasn't that I thought he was cheating on me with one of them or anything like that—it was that I had no idea what he saw in me when he had been with girls like that. The first time he stayed the night at my place I offered him some wine and had to give it to him out of a rinsed-out Diet Coke can because all my glasses and mugs were dirty. The next morning, I woke up bleary-eyed to find him already out of bed and scouring my stove top.

Some other things I liked about Tae:

The way my head fit on his shoulder.

That he was kind to old people on the street and strangers who asked for directions, even taking out his phone sometimes to google something for them that they could have probably looked up themselves, even if we were somewhere that was new to us, too.

How, when we were watching a movie and I asked him annoying questions about the plot and the characters and the actors, he never shushed me.

The way he did laundry, dutifully separating his clothes and sometimes even hanging them on his balcony to dry, so that they would smell of sunlight and wind.

How he looked whenever he cooked us dinner at my apartment, standing at my tiny electric stove with an apron wrapped around his waist and holding out a wooden spoon for me to taste from, always so anxious about achieving the perfect blend of spice and taste.

But being in a relationship with someone is kind of like navigating a giant house together. The trick is to try and be in the same room at the same time as the other person as often as possible, and the problem with me and Tae was that I was always stepping out of rooms too early or barging in at the wrong time.

When Tae asked me, during our third year together, what I thought of moving in together, I panicked. I called Yoonhee and we met for emergency drinks at Hattie's.

"What's wrong with you?" Yoonhee said impatiently. She,

along with Umma and everyone else in my life, loved Tae and thought I was incredibly lucky to be with someone like him.

"He's just too nice. And too clean. I can't live with someone like that." I didn't even realize I was picking the label off my beer until Yoonhee stopped me.

"You lived with *me* for several years," she said. "I'm nice and clean."

"That was different."

"Well, hopefully it'll rub off on you," she said. "I don't see what the problem is here. I would love it if James were cleaner."

"It's not normal," I told her. "Tae owns an ironing board. He changes his sheets every week!"

"Relax," she said. "You're acting like he kicks puppies or something."

Unlike Yoonhee, who had mostly had a string of monogamous relationships after college, I was not in the habit of meeting nice boys who treated me nicely. I was into short-term types of guys who were working on getting their web series or skateboarding company off the ground, or were veteran baristas entering their forties with nothing but a fancy grinder and a closet full of denim button-downs to show for it. I liked how expendable these relationships felt, how I never needed to worry about being some better version of myself around them. The guys I dated were always between things—relationships, jobs, apartments—and often slept among piles of dirty laundry on mattresses on the floor, which I sometimes rolled off of when I spent the night. Usually they had one smelly towel that I had to gingerly dry my hands on the corner of in the mornings.

I liked how, in comparison to them, my life felt stable, upholstered. Unlike them, I had a steady salary and a retirement account, even if I rarely contributed to it, and they never cared that I drank sometimes in the middle of the day, often alone, or that I sometimes went days without doing the dishes or taking the trash out or even washing my hair, just because I had suddenly and completely lost interest in doing anything remotely productive or healthy for myself.

But Tae cared, about all of it. And the more he cared, the more inadequate I felt.

"What if he realizes?" I said to Yoonhee, a little desperately.

She looked up from a text she was drafting to James. "Realizes what?" she said. "That you're a real person with problems and thoughts and flaws?"

"That we're nothing alike. That he probably needs to be with someone completely different from me, someone more like him. Someone who's good with kids and looks forward to the future and knows exactly what she wants."

She finished drafting her text, sent it, and sighed. "No one knows exactly what they want. Not even me, and I'm pretty close to it."

"I think he thinks I'm, like, a project. Something he can fix up."

"Well, do you want to be fixed?"

"Maybe," I admitted.

We were silent for a while. Yoonhee toyed with the paper wrapper of her straw and then said, out of nowhere, "You want to know what your problem is? You want to be fixed, but you also don't want anything to change."

"That's not true," I said, a little taken aback.

"I think you're scared," she said.

"Of course I'm scared," I said.

"But you're scared for the wrong reasons," she said. "If you'd just let someone in for once, you might be surprised at how okay it might be. You might be surprised at how happy it would make you."

"I am happy," I insisted. "I'm happy with the way things are."

"So that's why you called me?" she said. "Because you're so happy?"

I didn't know how to tell her or anyone else that the idea of living with Tae—even though we were sleeping over at each other's places all the time anyway—filled me with terror because it would involve having to be confronted with all my inadequacies every day. That sharing a living space together would mean he'd finally understand the full extent of my dysfunction and see that I wasn't just charmingly askew or a little bit sloppy from time to time. And I didn't know if I could take it, to see the look of tenderness in his eyes fade over time, to be replaced with the coldness and skepticism, the lack of belief in the other person's ability to change, that had characterized my parents' relationship.

"I mean, if you're not ready to live together, you're not ready to live together," she said. "But if you don't think this is something you'd want, like, ever, you should probably tell him."

"I can't," I said to him later. We were at his place, doing the dishes. He washed while I dried, studiously avoiding his gaze.

"Can't what?"

"I can't live with you."

"Okay," he said.

"I just, what if we regret it? Things are okay right now, right?"

"I said it's okay," he said.

"It's not that I don't want to be together. I just don't think I can plan a move or anything right now," I said, my words coming out in a rush.

"Ro," he said, taking the dish that I had dried three times now out of my hands, "it's okay. We can talk about it another time."

But we didn't, and things changed between us. That night he slept with his back to me, the way he did when he didn't want to talk, and I lay awake, staring up at the ceiling and the patterns of light that passing cars made. He always fell asleep as soon as his head hit the pillow, even after we'd had an argument or a tense night, which I resented. I listened to the sound of his breathing while I weighed the options in my head. I didn't want to break up, I knew. But a relationship is a straight road toward a destination, whatever that might be, and I could see, very clearly, that while Tae's road map was leading directly toward a future involving marriage, a house, probably kids, my own was much murkier and uncertain.

When I thought about the possibility of having a family of my own, all I could think about was listening to my parents scream at each other, to my mother telling my father that she wished they'd never met, that she wished she had never come with him to this country. And I remembered thinking that if that were true, if somehow my mother could go back in time and undo those choices she had made, unmarry my father, un-immigrate to the United States, zipping herself out of her wedding dress and into her travel suit and walking backward onto a plane that traveled backward all the way across the ocean to Korea, then I, too, would become unmade, shrinking into my body until I was nothing but a clump of cells, and then nothing at all. That perhaps my mother would have been happier if she hadn't stayed with my father and consigned herself to a life she didn't want. And what if Tae and I ended up just as miserable as my parents had been? Even at our happiest, I could hardly imagine a world in which that happiness might stay, take root, and become something that could stand on its own, let alone support something bigger than ourselves.

A year ago, when Tae first told me about the Europa program, about Arc 4's mission to Mars, I told him it was ridiculous. That it was not only unrealistic but also unseemly, arrogant, for us as a human race to jet off this planet in search of new worlds to ruin.

"Isn't life on earth already hard enough?" I asked him. "What's the point of trying to start all over again when we can't even fix what's happening here?"

He was surprised by my vehemence. "I'd think you'd appreciate what they're trying to do," he said. "It's the only way to save everyone."

"And you think everyone is going to get saved from global warming because some rich dudes decide we should build pods on Mars?" I said.

"It's better than putting our heads in the sand and pretending that anything is going to get solved that way," he said.

I've often thought that part of Tae's wanting to join the mission was an attempt to outdo his parents, who had immigrated from a Korea that was so vastly different from what it was today that it might as well have been a voyage through space and time. If the only thing he felt he could do in return, to prove that their journey hadn't been in vain, was to leave the earth itself.

The process for getting approved to join the Arc 4 mission was an extensive one. First, he had to apply by submitting a statement and a video essay explaining why he was interested in the mission. Then there were several rounds of interviews and fitness tests. In the weeks before his evaluations, which he had to fly to Los Angeles for, Tae woke up early every morning to run three miles. His meals became even more regimented—two lean proteins, two greens, and one protein shake between meals.

I mostly ignored these preparations of his, because I didn't know how else to deal with it. It seemed fantastical, anyway, to think that he would get in, with the program being so competitive. Arc 4 was accepting only twenty applicants out of the thousands who had applied. But as the rounds went on and Tae continued not to receive any emails that began with *We are sorry to inform you,* the possibility of his departure seemed more and more likely. Still, I never thought it would come true.

"So you're just going to let him go?" Yoonhee said, incredulous. "Are you going to, like, do long-distance or something?"

"It's not going to happen," I told her. "It's a very competitive program."

By then, things between me and Yoonhee had shifted, too. She wasn't responding to my texts or calls as readily, and whenever I did manage to get ahold of her, she was always busy. James had finally proposed earlier that year, in exactly the way she'd wanted (she was close with his younger sister and had told her when and how James should do it—on one knee, on a footbridge in the Brooklyn Botanic Garden with pink cherry blossoms falling all around them), and now that they had set a date for their wedding, she became increasingly unavailable. "Wedding stuff," she always said dismissively whenever she had to respond to a new text or email during our hangs, though I could tell she was buzzing with happiness.

"You'll be the maid of honor, right?" Yoonhee said anxiously. "You won't have to do anything. You can just show up, honestly. You know me, I'm going to plan it all anyway."

"Duh," I told her. "As long as I don't have to wear a dopey dress."

"I'm only going to make you wear a dopey dress," she said. "Everyone else can show up naked for all I care."

But I screwed up, like I usually do. When Tae was informed that his application had reached the final rounds of consideration, and all that was left standing between him and a spot on the Arc 4 mission was a few rounds of psychological evaluations and another series of interviews, I grew terrified. I stopped eating regularly and began drinking more. I couldn't sleep, thinking of how everything I'd thought would happen to us eventually—Tae realizing that he didn't want to be with me anymore and leaving—would be happening on a much more accelerated timeline than I had imagined, and that there was nothing I could do to stop it.

"I want to talk about this," he said one night when he was at my place. "Ro, please. You can't keep pretending this isn't happening, because it is."

"What's there to talk about?" I said, pouring myself another glass of wine. *If we don't talk about it, maybe it won't happen,* I thought. I queued up another episode of the crime show we had been watching and didn't look up when he left, not exactly slamming the front door but closing it with more force than usual. I heard him walk down the stairs and felt my heart stutter. On screen, the detective had found her killer and was closing in on him, chasing him down a dark street in the rain. Raindrops slashed against her face as she reached for her man, only to miss him by inches when she tripped and fell. *If Tae comes back up,* I told myself, *if I hear him knock on the front door, I'll let him in, and this time I'll ask him to stay.* But instead I heard his car start and drive off, and we didn't text or call each other for days.

Yoonhee asked if I could plan the shower for her. She said she knew it was stupid to care about the shower when she was already having a bachelorette and an engagement, but that she still wanted one, and I took one look at the Google Doc she had prepared of all the things she wanted and the people she wanted to include and closed it.

I opened my email, prepared to contact the other bridesmaids she had selected about possible venues, dates, and times, and then got so exhausted at the prospect of having to coordinate among these near strangers, of having to balance ten different people's schedules and foibles and come up with a theme, decorations, and ideas for the party, that I opened a bottle of wine and had it for dinner. The next morning, I woke up late for work and with a slew of texts from Yoonhee about what she wanted for the shower, which finally ended with "Never mind. I'll just do it myself."

I called her, but she didn't pick up. "I'm sorry," I wrote back. "Things with Tae aren't good. I'm just dealing with a lot right now."

"It's fine," she replied. "You do you."

After Tae finally told me that he had been accepted into the program and that he would be leaving for training camp in Arizona in two weeks, I felt calm, collected. It didn't matter anymore, I thought, because in a way I'd already lost him, the moment he decided to apply. He didn't seem to want to talk about it anymore, either. That night, when I reached for him in the dark, it felt as though, even when he was inside me, he was already far away, lost among the stars and planets, and that the only thing tethering him to earth was my need for him, as vast and silent as the night sky.

Later he had one of his nightmares. It always started with his shaking a little in his sleep, then crying out, saying something in Korean that was too garbled for me to make out. I knew from experience that it would be bad to wake him up, so I just held him, stroked his hair, and told him that everything was okay, that he didn't need to be afraid, until he stopped shaking and his breathing grew deep and even again. I never asked him what he dreamed about, and he never told me.

In the morning, I woke up before him, and I saw, tucked away neatly on the side table next to him, a small leather-bound notebook that he used to keep track of his to-dos and reminders—a charmingly analog habit of his that I'd never thought too much about. I flipped it open to a list he had made of things to take care of before leaving: buy batteries, buy thermal underwear, talk to landlord, quit job, sign paperwork, sell car. I ran through the items on the list, not even sure what I was searching for, until I got to the very bottom of it, where, in his neat, small handwriting, he had written, "Tell Ro." And, just like all the other items on the list, a line had been struck through it, a definitive line that told me what I was unwilling to admit to myself.

I got dressed and left quickly, making sure to take all the things I usually left at his place, like extra contact lenses and sweaters. I hesitated before grabbing the toothbrush he kept for me in the bathroom, and then finally dropped it into the garbage can on my way out. I took one long last look at his sleeping form, watching the way the morning light filtered in through the blinds and outlined each of the hairs on his arms in red and gold, and then I closed his front door behind me and left.

CHAPTER 13

When I was sixteen, I taught myself how to bake a cake from scratch for a boy. He was my first boyfriend, a tall, thin boy with a beaky nose whose name was, improbably, Michael Douglas, though he went by Mike. Mike wore all black and listened to bands with names like Metal Trash Mouth and Mother Slayer, all of which had album covers that scared me, though I pretended I liked their music to impress him.

We were too shy to do much other than make out in parking lots or at the mall, when we weren't chatting with each other endlessly on AIM, but when his birthday came around, I decided to make a cake for him. It seemed like the kind of thing you were supposed to do for your boyfriend. Yoonhee helped me pick out a recipe from the internet for a chocolate cake with peanut butter and coffee-flavored frosting—Mike seemed to subsist entirely on peanut butter sandwiches, and he liked coffee, which seemed like the height of sophistication to me back then—and I set to work. It was the night before his birthday, and I had decided to bring the cake with me to school the next day.

"What are you doing?" Umma said when she walked into the kitchen. She had just woken from one of the long naps she'd started taking after Apa disappeared and looked tired, the dark circles under her eyes making her face look gaunt. I was elbow-deep in flour and sugar and had even managed to get some in my hair.

"I'm making a cake for a friend," I said.

"You're making a mess," she said. She eyed the jars I had opened, the spillage across the counter.

When I was little, Umma baked all the time—cookies, cakes, coffee cakes, and banana bread every week, to bring to church. The other church ladies would coo over the baked goods and then ask me if I was as talented a baker as my mother was. For their anniversary one year, Apa had bought her a fancy stand mixer, which was her pride and joy, but after he disappeared, it mostly sat untouched in our kitchen, gathering dust.

"I'll clean it up, I promise," I said.

"You're not mixing the ingredients correctly," she said, looking over my shoulder into the bowl. "You have to fold the wet ingredients into the dry ones. And did you sift that flour?"

"It's just a cake, Umma," I said. "I think I can figure it out."

"Suit yourself," she said. She went to go read in the living room, but I could feel her judgment lingering in the kitchen long after she'd left. I mixed the batter and poured it into a cake pan, and then, while the cake baked in the oven, I made the frosting. It felt like magic, watching the peanut butter and instant coffee grounds mixing with the milk and confectioners' sugar—which, to my eyes, looked like freshly powdered snow—to alchemize into something sweet and thick and spreadable. I felt smug and invincible. "See?" I wanted to tell Umma. "Not everything I do is wrong."

But when it came time to take the cake out of the oven, I found to my dismay that the middle had collapsed in on itself, and although the outside of the cake was dry and crusty, the inside was underdone and soggy. Umma came in to take a look. "What did I tell you?" she said.

It was all too much. I didn't cry, not exactly, but I slammed the oven door shut and stared out the kitchen window into our backyard, at the bird feeder that Umma and I had constructed out of Popsicle sticks when I was little. A cardinal was pecking at it, and a blue jay came along and began shrieking.

Umma took out the canisters of flour and sugar that I had put away. "The longer you stand there and stare, the longer it will take to get this cake done," she said.

"I can't make it again," I said.

"You're going to have to, with all that frosting you made," she said sternly.

I watched as she sifted the flour into the bowl, cracked in the eggs deftly with one hand, added the rest of the ingredients, and mixed them using the stand mixer. We watched the bright yellow yolks of the eggs meld with the white of the flour and sugar, becoming something greater than the sum of their parts. "The trick," she told me, "is to let the ingredients breathe into one another, get to know each other. That's why sifting is important."

We discarded the bad cake I had made, and Umma popped the new one into the oven. She tried the frosting I had made and pronounced it "not bad," which made me thrill with excitement. When the oven timer went off and the cake was ready, it smelled heavenly. It was plump, soft, and most important, structurally sound. "Now we wait for it to cool," she said.

"If you put the frosting on it right away, it'll melt into the cake."

When it had cooled sufficiently, she showed me how to use her icing spatula, layering the frosting in swirls until it had covered the entire top of the cake.

"It's not Yoonhee's birthday," she said, looking up at me when we had finished. I realized that the entire evening had gone by with just the two of us laboring over this cake.

"No, it's not," I said.

"Must be some friend of yours, if you're baking for them," she said, and I was afraid she would ask, that she would divine it was for a boy, but she didn't.

In the end, the cake was a huge hit. Mike ate three slabs of it and pronounced it "awesome," and even Yoonhee, who was hard to impress and was also on a diet at the time, ate an entire slice. And while Mike and I ended up breaking up for some silly teenage reason a few weeks later—I think he lives in Philadelphia now and has a kid—the memory of that evening, when it was just me and Umma silently making a cake together, stuck with me. Not just because it was the most time we'd spent together since Apa disappeared, but because she had seemed, for once, excited about something I was doing. I still remember the look of surprise that had crossed her face when she'd tasted the frosting, and how the knots of tension in my shoulders had loosened at the sight of her smile.

When I get home from Rachel's, I dig around for the cake recipe, finally finding it in the back of one of my old diaries. *Cake for Mike's Bday* is written in my loopy high school hand-writing, and there are hearts drawn around the borders.

I go to the store to buy the ingredients and a cake pan, since I haven't baked in years. While waiting in the checkout line, I study the tabloid and magazine headlines, to see which celebrities have gotten married or divorced or have had babies or lost their baby weight.

An old white woman behind me notices me scanning the headlines and says, "I'm so happy for her." I realize with a start that she is referring to the blond celebrity whose smiling face I have been staring at.

"She's been through a lot," the woman says knowledgeably, as though we are talking about a mutual friend of ours. The woman is wearing a plastic visor, loads of makeup, and a T-shirt with kittens in a basket printed across it. She smells like cigarettes and chewing gum, a comforting smell, and though she seems hardy enough, she grips the handlebar of her shopping cart as though it is the only thing keeping her upright.

"She has," I agree.

"And she seems like such a nice girl," she says. Her voice is raspy, full of amusement. "That no-good husband of hers," she whispers conspiratorially. "I've never liked any of his movies."

Before I can agree again, it's my turn to check out. The girl behind the register gives me a bored flick with her eyes when I say hi and ask her how she is. At the last second, I throw in two copies of the tabloid that the old woman was talking about. "Here you go," I say, giving one of them to the woman.

"Oh!" she says. "Thank you, my dear." She waves goodbye at me when I leave the store, and I wave back at her as I hoist the bags out of my shopping cart.

I read my copy of the magazine at home, in between consulting the cake recipe. I sift flour, measure sugar, and crack eggs, all while reading about how one famous actress was abducted by aliens as a child and that's why her eyes never seem to focus correctly during close-ups; how another is the secret love child of the veteran director whose film she's currently starring in; how another has joined a lizard person cult and you can tell because of the way her jewelry choices have grown more conservative over the years. It's fascinating, the way these magazines seem to mine the smallest details and spin them out into something utterly fantastical.

When I was younger, I used to make small promises to myself all the time. If I counted three red cars on my way to school, that meant I would have a good day, or at least not a shitty one. If I opened a bag of Doritos and could correctly guess the number of chips inside, whatever boy I was crushing on at the time would like me back. If I could hold my breath and count to eighty, that meant I would get at least a 95 on my upcoming math test. If I could manage to cross the street before the light changed, that meant Apa would come back. None of these things were connected to what I wanted from them, but hanging my hopes on these small, nonsensical details felt to me like a way to make them come true, and it was almost enough to just imagine that they could.

I don't have an electric mixer at home, so I have to do everything by hand. Gradually my entire kitchen counter becomes covered in flour. Once the cake is in the oven, I finish reading the magazine. I get to the story about the actress the woman in the grocery store was talking about, who is apparently pregnant now via in vitro after years of trying with her ex-husband, an actor who used to star in action movies but is now primarily known for having an explosive temper on sets and throwing smoothies at production assistants. The actress is not revealing who the father of her baby is, and her face in the photo looks full and happy. The baby, the magazine tells me, is due sometime in January.

After the cake cools, I layer the frosting on in swaths. I lick a little bit of it off my knife and savor the sweetness on my tongue. I let the cake chill in the refrigerator overnight, and then I take myself off to bed, early for once, and fall asleep almost instantly, my nose full of the smell of chocolate and peanut butter.

The next morning, I wake up earlier than usual. The sun is barely up. I know only two people who are probably up this early, too. I imagine what Tae is doing. I check the Europa app and learn that the launch for the first stage of their mission is in just a few weeks. I shove down the feelings this brings up and instead focus on carefully covering the cake with tinfoil until it looks like a shiny bride.

I drive carefully, the cake in the front seat beside me. There are hardly any cars on the road. I pull up at a red light next to a car with a dog hanging out the window. The dog and I make eye contact, and she winks at me. I laugh, and I realize it is the first sound I have made today.

When I get to Umma's apartment building, the parking lot is full, so I have to park on the street. I buzz her door, waiting for her to get to the intercom. "It's me," I tell her, and I hear silence on the other end, before she lets me in.

The walk down the hallway to her unit feels like the moment from the other night being played in reverse. I hold the cake in my arms carefully, like it is an infant, and realize when I get to the end of the corridor that Umma's door is ajar.

"Hi, Umma," I say, and the door swings open.

She's wearing a fleece pullover and has her hair tied back, which gives her a youthful appearance, despite the gray at her temples. "What are you doing here so early?" she asks. A note of worry enters her voice. "Is everything okay? Are you in some kind of trouble?"

"No, I'm fine." I set the cake down on the kitchen table, where it seems to stare at both of us as we stand uneasily in front of each other. She looks thinner, smaller, and when I wrap my arms around her, she feels so tiny in my arms that I am afraid, for a moment, that I will crush her. She doesn't move at first, just standing there stiffly, and then I feel her hands patting my lower back, the way she used to whenever I had the hiccups at night and couldn't sleep.

"I brought you a cake," I say.

"It's too early for cake," she says, but she goes and gets us two cups of coffee from the kitchen, and we sit down and each eat a slice. The sweetness of the frosting is balanced by the darker notes of the coffee grounds, and the cake tastes, I notice with relief, like cake.

"I'm sorry," I say when we're done. Umma sits there, looking at her empty plate. I offer her more cake, which she accepts in silence.

"I want you to be happy, Umma," I say. "I want us both to be happy."

"Arim, you don't have to apologize. I understand."

"If Mr. Cho makes you happy, that's great."

"Mr. Cho is just a good friend," Umma says, but I know she's lying from the way she blushes. It's odd, seeing Umma act like a schoolgirl with a crush, but nice at the same time, like I'm getting a glimpse of who she might have been before she became my umma.

"This cake is good," Umma says, after a pause. "Where did you get this recipe?"

It occurs to me that she may not remember making the cake for me, all those years ago. "It doesn't matter," I say.

"I feel very guilty, Arim," Umma says.

"What, why? You don't have anything to feel guilty about."

"I wish we had been able to give you a brother or a sister." *We.* She hasn't referred to herself and Apa as a "we" in God knows how long. "I worried about you a lot, growing up all alone."

"I'm not alone, Umma."

"Who will take care of you when I'm gone?" Umma says, and she looks even more tired now. "I have nothing left to leave you."

"Umma, I'm fine. Or at least I'm going to be."

"I'm sorry if—" Umma pauses, looks down at her hands, which are placed on the table on either side of her plate, and clears her throat. "I know you were lonely after your apa disappeared."

I swallow hard, and I think about all the afternoons when I got home from school to find Umma in bed. The long blue evenings spent alone with my homework at the kitchen table, with only the TV for company. How sometimes I'd call the numbers they featured in infomercials for products no one wanted like ShamWow sponges or chia pets or goji berry supplements and pretend I was interested in buying them, just to have someone to talk to.

There are so many things that I could say now, but instead I reach across the table to hold her hand in mine. She hesitates just for a second before squeezing my hand.

"You're much stronger than I am," she says. "Just like your father. You were always so headstrong, so independent."

"I get that from you," I say. And we sit there just like that, hand in hand, our bellies full of cake, while the sun finishes rising, streaking the windows with orange-pink light that feels like the beginning of everything.

By the time I get back into my car and on the road, the first wave of rush-hour traffic has hit. I follow the other cars onto the stretch of highway that signals the turnoff for the Fountain. The building looks even more swollen and spiderlike than usual today, but the parking lot is relatively empty, as the mall isn't open yet. I try to spot red cars and count four.

I park and breathe in and out for a little bit. It still smells like coffee and peanut butter in the car. The radio is playing the Bee Gees, "How Deep Is Your Love," and the song fills up the car with its warm, buttery synths. I remember dancing with Tae to this song at one of his friends' weddings a few years ago, how he swept me onto the dance floor and spun me around, even dipping me at the end. "'Cause we're living in a world of fools, breakin' us down,'" he sang in a high, trembling falsetto into my hair while I laughed at him. I wait till the song ends before I get out.

Rick is at his podium and I wave hi. "You seem cheerful today," he says.

"Do I?"

"You look, I don't know, relaxed."

"I'm quitting today."

Rick's eyes widen. "Oh, man. Congratulations?"

I hand him my latest origami creation—a whale folded out of sleek indigo paper. It even has a small blowhole at the top. "You're getting better than me," he says.

"You're quitting?" Carl says with such disbelief that I'm not sure whether to feel flattered or insulted. He picks up the small globe on his desk and starts tossing it from hand to hand in quick, agitated motions. I note that he's lined up his stack of Post-it notes to be perfectly perpendicular with his stapler and mouse pad and resist the urge to knock them all off his desk.

"Yup," I say. *Don't speak into your chest,* I think to myself. Apa would have told me to straighten myself up and not to say things like *yup,* which he always said made a person sound uneducated. I arch my spine and tilt my chin upward, the way he was always telling me I had to in order to get white people, especially men, to take me seriously. "Yes," I say again, for good measure.

"I'm really sorry to hear that," Carl says. It sounds like he means it, too. "I don't think I have to tell you what an important member of this team you are, Ro."

I open my mouth to say something noncommittal and grateful in response, but then decide, *Fuck it.* "Actually, I don't think I've ever heard you express anything to that effect. In fact, I think most of the time you take me for granted."

Carl's eyes pop open, as though one of the animals in the aquarium has spoken.

"But that's not the reason I'm leaving."

"Is this about Dolores?" he says.

"It's not just that," I say.

"Then what is it? Ro, you're one of the best we've got. We rely on you," he says. He seems to be pleading with me.

"I just don't think I can stay here anymore," I say. "It's time I moved on."

"You're sure I can't convince you?" Carl says. "I can't offer you a raise right now—you know how it is—but I, well, *we* do need you. Maybe we can work something out with your vacation time?"

This is flattering until I realize that I'm tired of being needed but not valued. That I should have left the aquarium a long time ago—not because it's a bad place to be, but because it's keeping me from moving forward with everything else.

"Why don't you leave if you're unhappy?" Yoonhee and Tae had both asked me countless times before. But it wasn't that I was unhappy, exactly. It was just that eventually I started forgetting that I could do anything else.

What if you get stuck again, a small voice inside me screams. *What if you can't find another job? What if this is it? Take whatever he gives you and figure it out later. Be grateful someone wants you at all.* But then the image of Eriko snapping at her trainers and slamming into the other dolphins, all while continuing to circle her tank in tight, anxious spirals, comes to mind. I realize that the main difference between Eriko's situation and mine is that she never had a choice in her entrapment, but I do. I don't have to be stuck anymore.

I do some quick calculations in my head and decide that I have enough savings to last me for some time while I look for something else. "Thanks, but I'm pretty certain about this," I say, in what I hope is a firm voice. "I can give you two weeks but not more than that."

"Where are you headed?" Carl says. He is hunched over now, looking miserable. I catch sight of the corner of a framed photo on his desk. Carl is holding a small child and is standing next to a woman with dark blond hair.

"I don't know," I respond truthfully. I feel unmoored, light.

"I can't say enough about how sorry I am to see you go," Carl says.

"Thanks," I say. We sit there in silence, neither of us wanting to be the one to say something next. "Who's that in the picture with you?" I ask.

"That's my sister and her son. My nephew," he says, turning to look where I'm looking.

She looks like him but a bit rougher around the edges. She and Carl and the kid are all squinting in the sunlight, in what looks like a backyard. They all have the same wide grin and round forehead. I wonder what that must be like, to look so visibly like the people in your family, to have your kinship stamped in big letters across your features.

"I can tell," I say, and Carl beams with pride for a moment.

Over the next two weeks, I do my best to ignore Francine's prying, giving only vague, noncommittal answers about where I'm headed next. Carl suggests throwing me a goodbye party, which I immediately veto. I consider telling Yoonhee about quitting, but I don't. *Let her find out on her own,* I think.

On my last day, I run through my tasks quickly, saving Dolores's enclosure for last. When I get to her tank, she waves two of her arms at me. I close my eyes and imagine what it would be like to see her now with Apa by my side. What secret truths and hidden facts about her would he be able to tell me?

I've thought so many times about what questions I would have asked Apa, had I known he would be gone by the time I was fifteen. He looms so large in my memories. But even in my most vivid recollections of him, he never seems to be quite there; he seems to already be leaving us. He was always telling me to look at the world, to pay attention to it and take in its wonders, when all I ever really wanted was for him to see me. I feed Dolores and note her vitals. She seems active and healthy, as muscular as ever. I tap my hand on the glass, and she answers in kind, following the movement of my fingers. "You're going to have a really great life, Lolo," I tell her.

She stares back at me, her eyes large and skeptical. There is something about staring directly into the knowing iridescent eyes of a cephalopod—you can get a hint of the ancient knowledge that girds the strands of her DNA, the sense that the mechanisms that have been keeping her alive are so much older than anything else you know.

I dip my hand into the water and stroke one of her arms. She tendrils herself around me, and I feel the suction of the many cups on her arms, pulling gently at me. I tell her how beautiful and strange and wonderful she is, how anyone lucky enough to get to see her every day like I've been able to will have no choice but to fall in love with her. Ridiculously, I don't want her to see me crying, so I pull my hand out of the water and turn away, blinking until the world turns into streaks of light and blue water.

Dolores seems a little confused, if unperturbed. She dances through the water as I will my tears back into my eye sockets and wait for the pain to subside. I'm afraid that if I keep crying, I might never stop. It seems to me incredibly cruel that no matter how much has been taken from you, you never get used to the dizzying shock of losing something you love, the dull, crushing ache of it afterward. There's no way to rehearse for heartbreak, no matter how much you might walk around expecting it.

When I finally manage to pull myself together, Dolores has tired herself out and is sitting in a corner of the tank with her legs folded beneath her, like a very strange cat.

Apa told me that octopuses have three hearts. They all have to work in tandem—the first two hearts work to move blood to the octopus's gills, while a third, larger heart circulates it throughout the rest of the body. "That's why you usually see octopuses crawling," he said. "Because swimming actually causes that third heart to stop."

I've often wished that human bodies were as clever as those of octopuses. If we could divvy up the work of one heart among three, if we could have a semiautonomous brain in each of our appendages, perhaps we'd be more efficient with our time, less likely to waste it on grudges and hurts and all the things we feel we can't say to one another.

"I'm going to miss you," I say. And while I know that logically, no matter how smart she is, there's no way she can understand what I'm saying, it's enough to feel her silvery narrowed eyes on mine, to see them regard me, for one last time.

CHAPTER 14

Twenty years ago

My breath fogged up the window, and I wrote my initials across the glass with the tip of my finger. Windshield wipers danced hypnotically while snowflakes fell outside, flying like small white stars. It felt, when I looked out at the predawn darkness, like we were flying through space.

It was February, and we were on our way to the airport, to head to Hawaii for a rare family vacation. Apa had been invited to speak at a marine biology conference in Honolulu, and he had decided that we might as well make a trip out of it. I was ten years old, and I couldn't remember the last time we'd taken a trip together, though there were photos to prove that we had done so, including pictures of a road trip to Niagara Falls, when I was very little. In the photos from that trip, I'm about three years old, my face a grimace of discomfort as I cling to my parents. The three of us are wearing yellow ponchos, and we're drenched from the spray of the falls, which are a white blur behind us. Apa's glasses are fogged over from condensation, while Umma's perm is askew, but they're both holding on to me and each other and smiling.

Apa said that Hawaiian beaches were much nicer than the ones in New Jersey, which were all I had known. How the sand was softer in Hawaii—so fine, it felt like silk when you ran your hands through it. How the waters of the Pacific were so balmy they felt like bathwater. He had been there a few times before for research trips, but this was the first time he was taking Umma and me.

Apa was speeding a little. We hit pockets of traffic on the way to the airport, but for once, he didn't mutter to himself about the incompetence of the other drivers or groan loudly and lean on the horn if a car stopped short in front of him. Instead, he seemed upbeat and energetic, despite the earliness of the hour.

The airport was a blur of movement. I looked around, fascinated by how many people there were along with us. We passed harried-looking staff in crisp white shirts and several luggage carousels on our way to the check-in counter, while a persistent smell of coffee and warmed-over bacon followed us. While we were in line to check our bags, Apa left us momentarily, without saying anything. We were used to it—Apa had a habit of rushing off to go check on something or grab a snack or take a call somewhere without telling us in advance—but I could tell it put Umma on edge. She looked around nervously as we stood in line. A few minutes later, Apa came back holding two leaking paper cups of coffee for himself and Umma, and an orange juice for me. Umma took one of the cups wordlessly and sipped it, and I tensed myself for a fight, for her usual complaints about how he was always disappearing without a word. But instead she closed her eyes and uttered a small *ahh* of satisfaction before opening them again. "Thank you, yeobo," she said.

After checking in, we had about an hour before our flight. At our gate, Apa settled in for a nap, while Umma read a book and I drew pictures of the people around us. A pigeon had snuck in. It appeared to be waiting patiently along with us. I watched as a toddler stalked the pigeon, laughing delightedly while his mother warned him away from the bird in loud, authoritative Italian. I watched the three of them, the mother chasing the baby chasing the pigeon, and felt vaguely superior to the baby. I tried not to think of my baby brother that never was, and the fact that he and this baby would be about the same age now had he lived. *Ten years old is almost a teenager,* I told myself. I wrote the digits 1 and 0 in my notebook and doodled them in. I couldn't wait to be older. To be a grown-up seemed like the most dazzling thing in the world.

The sun began to rise after we boarded the plane. A weak orange light eked its way through the dirty gray clouds, and I could see patches of rapidly melting snow on the runway.

When the plane began readying for takeoff, I saw Umma's knuckles turn white and her lips start moving in a quick prayer. I caught Apa's eyes.

"You're not scared, are you?" he said as the engines roared. My stomach dropped just as I shook my head.

"Just like your dad," Apa said, chuckling.

I smiled back and tried not to panic as the world went diagonal and we were all knocked back in our seats. The flight attendant's calm voice came on the intercom, telling us to keep our seat belts fastened until further notice. I checked and double-checked mine, imagining that if it were not secured, I would suddenly go flying out of the plane, sucked out through an errant open door.

Once the plane had righted itself in the air, I had a chance to notice just how brilliant the colors in the sky were. The light up here seemed clearer and brighter, and it was turning the clouds gold and peach. Far off in the distance, the parts of the sky that the light had not yet reached lightened from indigo to ultramarine. Next to me, Apa was asleep, as though we hadn't just left the earth to launch ourselves into the sky.

Hawaii was hot. Once we landed, I immediately shed the layers I had been wearing, tying my sweater around my waist and stuffing my jacket into my blue carry-on backpack. We were shuttled into a cab, which took us to a small motel in Honolulu. It was close to the ocean—just a five-minute walk away from Waikiki Beach—but the room smelled of bleach and cleaning products, and the brown carpet felt scratchy under my bare feet. Dead flies dotted the fluorescent lights of the bathroom.

"Pretty good deal for the location, eh?" Apa said. I nodded, trying to hide my disappointment. He turned on the air conditioning and it slowly whirred to life. Umma began unpacking, putting our clothes and belongings away in deft, sure gestures. I wanted to tell her that I could put away my own things, but she seemed determined to do it herself. I sat down on the bedspread, suddenly tired out from our journey, and fell asleep curled on the edge of the bed.

When I woke, it was the next morning, and my stomach was growling. Umma was washing something in the bathroom. I walked in to find her scrubbing at a coffee stain on the blouse she had been wearing on the plane. I was startled by the sight of my mother in just her bra. The gold cross neck-lace she always wore shone underneath the fluorescent lights. "Where's Apa?" I asked.

"He had to go to his first session," she said. "We'll meet him for lunch later."

I noticed that among the many things she had brought, Umma had packed a small rice cooker, which stood on the dresser, along with containers of seaweed, cans of Spam, and Tabasco sauce, as though we were going camping.

I changed into a sundress that Umma had laid out on the bed for me. I always felt silly in it, because it was ruffly and full-skirted in a way I didn't like, but Umma nodded with approval when she saw me wearing it. "See how nice you look when you actually wear the clothes I get you," she said.

It wasn't a long walk from our motel to the much larger, nicer hotel where the conference was, but by the time we got there, the sweat underneath my armpits had pooled out onto the fabric of my dress, and I was worried that I smelled. Ear-lier that year in school, we had learned about periods and deodorant, the latter of which our teacher had stressed the importance of. I was too nervous to ask Umma about deodor-ant, because as far as I could tell, she didn't wear any. I had noticed, however, that I was starting to sprout wiry black hairs on my arms and legs, as well as on my crotch, and I felt both thrilled and horrified by this development. I had hesitantly brought up the possibility of starting to shave with Umma, and she immediately dismissed it. "The more you shave, the more you'll need to shave," she said, which sounded like a riddle to me, the kind that had no answer.

The hotel was full of people there for the conference—mostly academics and some field experts, all wearing multi-pocketed khaki shorts and vests. Apa emerged from a crowd of people leaving one of the sessions, dressed in a wrinkled blue button-down that didn't seem to have survived the flight very well and that looked out of place among everyone else's much more casual attire.

He waved us over and introduced us to another man he was engaging in conversation, but it was clear, at least to me, that the other man, a professor at UC Berkeley, wasn't very interested in talking to Apa. Every time the professor began to try to make his excuses, Apa would launch into another question about the session, which, I gathered, had been on coral reef ecosystems and how to save them. "I'd love to read your paper," Apa kept saying until the man reluctantly agreed to give him his email address. I squirmed, my toes curling upward in their sandals. It was not a nice feeling, my embarrassment at Apa's eagerness to please and his obliviousness.

"I think that went really well," Apa said cheerfully over lunch. We were seated at a restaurant that the hotel concierge had recommended, and although Umma winced at the prices on the menu, Apa waved away her concerns.

"Everyone I've spoken with has been incredibly interesting and helpful," he said. "My presentation is tomorrow, and I'm sure it will be well attended." He said all this as if it was guaranteed, as if saying so was enough to make it so.

Umma cut up her mahi-mahi steak, which was something she wouldn't normally have ordered, but Apa had insisted she get it. "I'm glad to hear this has been worth it so far," Umma said. There was a slight edge to her voice, and I couldn't tell if it was from having to eat fish, which she disliked, or from something else.

I pushed my food around on my plate while I listened to them have another of what I called their tiptoe fights. Tiptoe fights were when neither of them wanted to come out and say the thing that was bothering them outright, and it was a kind of competition until someone finally exploded or left the room, whichever came first.

"I'd say the North American Biology Association conference is worth it, yes," Apa said mildly.

"The university would have covered our travel expenses. Where you work now doesn't," Umma said.

"I don't work at the university anymore. Where I work now pays our bills," Apa said.

"Can you both just stop?" I interjected. They ignored me, except to shoot warning glances in my direction.

Then Umma sighed. "She's right," she said, turning to Apa. "I'm tired. Let's just try and enjoy ourselves." I watched with astonishment as Apa relaxed as well. The moment passed, and we continued eating.

Afterward, we walked along Waikiki Beach, which was crowded with the pale, glistening bodies of tourists. Surfers carrying brightly colored boards walked past us, their hair wet and their bodies taut and lean. The sky was a delicious deep blue, though the sun was beginning to sink. I took my sandals off and waded into the water. Apa was right—the ocean here was warm, like stepping into a nice bath. Palm trees danced gently in the wind. It was hard to believe that just a few hours ago, we had been driving through snow flurries in the dark to the airport.

I found a flat, shiny green disk in the wet sand, along with a small pink crab that had been turned onto its back by the waves. I gingerly picked up the crab, the way Apa had shown me, turned it right side up, and deposited it on higher ground, where it scurried away. I traced the edges of the disk, marveling at its smoothness. I held it up to the sun and watched how the light filtered through it and became something wobbly, almost magical.

I wanted to show Umma and Apa what I had found, but I decided to keep it to myself, slipping the disk into my pocket. Apa would give me a lecture about seashells and shore erosion, and Umma would say that it was a piece of common sea glass, a fragment of someone's smashed beer bottle that had been pounded and flattened by the beating of the waves, but to my eye, it looked like a gem. And maybe, I thought to myself, it was even cooler if that was all it was—a piece of trash transformed into something beautiful.

We walked back toward the hotel in single file, with Apa at the lead, then Umma, then me. The air, away from the beach, smelled of fried food, cigarettes, beer, and motorcycle exhaust. The crowds by the oceanfront bars grew larger as the sun got low in the sky and the streetlights turned on, one by one. A gray cat with pale eyes and a crooked tail followed us for part of the way. I clucked at it and petted it for a few seconds, while Umma and Apa's backs were turned, and then ran to catch up with them before they disappeared around a street corner.

The next day it rained. We had made tentative plans to go to a history museum while Apa was at the conference, but Umma had a headache and needed to lie down with all the lights turned off. I fetched her cold bottled water from the vending machine on our floor, and then, when I was sure she was asleep, I changed into my swimsuit, put on a pair of shorts and a T-shirt, swiped the plastic room key from the nightstand, and clicked the door shut behind me.

The motel was a small one, only six floors. I wandered the halls of all of them, taking the elevator up and down until I started getting suspicious looks from the other guests, who were mostly young or older couples. On occasion a large family would walk in, all dressed in matching outfits and with sun block swiped onto their noses, even though the sun wasn't out. Everyone except for me seemed to have a definitive plan for the day.

"Are you lost, sweetie?" a woman with a tower of red curls that peeked out over the top of her sun visor asked me.

I shook my head. "I'm just waiting for my mom," I said, which wasn't entirely untrue.

Finally, I got bored enough to contemplate the tiny pool in the outdoor courtyard of the motel. NO LIFEGUARD ON DUTY, a sign proclaimed. The rain had slowed, but the sky was still a dark, stormy gray. I dipped a toe into the pool water and determined that it was okay for swimming in. I secured my goggles to my face and cannonballed off the diving board into the deep end, startling the lone swimmer in the other lane, an old man doing a few sedate laps back and forth.

The water was much colder than I had anticipated. I watched the bubbles from my nose float upward to the surface, and then I let myself shoot up like a champagne cork, theatrically gasping for air once I broke through the water. I thought about scuba divers, how Apa once told me that they had to be careful when they ascended to the surface because of something called the bends. He told me it was due to sudden changes in water pressure—that gas bubbles could form in the blood if divers rose to the surface too quickly or stayed too long at depths that they couldn't tolerate yet, and could make them feel sick or dizzy or, in the worst cases, lose consciousness or feeling in their limbs.

It made sense, I thought. Get used to anything for too long and the opposite of it starts to feel like a shock. It was better to be prepared for the worst at all times.

We developed a routine during our stay in Hawaii. While Apa was at conference sessions during the day, Umma and I would walk around downtown Honolulu. She was different in Hawaii, I thought—she smiled more and moved more slowly, seemed less likely to scold me for minor infractions like chewing with my mouth open or scratching myself in public. We would duck into tacky tourist shops and she'd let me buy things we didn't need, like plastic figurines or postcards or sunglasses. Then we would sit on the beach, and I would look for bits of sea glass or shells to take back and Umma would read or nap. Afterward, we'd meet Apa for dinner, and then we'd go for a drive in our rental car along the sea cliffs, with all the windows down. Umma took to tying her hair back in a cheap polyester scarf she'd bought in one of the gift shops, and when she wore it tied around her face, with her sunglasses on, she looked like a glamorous old Hollywood star.

We bought boxes and boxes of sliced pineapple to take back to the room or to eat on the beach. Umma and I couldn't get enough of it. Apa joked that we would both turn into pineapples ourselves, the way we couldn't stop eating them. Their golden cubes tasted like heaven. I wondered who had first thought of cutting open and eating a pineapple, a fruit that looked so hostile and tasted so sweet.

At night, we ate in restaurants that either had outdoor seating or were right on the beach. One of those nights, a live band consisting of two ukulele players, a keyboard player, and a saxophonist set up near the restaurant where we were eating and began playing. I listened, enthralled, as they launched into a heartfelt rendition of "Hotel California." When they got to the chorus, I saw that Umma and Apa were looking at each other and singing the words, smiling at each other. "You know this song?" I said incredulously.

"Of course," they said. "It was very popular in our youth."

All around us, older white couples, dressed in their printed T-shirts and halter-top dresses, were dancing in the sand. Their pink sunburns gleamed in the flickering light from the tiki torches set up around the restaurant.

Apa turned to Umma and held his hand out. "Shall we?" he said.

I sat in my seat, mortified and fascinated, as they swayed gently to the music. They held each other stiffly, like self-conscious newlyweds. At the end of the song, everyone turned to the band and clapped, and my parents returned to their seats, a little flushed.

"Can we get dessert?" I asked, deciding to take advantage of the moment, and they agreed. We ordered deep-fried ice cream, something I'd never even heard of. As the ice cream melted in my mouth and on my plate, I found myself wishing things could always be like this, that we could always allow ourselves to be a family in this way.

The day before we left, I knew something bad was going to happen. All day, the weather had been off, the sky a flat, humid gray and the light a terrible greenish orange. The ocean was choppy, and even the birds that scavenged for food scraps along the beach seemed sluggish.

I woke up from an afternoon nap soaked in sweat, to hear my parents arguing in fierce whispers.

"I would just be staying for a few more days," Apa said.

"We can't afford it," Umma said. "And you're expecting me and Arim to fly back alone in the meantime?" My skin prickled all over.

"You know how important this is for me," Apa said. "It's not every day that I get to present my research findings to colleagues in my field."

"This isn't even for a book," Umma hissed. "You said this meeting is for a research article. I don't see why you have to extend your stay for something as inconsequential as that."

"Are you stupid?" Apa said, trying to sound calm. I hated when he called Umma that. "This could be an important connection. The editor mentioned they're looking to commission some books as well."

They went on like that until their whispers grew louder and louder and I could no longer pretend to be asleep. "Are me and Umma going back alone?" I said, sitting up.

They both fell silent. "That's what we're discussing now," Apa said.

"No, we're not," Umma said. "What kind of family vacation is it if we can't even leave together as a family? You tell this editor that research article or no, you can catch up with them another time." Her lips were pressed into a thin white line.

The rest of the day was tense and silent. For dinner, we opened one of the Spam cans and had some of that with the rice and seaweed. Apa and Umma didn't speak to each other all throughout the meal. Our flight was early the next morning, and Umma told me to sleep in the clothes that I was planning on wearing to the airport, so that we wouldn't have to spend too much time getting ready in the morning.

I woke in the middle of the night to the sound of shoes being put on and then the door clicking shut. Umma was still sleeping, but Apa was gone.

He's finally left us, I thought, dazed. And then I thought, *I won't let him.*

I managed to find my sneakers in the dark and slide my feet into them, and then, grabbing Umma's key card from her nightstand, to slip out the door after him.

The hallways were empty, but I heard the elevator ding, which meant he had just gotten on. I hurried down the stairs and managed to get to the lobby just as I saw Apa exiting the building. I followed him from a distance and watched as he skillfully dodged the drunks and panhandlers surrounding the motel. They mostly ignored me, though one guy tried to hassle me when I told him I didn't have any money on me. I kept my voice steady, even though my hands shook, and I ducked into a McDonald's for a bit until he had gone away. When I emerged, I thought I had lost Apa and that I should just go back to the room, my throat filling with panic, until I caught sight of him again, walking toward Waikiki Beach.

Waikiki Beach at night felt different, the walkway and the sand awash in neon colors from all the late-night beachfront bars. Everything was louder, more exciting, but also a little scary. I walked past a couple kissing on a sand dune, their arms and legs tangled around each other so that they looked like some kind of weird alien organism. I narrowly avoided stepping in a puddle of someone's vomit. Apa kept striding onward, heading toward the water. *Where the heck is he going?* I wondered, and then I finally saw it.

What I had thought was just the reflection of the city's lights on the water was actually waves of warm bright blue. The ocean was aglow with light. Each new wave that rolled and crashed toward the shore was the brightest, purest blue, like the color of a gas flame or of Powerade. Above us, a calm white moon presided.

Apa had stopped near the edge of the water. I saw, as I got closer to him, that he had taken his shoes off and was holding them in one hand. His pant legs were rolled up, one higher than the other. I took off my shoes, too, and dug my feet into the cool sand.

"Apa," I called to him. He turned around, and instead of scolding me for following him or for being out of bed alone, he smiled.

"Isn't it incredible?" he said, gesturing at everything—the stars, the bright blue bioluminescence of the incoming tides.

The last thing I remember from that trip is the sight of my father standing there, ankle-deep in the water, where the sand and sky seemed to converge at the edge of the shore, surrounded by the vast, shining sea. How relieved I was that he wasn't leaving us in the night after all; how in the end, he had simply gone outside to look at something beautiful.

But best of all was the look on his face when he turned to see me. He looked at me as if I was more marvelous than all the stars in the sky and all the wonders of the sea put together, as if I was the best thing he had ever seen. "Come here, Acorn," he said, holding out his hand. I ran toward him, my heart as bright and buoyant as the foam on the waves.

CHAPTER 15

At the end of my last day at the aquarium, I collect my things from my desk, and it's just a little depressing when I realize that the only things I have to take with me, after all my years here, are a stained coffee mug and a small fake plant I bought on a whim once.

I walk through the hallways of the mall, abuzz as usual with shoppers. I walk past a little girl holding a balloon, and her mother, sitting on a bench. The mother is talking on the phone. "No, that's not what I said at all," she tells the person on the other end sternly. "You need to listen to me."

"Be good, okay?" the girl tells the balloon just as sternly. "Sit still, and no wandering off." The balloon seems to nod back at her.

When I get home, I do what I always do when I'm at a loss: contemplate the contents of my fridge. Inside, there are two bottles of artisanal mustard, a few packets of soy sauce, and some IPAs, the kind that Tae used to drink. I used to buy them for him, because despite the fact that I'll drink almost anything, I have never been able to get used to hoppy beer.

The day Tae left for Arizona, I found an old six-pack of them in the back of the fridge. I drank them all in one sitting, puked them back up, and then, the next day, went out and got another pack that I haven't touched since then. I open one of the cans now and take a small, hesitant sip. As usual, it tastes like garbage to me, but the more I drink, the more the bitter carbonation makes me feel like my skin is unzipping itself, and the less I hate the taste of it.

I spend the rest of the evening watching nature documentaries and reading articles about Mars on my phone. I learn that on Mars, gravity is weaker, meaning that if you jump on Mars, you can jump three times higher in the air than you'd be able to on Earth. And a day on Mars is an extra thirty-seven minutes long. What would I do with all that extra time? I wonder as I crack open my third beer. Probably nothing, I decide.

Eventually I fall asleep in front of the TV and dream about kangaroos on Mars, their big feet bouncing off of the dusty red surface of the planet as they bound toward the horizon. Two moons hang in the sky, and the kangaroos are jumping so high it almost looks like they'll graze the edges of those moons. When I wake up, my neck is spasming and the doorbell is ringing.

"You quit?" Yoonhee says, incredulous, when I open the door. "I can't believe you didn't even tell me today was your last day." It is late, and she looks pissed.

"What time is it?" I say groggily.

She brushes past me without asking if she can come in, and

I remember, almost as if it happened to another person, that once upon a time, she and I lived here together. "Gee, vacuum much?" she says, wrinkling her nose, but she still sits down at the card table.

"Not really," I say. "It's not like I have much company."

"God," she says, looking around. "It feels like it was a million years ago when we first moved in. I can't believe you still have that couch."

"Leave her alone," I say. "She's just trying her best." Yoonhee laughs once, and then we fall silent.

"What are you doing here?" I say.

Yoonhee doesn't answer at first. She grabs one of the beers from the pack and pops it open, takes a long swig, and winces. "This is disgusting," she says.

"I know," I say. "Tae liked them."

"I came by to apologize," Yoonhee says. "For what I said the other day. I know everything's been hard. I wasn't being fair."

"You were right," I say.

"I know I was, but I shouldn't have said it," she says.

"Let's get back to the part where you were apologizing," I say.

"Sorry," she says. She takes another sip of the beer and makes the same appalled face.

I don't know who's more surprised, Yoonhee or me, when she begins to cry. I hand her a roll of paper towels and watch as she pulls off sheet after sheet, blowing her nose theatrically. Yoonhee has always been a pretty crier, and afterward, her eyes are bright and her cheeks are flushed, as though she's just touched them up with blush.

"It's been hard, lately," she says. "And I miss you."

"I miss you, too," I say.

"I should have been here more," she says. There is a pause before she continues. "But you should have been there for me, too."

"I know," I say. I try not to look at her directly, because if I do, I'm afraid that I'll see something in her eyes that'll tell me what I think I already know—that I'm a shitty friend, that I don't deserve anything good.

But instead, when I do look up, she just looks like Yoonhee, like my best friend, just pissed off. Her eyes say, *That's it?*

So I try again. "I really, really fucked up."

"Ro, it's my fucking wedding," she says. "I needed your help."

"I know," I say. My voice wobbles. "I want you to be happy, Yoonhee, I really do. But it was all happening right when everything with Tae was turning to shit. I know that doesn't make it right. I know I'm a bad person for feeling that way."

"That's what it's all about. Being happy for people even when you don't want to be. Being there, even when it sucks. And celebrating when it doesn't."

I wipe my snot away with the back of my shirt sleeve, which Yoonhee pretends not to see. She hands me the roll of paper towels.

"You didn't have to be that way about Dolores, though," I say. "Even if she will have a better home with that guy."

There's a pause. "Actually, she won't," Yoonhee says. "That's what I came here to tell you. He's not buying her anymore."

"What?" Suddenly I am outraged. "That asshole."

"He decided the home renovations he was making weren't worth it. To be honest, I think he got freaked out when he saw her. I guess she's much bigger in real life than she seems in photos."

"What are you going to do?" I ask. My heart is thudding.

The confusing mix of rage and relief that I feel is making me nauseous. Or maybe it's just the beers.

"I guess we'll figure out another way to keep the place open," she says. "Also, I can convince management to let you come back. They need you."

I consider this. I think about another year or so of doing the same work I've done for the last eight years, but then I think about what Apa would have wanted for me, what he'd say if he could see me now. I'd like to think he would have wanted to see me happy. I remember that long-ago night in Hawaii, how we watched the ocean glow until the stars began to fade. Whatever I do next, I don't want to forget the way it made me feel, like the world was so much bigger and more beautiful than I'd ever thought it could be.

"I need the time away," I say finally. "I'm thinking of going back to school."

Yoonhee's perfectly shaped eyebrows shoot up. "Since when?"

"Since just now," I say.

"You know," Yoonhee says, "I was always jealous of you. When we were kids."

"What? Why?"

"You just seemed to have such a definite idea of what you wanted. What you were interested in, your likes and dislikes. Once you set your mind on something, that was it." She shrugs. "I've always admired that about you."

"I don't feel that way anymore."

"But you'll figure it out," she says.

"What if I don't? What if everything is just this, forever?" I gesture around the apartment. I know I'm being dramatic, but I really need someone, anyone, to tell me that someday it won't hurt every day just to wake up, to tiptoe around the holes left behind by everyone who's ever left me or is in the process of leaving me.

"Nothing is forever," she says.

"That's not exactly comforting, either," I say.

"Okay," she says. "But why does it have to be all or nothing? Forever or never?"

"Because everyone leaves in the end," I say. "Because nothing good that happens to me ever stays."

"Wrong," she says, and now she sounds furious. "You're so busy trying to anticipate every bad thing happening to you that you can't even get it together long enough to fight for it. You want things to leave you so you can sit there and feel sorry for yourself when they don't work out. That's what happened with Tae and that's what you're doing with me now. And I'm not gonna let you."

The blood rushes to my face. We glare at each other.

"Look," she says, "I want you in my life, okay? I want you to be the fucking weird aunt to my adorable children and be a bad influence on them and look out for them when I'm too tired to be a real person. I want us to get old together and knock back shots like we're twenty-two again and talk about all the stupid things we used to do and have really bad hangovers together. I want to go on a dumb cruise when we're, like, seventy-five and wear matching bathing suits. But if you don't want all that, that's fine."

"Cruises are really bad for the environment," is all I can think of to say. She looks at me, exasperated.

"You know what I mean," she says.

"I know," I say. "I want all those things with you, too." And I realize, once I say it, that I do. It's hard for me to imagine getting old at all, but if there's anyone I'd want to do it with, it's

Yoonhee. It's always been her. And just knowing that somehow feels like enough for now.

"Okay then," she says. She shakes her head, as though she thinks I am probably the dumbest girl on earth, but when I ask her if she wants to help me finish the rest of the beer and watch a documentary about cave paintings, she says yes.

A clipped British voice narrates in voice-over, telling us that these paintings, which have just been discovered in a cave system in France, have not been seen by other human beings, other than by the team that is excavating them, in thousands and thousands of years.

"What compels us to capture movement and light?" the voice-over says. "For millennia, human beings have sought out the answers to our existence in the natural world, seeking solace and meaning in the patterns of nature. It is perhaps in creating such images that we find ourselves."

We are inside the cave now with the camera crew, and for a moment, the crew extinguishes all its light sources, and we get to experience, along with the explorers, a moment of pure darkness. The only thing we can hear is the sound of their breathing. "This is giving me anxiety," Yoonhee says.

And then the lights come back on, and the caves are awash in warm, rich colors. Stout-bellied horses gallop in yellows and reds across the walls, while the silhouette of a brown cow lowers its head, aiming its horns at a crowd of stick figures with bows and arrows. Graceful, swirling lines undulate and stretch among the images, suggesting movement. Handprints in rust-red and bone-white dapple the walls. It feels as though the cave itself is alive.

Sometimes, when I was little and Umma had to copy sheet music for the choir at our church, she would take me along with her. When she wasn't looking, I would xerox my hands on the copy machine, enjoying the feeling of the warm green light as it memorized my palm prints. My hands looked like ghosts, floating on a black field. I xeroxed my hands over and over again, layering new copies on top of old ones to create an effect of repetition. I thought that this was what hands from another realm might look like, if they could push against the thin membrane that separates our world from theirs.

I imagine, still, that this is what it looks like when the ones we've loved and lost are trying to reach us. When they are able, however briefly, to tell us that they are there and that we are not alone.

By the time Yoonhee leaves, it's past midnight. She gives me a hug at the door and makes me promise to meet her for lunch later this week. "I need your help," she says. "I still haven't picked out the damn dress."

"I thought you had one," I say.

"I returned it," she says, despondent. "I've tried on so many dresses, I'm starting to get to a point where I don't even know what I look like anymore."

"You know James wouldn't care what you wore, right? You could show up in a garbage bag and he'd still be ecstatic."

"Of course he doesn't care," she says impatiently. "The dress isn't for him, it's for me!"

A few weeks go by, during which I apply to jobs, most of them odd ones. I apply to tutoring agency positions, including one for tutoring middle schoolers in biology. I interview with a woman who seems overly impressed by my background and basically hires me on the spot. I meet with my first student, a hard-to-impress eleven-year-old who won't even look at me through her bangs until I start doodling and labeling the parts of her cell diagram for her and drawing faces on the different parts of the cell. I find that this information comes back to me easily, even though I'd thought I'd forgotten most of it. *Ribosome. Mitochondria. Nucleus.* After I label each component of her diagram, I ask her to explain its function to me. The hour is up before I know it, and the woman asks me to come back next week.

Yoonhee buys an ivory-colored dress with a lacy bodice and a long, sweeping skirt. I pick out the least offensive bridesmaid dress in the shop, a navy blue one with thin straps and a V neckline that Yoonhee says will look nice against the peach and white flowers she's picked out. I send a picture of me in the dress to Umma, who texts back that she approves.

I take another job, reviewing English subtitles for foreign documentaries. I spend hours in front of my computer with my headphones on, making corrections on a sheet that the film production company sends me. I learn about the top twenty volcanic eruptions in the history of the world, train tunnels in Norway, papal corruption scandals in the Middle Ages, and the production of lipstick.

One day I'm about to queue up a documentary on the world of fungi when I get an alert on my phone. ARC 4 LAUNCH TODAY AT 2PM ET, it tells me. SWIPE TO GET A REMINDER FOR THE LIVESTREAM. I comply, and then I realize that my hands are shaking.

A few hours later, when I've finished the documentary and

started another one, on the natural world of Iguazú Falls, I get a call from Yoonhee. "Are you watching the livestream?" she asks. "It's happening now."

I queue up YouTube and listen to the commentators talk excitedly about how unprecedented this launch is. How, if all goes well on the mission and during the first few months of their time there, the participants, selected from a pool of hundreds of thousands of people, will be responsible for settling the first human colony on Mars.

There are endless interviews with talking heads, representatives from Europa, including Rob Houck, who looks like a taller, more freckled version of Phil Houck. "We couldn't be prouder," Rob says. "This day is the culmination not just of our dreams, but also of the dreams of our entire planet." Yoonhee snorts, still on the line.

But it's hard not to feel reverent, not to feel a thrill when the crew strolls out onto the tarmac to the sound of cheers from the crowds. I try to spot which one of the small figures might be Tae, and I think he's the fourth person to get on the ship, which looks like a sleek silver needle. He looks around briefly, then waves to the crowd, which goes wild again. The doors close, and then amid more useless commentary, the countdown begins. For a moment, I imagine the worst, the rocket exploding into shards of metal and clouds of flame. But then I tell myself I don't need to do that, that envisioning the worst possible thing isn't the same as being protected against it.

"They're saying this is just the start of it," Yoonhee says. "Maybe in just a few years we'll be able to go visit."

They reach the final stretch of the countdown, and then it happens. Rocket propellant belches orange and dark gray clouds as the silver needle lifts itself off the ground. A long tail of flame follows it as it heads farther and farther up into the clear blue sky, like a dragon bound for the stars. "Wow," Yoonhee breathes, and the two of us and the crowd on the livestream fall silent, as we watch the rocket climb higher and higher, until it disappears from view.

I imagine how Tae must be feeling, strapped into an other-worldly contraption that is shooting him straight up into the upper layers of our atmosphere and beyond, millions of miles away to a place where no one he knows has ever gone before. I wonder if he feels scared or excited or both. I wonder if this is how Apa felt the first time he left for the Bering Vortex, or if Umma felt this way, too, when she first took off in an airplane for the United States.

I think about all the people I've ever loved who have dis-appeared, who have gone and not returned. Of the ones who stayed and the ones who have been here all along.

And as the livestream fades out and the sky darkens to a deep, steely gray-blue in the wake of the rocket's trajectory, I wonder what's coming next.

CHAPTER 16

A few weeks later

By the time we arrive at the aquarium, it's crawling with families. Hailie, who gets anxious around other kids, reaches for my hand as we walk through the doors. We're both still sweating from the June humidity outside. "There are so many babies here," she says, annoyed, as toddlers dressed in bright colors walk by us, shrieking and trying to evade their tired parents.

I remember how it felt to be her age, how I always felt so much older than I was. "You were a baby once, too," I say. "I remember when I first met you. You were so tiny." It's true—Hailie was premature. Rachel let me hold her in the hospital, and when she opened her small mouth to yawn, her pink tongue was as small and delicate as a kitten's. I'd been so scared of dropping or smothering her that I'd sat completely still, unable to move. *How can anything be so small and still survive,* I'd thought.

"I wasn't *that* small," Hailie tells me.

"Oh, really?" I say. "I'm pretty sure your mom has the pictures to prove it."

"I was there," she says authoritatively. "I remember it."

"That's scientifically impossible, Hailie," I say, paying for our tickets and smiling at the guy behind the desk, who looks new. An intern, maybe. It's a Saturday, which is usually the Fountain's busiest day, and I wonder if I'll run into any of my coworkers. If it'll be weird.

"No, it's true," she insists. "You smelled like cinnamon."

"Okay," I say, because it's easier to just agree with Hailie when she says things like this. I feel the urge to wrap my arms around her and hug her. Instead, I hand her the floor map. "You're our guide for today," I say. "We can go wherever you want."

"Really?" she says, like I've just offered to let her drive us home. "Mom never lets me pick what I want to see first."

"Well, she's not here today, so we get to make the rules."

Rachel had asked if I wanted her to come, too, when I called and offered to take Hailie to the aquarium. "She can be a handful," she said. "As you know." But I told her she needed the day off from being a mom, that she should take herself out somewhere, visit a spa, get her nails done, or go get wasted at two o'clock in the afternoon and pick up a stranger at a bar, whatever she wanted.

"Great—not you, too, getting on my case about meeting people," she'd responded, but I could hear her smiling while she said it.

Hailie decides she wants to see the tide pools first. I help her reach into the cold water of the open tanks to gently stroke the spines of the sea stars. She giggles at how strange they feel. "Does it hurt them? Can they feel me?" she asks.

"They don't really have brains, but yes, they can feel things," I say. It's easy to assume that just because something is inert, it doesn't feel or experience pain, or to want to become numb yourself. I think about all the times I've wandered through the aquarium, trying to stop feeling anything at all, imagining my body turning to water and salt. And then I think about how lately I've been wanting to feel as much as I can of everything.

She spreads her arms and legs wide and staggers around. "I have no braaaaaains," she says. "You do it, too, Auntie Ro."

We walk around like that, two zombie sea stars, until we attract a crowd of tiny children who decide to follow suit, much to their parents' amusement and annoyance.

Hailie loves the seals, the slippery smoothness of them and their bright doglike eyes. "They're so big," she says. We watch a harbor seal—Mindy, I think her name is—bob up and down peacefully on her back, her belly forming a dome over the surface of the water. At first it looks as though she is alone until she shifts and we see her baby floating next to her. "Ohhh," Hailie says, her breath forming a mist on the glass. We watch the two of them move gracefully around each other, in a kind of dance, until Mindy decides she's had enough of us gawking at her and dives down to the bottom of the tank, the baby following in her wake.

Hailie reaches for my hand, and I wonder how long it will be before she gets too old to take to places like the aquarium, before she stops instinctively reaching for a hand to hold when a moment feels too big to keep to herself. If this day will stand out in her memory at all, when she's my age or older. It seems unfair to me that we don't get to pick and choose the memories that stay with us—which memories become embedded and bound into the sinews and seams of who we are, and which we lose.

We move on to the penguin enclosure, which is a flurry of activity, as usual. A few of them are swimming, while others are gathered on the rocks in clusters. Sonata and Arpeggio are still together, it seems—they're standing next to the water, grooming each other with a tenderness that it's hard not to feel moved by.

"Look at that one," Hailie says, pointing at one penguin standing apart from the others, up on one of the highest rocks in the enclosure. It's Coda, stretching out her wings and wiggling them back and forth, like she's dancing.

"Why is she all alone?" Hailie asks.

"She's not," I say. "See?" Coda clicks, making a soft squawk. And pretty soon she's joined by a few of the other royals, who hop up on the rock next to her. A warm patch of sun illuminates them like a spotlight, and they stretch their necks contentedly.

It's quieter in the invertebrates section of the aquarium, as though the sound is more muted back here, away from the main halls. We marvel at the pale moon jellies drifting like ghosts through the bright blue of their tanks, as well as the sea nettles with their long, trailing tentacles, glowing like hot-air balloons made of neon. Hailie is entranced, her nose pressed right up against the glass, and I take a picture of her on my phone to send to Rachel.

"Do you want to see my favorite part of the aquarium?" I say to Hailie, and she nods. We walk over to where Dolores's tank is, almost in the very center of the invertebrates section.

Dolores is pressed right up against the glass, the way Hailie was over by the sea nettles, as though she is intent upon catching every detail of the aquarium, just as we might be watching her. When she sees us, she turns a pale creamy orange and her eyes narrow. I tap the glass gently.

"Is that her?" Hailie says. "Is that the octopus your dad found?" The memory of the first time I ever saw Dolores, when I wasn't much older than Hailie is now, wells up in my mind. I remember how it felt to have my hand in Apa's, the delicious chill that rushed down my spine as I watched Dolores's arms move through the water. I remember feeling happy that day, even in the aftermath of Umma and Apa's fight, in a way that was harder to come by after he disappeared. But even though Apa is gone, Dolores is still here, and so am I.

"She is. Isn't she amazing?"

"She's kind of scary," Hailie says, unable to tear her eyes away as Dolores unfurls her arms and coils them up again.

"She is at first," I say. "But she's actually really friendly."

"Ro?" I turn around to see Francine, who walks over as though she's been waiting for us.

"Francine," I say, "it's good to see you." And to my surprise, this is not a lie. Any jitters I may have felt about running into people I used to know seem to have faded, the calm blue of our surroundings suffusing my thoughts.

"I guess you missed us, huh?" she says.

I decide not to answer that one. "Hailie, meet Francine. Hailie is my cousin's daughter," I add before Francine can pry.

"Is this your first time with us, Hailie?" Francine asks, and Hailie, engrossed in Dolores, barely looks up to nod.

"Francine, I have a favor to ask," I say, but before I can say what it is, she asks me, or rather, asks Hailie, "Do you want to come meet her?"

"Is that cool?" I say.

" 'Course it is. I was just about to feed her anyway," Francine says matter-of-factly. "Besides, she misses you."

I help Francine lift the lid of the tank. Dolores shoots up toward the surface, and Hailie gapes at the way she uses her suckers to grip the walls and rocks of her tank to get closer to us. We watch her lunge toward the food that Francine sprinkles in, shoveling bits of shrimp and squid into the cavity where her beak is.

One of the things I've missed most about working at the aquarium is getting to feed the animals. There's something so simple and pleasurable about watching an animal eat, witnessing the matter-of-fact alchemy of turning food into energy. When an animal eats, it's not thinking about anything but the food at hand; it's simply trying to absorb it as quickly as possible. There isn't much time, out in the wilds of nature, to wonder too much about anything other than eating, hunting, mating, and surviving.

But Dolores, as soon as she's done eating, wants to explore. I stick a tentative hand into the water and close my eyes as I feel her curl one arm around my wrist. Octopuses can recognize the distinctive tastes of everything, including of different people, and I wonder what I taste like to her, what she remembers about me.

"I want to try," Hailie says, and so, with some guidance from me and encouragement from Francine, she dips her hand into the water, too. Dolores wraps herself around Hailie's wrist, as curious as she is tenacious, and the look on Hailie's face is one of confusion and wonder. "She's getting to know me," she says.

"Yes," I say to Hailie. "She's figuring you out."

"I'm figuring her out, too," Hailie says. "What's her name?"

"Dolores," I say.

"Ow, that hurts a little," Hailie says, frowning as Dolores tugs harder with her suckers. "I don't think I like this anymore."

"Just relax," I say. "She won't hurt you." Hailie breathes in through her nose and out through her mouth, a technique that Rachel said the counselor at school recommended.

I squeeze her shoulder. "You're doing great, Hailie. Why don't you try talking to her?" Apa always said that talking to the things we didn't understand or felt afraid of was helpful, because it made them seem less far away from us.

I wonder what Apa would say if he were here, what he'd tell Hailie about giant Pacific octopuses and their importance to his research, their beauty and magic. What did he see out in the Bering Vortex that drew him to it again and again? And if he had returned from the Vortex on his last trip, would he have finally stayed home for good?

In the end, I know, no amount of wishful thinking can ever bring him back, and nothing we say or do or promise to one another can inoculate us against loss or leaving. But in the meantime, there is still so much of this world to see and hold on to, to care for and care about, to love in spite of—or because of—the fact that none of us are here for very long.

"Hi, Dolores," Hailie whispers into the water. "It's really nice to meet you."

As if in response, Dolores spangles herself gold. Then, when she's ready, she gently lets go, and something inside me loosens, too. She sinks back into the water, as bright and burnished as a falling star.

ACKNOWLEDGMENTS

There are so very many people in my life to thank. Without them, I would not be here, and neither would this book.

Vanessa Chan and Katie Devine, my first and best readers: for the countless pep talks, conversations, and mutual hype sessions, and for believing in me and this book. It is among the greatest joys of my life to write with you.

Mira Jacob: for all the phone calls and voice notes, for your generosity and graciousness. I am forever indebted to you for seeing me and for seeing this book, before I even knew how to see it.

Kate Tooley: for every octopus fact and clip, for your incisive feedback that cracked open everything, for letting me share all my weirds with you.

Lauren Browne, Victoria Dillman, John Kazanjian, and the whole New School crew: for being my friends and comrades during unimaginably strange and difficult times, and for reading the first few pages of this novel and encouraging me to keep going.

Jemimah Wei and Grace Shuyi Liew: for being incredible cheerleaders, for all the celebrations along the way.

Marie-Helene Bertino: for teaching me how to find and protect my magic.

Danielle Bukowski: for that first note from you that changed everything, for being the best champion of my work I could have ever hoped for.

Caitlin Landuyt: for loving Ro and Dolores and their world, for your kind, careful questions and encouraging notes that made this book so much more than I could have achieved on my own.

The wonderful team at Vintage—Barbara Richard, Eddie Allen, Quinn O'Neill, Nick Alguire, Austin O'Malley, Nancy Inglis, Annie Locke, Julie Ertl, Anabeth Bostrup, and Mark Abrams: for helping to usher this book into the world.

Leo Hijikata and Reggie Oey: for your invaluable insights into the inner and outer lives of aquariums.

The Center for Fiction: for the time, space, funds, and resources I needed to push through edits on this novel and begin my next.

Daniel Gibney and Princess Ikatekit: for the immeasurable gifts of your friendship and time, and for all the octopuses, both real and symbolic.

Alex Garcia: for your care and support.

Michelle Smith: for telling me, "because I want to read it."

Dorothy Wang: for teaching me how to value myself and my work.

My writing teachers from over the years—K-Ming Chang, Kali Fajardo-Anstine, Ann Hood, Wayétu Moore, Bushra Rehman, Jim Shepard, Weike Wang: for your encouragement, your wisdom, and your words.

Yuna Chung: for the social media lessons, for your grace and wit.

My Umma and Apa, Soonhee Kim and Kwang-Hyun Chung: for your fierce love and protection, and for the language and stories that make up who I am.